TWICE THE HOT LEAD, TWICE THE HOT LOVIN' IN A GIANT SPECIAL EDITION!

HIGH STAKES

On Buckskin's third deal the man with the cigarette dropped his cards and lept to his feet. His hand streaked toward the six-gun on his hip. Buckskin eased upward and the edge of the table splintered six inches from where the man stood, still trying to get his gun cocked and aimed.

The sound of the .45 round exploding in the room caused four of the men to clamp their hands over their ears to shut out the bouncing thunder of the shot. The man with the hand gun slowly let the weapon swing down to the floor, then he dropped it and he began to shake all over.

The house man picked up the six-gun and helped the man out of the room. He had only ten dollars left in his chip box. One of the other players pushed the ten dollars into the pot and when the house man came back he nodded at Buckskin.

"I think it was your deal," the house man said.

The *Buckskin* Series from *Leisure Books:*

#42: MORGAN'S SQUAW
#41: GOLD TOWN GAL
#40: SIX-GUN KILL
#39: BLAZING SIX-GUNS
#38: DERRINGER DANGER

Double Editions:

.52 CALIBER SHOOTOUT/TRICK SHOOTER
TOMBSTONE TEN GAUGE/DEATH DRAW
RETURN FIRE/RIMFIRE REVENGE
SCATTERGUN/APACHE RIFLES
LARAMIE SHOWDOWN/DOUBLE ACTION
COLT CROSSING/POWDER CHARGE

Giant Editions:

CRIPPLE CREEK SONGBIRD
SHOTGUN!
BAWDY HOUSE
MUZZLE BLAST

SIX-GUN JUSTICE

Kit Dalton

LEISURE BOOKS  NEW YORK CITY

A LEISURE BOOK®

May 1996

Published by

Dorchester Publishing Co., Inc.
276 Fifth Avenue
New York, NY 10001

Printed in the United States of America.

BUCKSKIN
SIX-GUN
JUSTICE

Chapter One

Sherry Crawford sat in the back room of the Criterion Saloon and smiled softly. It was the highest-stakes poker game in town and she didn't mind at all that she was the only woman at the table. She had just dealt herself four jacks in a game of five-card draw and she kept her usual poker-face polite smile firmly in place as she looked at the four men still in the game.

Sherry let her short black hair swirl from side to side as she turned her head. She leaned forward just a little to show more cleavage under her white blouse with a scoop neckline. An interesting two inches of the tops of milk white breasts showed even when she sat up straight.

Sherry looked across at the man with the cigar clamped in his teeth. He had been a moderate winner all evening. The time was a little after one A.M. and most of the players had dropped out, gone to sleep in chairs at the side or left for home.

"Mr. Potts, I believe the bet is up to you since you opened," Sherry said in her soft voice with the suggestion of a whiskey huskiness. He looked up, scowled and preened his beard with his left hand. Then he grunted and pushed a hundred dollars' worth of chips into the pot.

"A hundred," he growled. Potts was a shrewd poker player who knew when to bet and when to fold. Sherry respected his bet. He was clean-shaven with sharp black eyes and a thick body. She almost giggled when she bet with herself that he would have chest and back hair thick as a bear. She pinched her eyes a moment to get back in the game.

Sherry had missed the man's name next to Potts. He had lost half his stake and was far from pleased. He squinted at his cards, held tightly together. He spread them a quarter of an inch to check each pasteboard again, shook his head and tossed his hand face down on the table.

The next man at the table snorted and pushed in 200 dollars in chips. He was Nate Hill, who owned the Criterion Saloon. Sherry knew Nate well. He was a firm, trim man in his thirties with lots of blond hair, a darker moustache and a weakness for gin and milk. He looked at her, pinched his forehead into a row of wrinkles, then sighed.

"A hundred and bump you a hundred," Hill said.

Sherry came next. She met the bet and raised it a hundred, adding chips worth 300 dollars to the pot.

"Three hundred to you, Mr. McIntosh," Sherry said with a smile. The fifth person at the table was Cyber McIntosh. She had not played with him before in this Friday-night game during her more than month-long stay in Yankton, Dakota Territory. He was medium height, wore a farmer's hat, and his face was sunburned and weathered. He showed a six-gun on his right hip, but seemed polite and reasonable. He scowled as he studied his hand, then looked up. As he did, Sherry leaned forward and arranged her stack of chips. The routine move let her blouse flare open. McIntosh stared at her breasts. She wore nothing under the white blouse. He saw the large rounded orbs, the wide pink areolas and the darker red nipples, and sweat popped out on his forehead. He didn't look away. Sherry studied her chips a moment more, then without looking at any of the men, leaned back so the fabric returned to its proper position and covered her breasts.

"Three hundred to me?" McIntosh asked, stammering slightly. Potts assured McIntyre it was 300. He wavered. Then he swore softly under his breath and pushed 300 dollars' worth of chips into the pot. Sherry knew that her chest show had been enough to fluster the man. It had worked so often before.

"That's two hundred more to you, Mr. Potts," Sherry said.

He frowned. "I can count, damn it!" He slid in another two hundred. He'd had the benefit of her show of tits too. Sherry only smiled benignly.

"And a hundred more for me," Hill said. He looked at his cards and shook his head. "Damn, I'd like to know what you have but I'm not going to mortgage the place to find out." He dropped his cards face down and leaned back.

"Looks like you're called, Sherry," Cyber McIntosh said. He stared hard at her. "Let's see what you've got."

She laughed. "Really, Mr. McIntosh, not right here."

The other men roared.

"Damn it, let's see your cards," McIntosh snapped. "I never did like playing poker with a damn woman."

"Then I hope you like these." She laid down her hand of four jacks and the six of clubs.

"Damn!" Potts said, tossing his cards face down onto the table. "Beats me."

"Can't be!" McIntosh bellowed. "I've got four sevens. Do you know what the odds are of two hands in five-card draw coming up with four-of-a-kind? It's impossible. You cheated. Damn you, woman. You cheated." He stood suddenly, pushing the table toward Sherry and tipping his own chair over backwards. He clawed at the six-gun on his hip but he was no fast-draw artist. After fumbling for a moment he pulled the weapon from leather on his right hip.

Before he got the gun up and cocked, Sherry lifted a .38 short-barreled revolver from her lap and, holding it with both hands, shot McIntosh twice in the chest. He stood there a moment, then his hand fell from his gun, he turned sideways and crashed to the floor.

Nate Hill pushed off his chair and knelt beside

McIntosh who lay sprawled on his side. Hill pinched the man's nose. No breath. He felt for a pulse at his temple but found none.

"I'm afraid he's dead," Hill said. "Potts, would you go bring the sheriff? McIntosh drew first. You all saw it. A case of self-defense." Potts nodded and hurried out the door into the saloon.

The man who had dropped out of the hand early sat as if frozen in his chair. He shook his head and looked at the dead man, then back at Sherry. "You're a fair to middling shot with that little gun."

"Sometimes I need to be. I can shoot as good as most men." She scraped the pot of chips into the small basket the cashier had provided her and went to the cage at the side of the room where the chips were exchanged for money. The last pot had 1,200 dollars in it. She had about 500 she didn't bet which made 1,700 dollars. Not a bad night's work. Of course it wasn't all hers. She looked back at Nate Hill who motioned to her.

"Miss Sherry, you need to stay to talk to the sheriff. He'll want a signed statement by you as well as the other players at the table. He's a stickler for paperwork."

The barkeep must have heard the shot because he hurried in with a tray of free cold bottles of beer. He passed them out to anyone who wanted one. There were nine men in the room. Two who had been sleeping woke up. Two other men not in the game came forward talking about the shooting.

Sherry sat away from the others, drinking a beer and smoking a long, thin cigar. For just a moment after shooting McIntosh she'd had a twinge of conscience. Then her better judgment took over and she knew the man had tried to kill her. She frowned. She didn't enjoy killing a person. Nor did she think it was some terribly wrong thing to do. She'd been defending herself and her crotch ever since she could remember. She had grown up pretty and big-busted, and from the time she was twelve she had been fighting off boys and then men.

Well, she didn't fight them all off. When she acquired a little experience, she made sure it was her choice, not just some sex-crazy male grabbing for her breasts.

The sheriff, Henry Brown, arrived. He had two deputies and was working the night shift for one of them. He looked like a western sheriff. He stood just over six feet tall, slim-waisted with a gun slung low, a craggy face and piercing blue eyes. Some thought he'd been a gun sharp farther west when he was younger but nobody had the nerve to ask him. He talked to the saloon owner, Nate Hill, then came over to Sherry.

"So, Miss Sherry. It happened again. Twice so far as I remember."

"He tried to kill me. Had his six-gun out of leather and was pointing it at me. I didn't give him time to cock the hammer."

The sheriff grunted and sat down in a chair. "About what the other witnesses have said. I'll want you to write out a statement for me and sign it. Want to do it now, or down at the jail tomorrow?"

"Now. The poker game seems to be over."

A half hour later, the statement was written, signed and witnessed, and the sheriff had statements from two other witnesses. Then he released everyone.

When the others had left, Sherry gave the wicker basket with the money in it to Nate Hill.

"Nate, take care of this for me, will you?"

Nate took the basket, folded the bills in his pocket and nodded. "I think I should walk you to your hotel. Not safe for a lady to be out alone this time of night."

"It isn't even two A.M. yet," Sherry said, but the challenge had gone out of her voice. She took a deep breath. "Yes, maybe you better see me to my hotel room. It's been a long day."

Halfway to the Wayfarer Hotel on Main Street she caught Hill's arm and clung to him. All at once she found it hard to walk.

"Suddenly I'm not as brave as I was back there facing that ugly old forty-five. I didn't mean to kill the man, but what else could I do? I knew he was going to shoot me dead."

He held her up for a few steps until she regained her strength and walked more easily. He slowed the pace.

"Nothing you could do. Of course, that naked display of your fine superstructure didn't do much to help calm the man down. I know, I know, it's one of your best weapons, but I want you to use them sparingly in the future. Blouses a little tighter might not hurt."

She said nothing and he cleared his throat. "I'm making new rules for the back room. All high-stakes poker games will require that all participants and observers check guns and knives at the door.

I'll hire the biggest man I can find in town to be the enforcer. Check them at the door or you don't play. I'd say about one more killing by you at a card game in this county and you'd get a free ticket downriver on the next sternwheeler steamer."

She watched him, the weariness showing around her light green eyes. "Yes, I think you're right. Sheriff Brown was a little out of sorts with me. That no-gun rule for the back-room games is a good idea. Only five more months."

He didn't reply, just led her into the hotel, up to her room on the second floor and said good night to her all gentlemanly and proper.

Sherry closed the door, found the matches and lit a lamp, then locked the door and leaned against it.

"Bastard," she shouted.

Buckskin Lee Morgan eased up to the desk at the Cherry Street Hotel and looked at Box 305. He hadn't shaved for a week, his jeans still had miner mud on them, and his shirt was torn in two places. Only his holster was clean and oiled and the Spencer Carbine over his shoulder was spotless.

The clerk behind the desk was new to Buckskin, a tall, thin kid just out of his teens and uncomfortable in his white shirt and tie.

"I'd like the key to room 305," Buckskin said.

"Yes, sir," the youth said and reached for the box. He came down with the key and a long white envelope. He looked at the writing on it, then handed both to Buckskin.

"Sir, you're requested to contact our guest facilitator, Miss Clarice Johnson, at your earliest convenience."

"Guest facilitator?" Buckskin asked. "What the hell is that?"

"It's what we've needed around here for a long time to keep riffraff like you out of our fine establishment, Mr. Morgan," a soft voice said from behind Buckskin. He turned and grinned.

"Another promotion, Clare? You're gonna be the manager of this flea trap before long."

The lady behind him was short with dark hair, brown eyes and the sweetest face he'd seen in months. She wore a dress that was long and slim without a belt and reminded him of a fancy Chinese gown.

"Morgan, you be good and I'll buy you supper in the dining room tonight. We've got something to talk about." She turned to the desk clerk. "Charles, will you get the box of mail from the back office marked Buckskin Morgan? It's quite full."

"Yes, Miss Johnson," the clerk said and left.

Morgan grinned. "Cracking the whip like a teamster. What's our big dinner conference all about?"

"Wait until you have a bath, find some clean clothes and relax a minute. I'll see you down here at six o'clock." She grinned and he could see the little homeless waif he'd known six years ago. "Don't you dare be late. In my new job, I don't like to wait for people."

She carefully pecked a kiss on his cheek, then hurried away.

Buckskin took the cardboard box of mail that Charles brought and walked up to his room on the third floor. This was his home base, his office, his mail drop, his only roots. Seven years ago he had foiled a robbery here at the hotel and kept two guards from being killed. He earned the undying gratitude of the hotel management. They offered him a free room for the rest of his life. He could use this address for mail and utilize the room whenever he was in town. Maid service and free meals in the dining room were included. He accepted.

Ten minutes later he had sorted through the mail on the double bed and put it in three stacks: Urgent, Do It Soon, and Sometime. He looked at the urgent pile. There were letters from what he guessed might be potential clients. He'd get to them just as soon as he had a bath.

In the bathroom at the end of the third-floor hall, he discovered that in his absence they had installed hot and cold running water. He simply turned on a faucet for hot water. He found towels and locked the door and settled in for an hour-long hot-water soak.

He cut it to a half hour and came out scrubbed hair to toenails, pink and glowing. Running hot water? What would they think of next?

Back in his room he looked at the urgent pile and found two envelopes with the same stationery. Both were from the Harold Evans Real Estate Co. Inc. Harold Evans was said to be the richest man in town. Somebody figured he owned half the city. Buckskin opened one of the envelopes and read the letter.

Mr. Morgan,

I am in need of your services. If you are in town and available, please contact me at the earliest possible time. The matter is pressing. Your fee is no problem. I'm desperate.

Harold Evans, President

He tore open the second envelope and read he letter on the fancy stationery.

Dear Mr. Morgan,

It is a week since my first letter. If you are in town I would appreciate a visit at your next available moment. My wife is missing and I want you to find her. Cost is no object. I will pay $10,000 or more for your assistance. Please contact me.

Harold Evans, President

Buckskin's home room was the largest the hotel offered, with a double bed, big dresser, and a section to one side with a desk, a file cabinet and two chairs.

He put the two letters on his desk, dressed quickly and checked his watch. It was slightly after four. He might have a chance to catch Harold Evans today. He wore his usual town clothes, brown trousers, cowboy boots, a long-sleeved western shirt with a tan vest and his Stetson.

A cab picked him up in front of the hotel and five minutes later he stood in the lobby of the Harold Evans Real Estate Office building on Colorado Street.

A receptionist looked up from her pad of paper and brightened.

"Yes, sir, may I help you?"

Two minutes later he had been hurried into the second-floor office of Harold Evans himself. The office was five times as big as Buckskin's hotel room. Huge widows looked out over Denver and the furniture would better suit a living room than an office. To one side, a large desk in quarter-cut oak commanded the scene. A high-backed swivel chair behind it held a small man in his fifties. He turned and stared at Buckskin as soon as he came into the room.

"Mr. Morgan. I'm glad to see you. Sit down. Would you like a fine cigar? You and I have business to talk over."

Evans didn't waste any time.

"My wife is missing. No, I don't think there was any foul play. She evidently tired of me and ran away. I could have sent the police after her since she took some bearer bonds that were mine, not hers, but that's not important. I want her back."

"When did she leave, Mr. Evans?"

"Left home the morning of August fourteenth, this year, 1881. Yes, nearly a month and a half ago. I thought she would come back. The money she had must surely have run out weeks ago. She had only two thousand dollars with her and she spends money as if it's leaves from some tree."

"Any idea where she is?"

"Yes, I do. I've had a report that she, or someone who looked a great deal like her, was seen a week ago in Yankton, Dakota Territory."

"That's a long way from here, Mr. Evans. Is this sighting reliable?"

"Extraordinarily so. It's by a former employee of mine who knew Dawn well. That's her name, Dawn Evans."

"Do you have a description, a picture, any way to positively identify her?"

"Yes, it's all here in an envelope for you. I'd suggest you study this material tonight, come see me at eight A.M. tomorrow, and I'll answer any questions that you have."

Buckskin stood and prowled to the window and looked out, then meandered around the room.

"What is troubling you, young man?"

"What if I find her and she doesn't want to come home? She's an adult. I have no police powers. I won't kidnap her and return her to you against her will."

"No, no, of course not. Such contingencies are spelled out in the briefing and instructions in the envelope. In such a case I have detailed several plans to entice her back including a new wardrobe, two trips to Europe a year, riding lessons, and to create a dance company for her to dance in and to direct when she's ready. I have offers here that I think she will jump at once I find her."

"I'll read the material over and give you my decision about taking the job tomorrow."

Evans looked startled. "You mean there's a chance you might not take it?"

"Yes. I don't like this kind of search for a runaway who is an adult. How old is your wife?"

"That's part of the problem. She's twenty-five and

I'm fifty-five." He paused and stood. Now Buckskin realized that Harold Evans was no more than five feet, three inches tall.

"I'll start my offer at ten thousand dollars and expenses if you want to take the job. If you bring her home safely and she stays here, you'll get an additional five-thousand-dollar bonus." You must realize how much money that is. A clerk in a store makes forty dollars a month, less than five hundred dollars a year. This offer amounts to that clerk's salary for thirty years."

"I've been poor most of my life, Mr. Evans. I know the value of a dollar." Buckskin stood.

"Mr. Morgan, my first wife died in a typhoid epidemic four years ago. I've been married to Dawn a little over a year. I miss her terribly. My whole life is upside down. My business and my successes mean nothing without her. I hope you can help me. They told me you're the best detective in Denver. I've approached no one else."

Buckskin nodded again, then looked at his Waterbury. "Thank you. I'll contact you in the morning. I appreciate your concern. This sort of case is never as easy as it looks. I still have some reservations. I'll study your material. Now, I'm afraid I have a social engagement."

Buckskin shook the man's extended hand and found it soft and limp. When Buckskin reached the door Harold Evans spoke again.

"I hope you'll find Dawn for me. Without her my life is a total waste, a ruin, a desolation."

Buckskin waved and hurried outside. He didn't want to be late for his dinner with Clare Johnson. What did she mean she had something to talk to him about? It could prove interesting.

Chapter Two

For dinner they had fried oysters and clam strips surrounding the biggest halibut fillet Buckskin had seen since leaving Alaska. The seafood plate was accompanied by a variety of sauces and side dishes of baked potatoes and cheese, broccoli, carrots, three kinds of salad, hot dinner rolls and coffee.

"New chef?" Buckskin asked when the pre-ordered dishes arrived at the only dining room table that looked out over half of Denver.

"New and wonderful," Clare said. "I'm afraid I'm going to get fat if I eat here too often."

"So what's the big news?" Buckskin asked.

Clare smiled, hid her face behind one hand for a moment, then sighed. "You don't believe in letting a lady set the scene, ply you with a good food and wine and then build up to the big moment, do you?"

Buckskin grinned. "I messed up again, huh? Sorry. Okay, let's enjoy the food, and the wine is fine. Where do you get clam strips in Denver?"

When the food was gone and the wine bottle almost empty, they looked out at Denver as the lights started coming on in the downtown section. Clare cleared her throat. The whole dinner had been taken up with small talk, about how his last job went, about whether or not he was going to take the case from Evans Real Estate, about her work at the hotel. Then she sobered.

"Buckskin Lee Morgan, I think it's high time that we became a bit more serious. I've known you for six years now. You've seen me at my worst, and now at my best. Since I don't think you'll ever ask me, I decided in this modern day and age that it's up to me to ask you.

"Buckskin, I want to marry you."

Buckskin leaned back in his chair and studied her a moment. She was serious. For a fraction of a second he knew he showed surprise, then he masked it with his poker face and let the chair down slowly.

"Clare, I certainly am flattered. I—"

"Before you say anything else, let me charge on here. I know that you and I spent quite a few nights together. You saved me and I was grateful. But I haven't been inside your room for over a year, if you'll think back. I've wanted to be more than just a bed warmer for you.

"Now, say you keep doing your detective work and go traipsing around the country. I can live with that. But I'll be here true and solid when you get home. I can keep my job here and take care of your mail and be a kind of secretary for you, and then when you come home it would be a real home and . . ." She let her voice trail off.

A tear crept down her cheek and she wiped at it. Then she shook her head and stared hard at him.

"I love you, Buckskin Lee Morgan. I tried not to, but no way could I avoid it. Like the measles, I guess. I caught it bad."

Buckskin picked up her hand and held it tenderly in both of his. He reached in and kissed away a tear that rolled down her cheek.

"Hey, little girl, don't cry. I hate it when you cry. Turns things all around. Clare, you know I'm not good husband material."

She shook her head and touched his cheek. "Hey, once I get a halter on you you'll be the truest, the most loyal and finest husband any woman ever had. You're just a little wild yet, like some range stallion who's been running free all his life. One good halter and an altar and I swear you'd be the best husband in two hundred counties."

"Sweet, wonderful Clare, you're not thinking this out well enough. Like today. I came into town about two o'clock after being gone for over a month. I read my mail and there's a new client, a man highly interested in hiring me to find his wife. He'll pay me fifteen thousand dollars if I can find her and bring her back.

"I'll probably take the job, and that means I'll be on the train by noon tomorrow heading as close as it can take me to Yankton, Dakota Territory. What kind of a marriage would that be, a day here and a day there every month?"

Tears came freely now but she made no crying sounds. "It would be a better marriage than what I have now. At least I'd have you for one day a month."

She stood and walked away. He followed her. She went out of the dining room, through the lobby and to the stairs. Without looking back, Clare went up the steps. Buckskin was at her side. She went to the third floor and stopped in front of his room.

"If you won't marry me, Buckskin Lee Morgan, may I please be with you tonight?"

He unlocked the door and they went inside. He lit the lamp he had left near the door. She looked at the mess of mail on the bed. Then she put her arms around his neck and pulled his face down and kissed his lips hard.

"I want to be with you tonight."

"Like a sister? Like when you were fifteen and I found you shivering in that rain storm and let you stay in my room?"

"And you never once touched me. You said I was your little sister and you protected me. For three years you were the best friend I had. You found a room for me and got me a job here at the hotel. Such wonderful, sweet memories."

She kissed him again. "But tonight I want to be with you like a wife. I want to remember how good it is with you deep inside me and the surge of joy and the wonder and the rapture. If you won't marry me, just pretend to love me tonight, and I'll be able to struggle along without you tomorrow."

That night it was better than it had ever been before for both of them.

The next morning, Buckskin spent an hour reading the material in the envelope about Dawn Evans. Evidently she had been a handful for her older husband. Twice the police had found her drunk and disorderly and brought her home. There was a complete description, four different pictures of her and a positive identification: Dawn Evans had three small moles forming a triangle on the underside of her right breast.

Buckskin walked into Harold Evans' office promptly at eight and agreed to take the case. A handshake sealed the agreement and Evans gave him a thousand dollars in twenty-dollar bills in a money belt for his expenses.

"If you need more, send me a telegram. I assume that this Yankton, Dakota Territory, will have a telegraph. If not, a letter on the steamer to the rail line will work. I know you'll do your best. I suggest you be on the noon train east. You can take the train into Omaha and then go by sternwheeler up the Missouri River to this Yankton, which is high up on the northern Nebraska border. I wish you luck."

Buckskin hurried back to the hotel, packed, and told Clare goodbye. She was tight-lipped as she kissed him on the cheek.

"Have a good trip and a successful hunt." She sighed and shook her head. "Damn, I wish you'd marry me."

Buckskin grinned. "Little lady, you might just corral me yet, who knows? Right now I'm off on a hunt." He bent and kissed her lips which responded immediately. Then he waved and hurried out the door to catch the 12:04 heading for Omaha.

Behind him, Clare Johnson's face showed a grim little smile. "You just wait, Buckskin Lee Morgan. Next time you get home I'll do a better job of persuasion."

The train ride to Omaha was uneventful. He wired ahead and had a reservation on the next sternwheeler heading upstream after the train arrived in the Nebraska city.

He'd never been on a sternwheeler. They were different from the big sidewheelers that plowed up and down the mighty Mississippi River. The sidewheelers worked fine in the big wide river, but when the Missouri narrowed and shallowed out, the bigger boats couldn't get far upstream.

The sternwheelers had another advantage over the side-powered boats. They were narrower, and with the power wheel in the rear, they were less prone to hitting snags and submerged logs in the river. Snags caused more river boats to go down than any other problem.

Buckskin carried his carpetbag and stared at the *Far West* where she had tied up at the Omaha dock on the Missouri. The ship was nearly 200 feet long from bow to the last paddle on the stern wheel. He had a pamphlet that said the ship could carry 200 tons of freight and 30 passengers in its cabins. More passengers could rough it on the cargo deck, which would be sometimes dangerously close to the waterline.

With all of this weight, the ship would still draw

only three feet of water, and would go upstream far into some of the smaller tributaries that fed the Missouri.

Eighty percent of the ship's structure sat above the waterline. The main deck housed the fireboxes and steam boilers at about the one-third point of the ship. Nearby was the necessary stack of cord wood to fire the boilers.

Over the main deck was the boiler deck where the cabins for the richer passengers were located. This deck had a railing around it and a promenade where the richer passengers could stroll. Amidships and built on top of the cabins was the square wheelhouse, fully enclosed by glass windows for an all-around view of the always dangerous river.

Steam from the boilers went through a pipe to the rear of the ship where the engine drove a pair of giant connecting rods that powered the large stern wheel that propelled the ship across the water.

Buckskin stared at the stern wheel. It was little more than a wooden cylinder 18 feet in diameter and 24 feet wide and belted with cast iron. Twin steam-powered engines turned the wheel twenty times a minute. That meant that the thirteen paddles across the 24-foot wheel dipped into the water a total of 260 paddle dips a minute to push the ship up or downstream.

The *Far West,* like most of the sternwheelers, had twin smokestacks that belched smoke when the boilers were fired up. As Buckskin watched, he saw smoke start to seep from the twin stacks, then come on with a surge. Half a dozen passengers moved to the gangplank, and he hurried so he wouldn't be left behind. He gave his ticket to the purser at the plank and walked on board. They told him they would be making about ten miles an hour against the current, so it would take about twenty hours to make the trip. With the crooks and turns of the Missouri, a land distance of 150 miles stretched out considerably farther than that on the water.

The *Far West* left the dock in Omaha slightly after three P.M., and the word was that with the high water and the number-one pilot, the ship would travel at night as well as during the day. Night trips were more frequent now as the pilots became more familiar with the changing river.

Buckskin had engaged a cabin and found it to be small but adequate. The single bunk bed built against the wall looked most inviting. With a twenty-hour trip ahead of him he'd be needing a good night's sleep. He reread the material on Dawn Evans. He'd seen the type of woman before, self-centered, spoiled, too much money and nothing to do except spend it. Only now her supply of money must have been cut off.

She could always go to the cribs, but from the looks of her, she wouldn't do that. She'd find some other way to make her expenses. Why did she alight in Yankton, Dakota Territory? Maybe that's where she ran out of money.

He put his bag away, checked the key and lock on the cabin door, then took a stroll around the promenade deck. Not a lot of fashion plates on board this run. Some businessmen, a pair of middle-aged widows out for a lark, an earnest young couple who looked as if the two of them might be working out the answers for the problems of the world.

He watched the operation of the ship. The mechanical parts of it were so simple it was almost ludicrous. But they worked. The wood was burned to create steam, steam shot back to the stern where the two small engines converted the steam into forward and back motion to power the connecting rods on the big drive shaft that turned the mighty paddle wheel.

He completed his trip around the ship and headed back to his cabin. A few doors away he stopped. A young woman paced up and down in front of his cabin door and kept looking both ways. Odd. No one except Clare and Mr. Evans knew he would be on this ship.

He walked by, looking away from the girl so if she had recognized him before, she couldn't now. He glanced at her when she walked away and felt certain he didn't know who she was.

He walked back to his cabin 22, but before he could get the key in the lock she approached him.

"Mr. Morgan. I know you must be busy, but could I speak with you for a few minutes? I need some advice."

"Do I know you?" Buckskin asked.

"No. I'm from Denver and I've seen you and read about your detective work in the newspaper. When I boarded I was sure it was you. I really need some help."

He had seen a bench near the bow end of the promenade near the stairway to the lower deck. He suggested they go to the bench, and they sat there watching their progress up the broad Missouri.

"You said you have a problem?"

"Yes, my sister. She's a year older than I am. Self-confident, knows exactly what she wants. She's a singer and a good one. Not a dance hall girl, but she has sung in some of the better saloons. She's not a whore. She sang in Omaha for six months, then wrote me that she was going to go upriver and work some of the larger towns. I had one letter from her in Yankton, up in the Dakota Territory. She said she had a good job, and the manager was a fine man. That was the last letter I got, over two months ago. I just know that something terrible has happened to her. Will you help me find her?"

"Miss, I'm sorry, but I'm already on a case. I'm just starting it and it's not going to be an easy or a quick one. I'm sorry."

"I don't have much money, but I could pay you ten dollars a week. It's from my inheritance my mother left me. I get twenty a week but I can give you ten. Will you do it for that?"

Buckskin stood. "I'm sorry, miss. I thought you understood. I can't possibly take on another case right now. I'm sure you'll find somebody to help you."

"She vanished in Yankton. I know that's where you're going. You can get into places where I can't. Like the saloons. I'm sure that's where she was kidnapped. She must have been kidnapped or she would have contacted me."

Buckskin stood. "I'm sorry, miss. I simply don't have the time to help you. I wish you good luck in finding your sister. Now I have to go." He moved off at a fast pace, went to his cabin, unlocked the door and hurried inside. He breathed a sigh of relief. Some people found it hard to accept no as an answer.

He went over the rest of the background material on Dawn Evans. Before she married Evans, she had something of a reputation as an expert poker player who sometimes played in high-stakes games. Interesting.

He opened the door and looked out at the darkening skies. He'd heard that the boat would slow down as night fell, then if there was a full moon, the speed would pick up a little as they worked through the easier stretches of the river.

He'd heard that some of the shorter sternwheelers had worked all the way into the Yellowstone River and even down the Little Bighorn River way out in the middle of Montana. They were amazing craft.

He started to close his door when a figure darted past him and into his cabin. He turned, reaching for his six-gun, which he had strapped on once the boat left Omaha. Then in the pale lamplight of his cabin he saw that the intruder was the girl who wanted him to find her sister.

She wore the same sheer white blouse and long white skirt and stared at him with angry eyes.

"Mr. Morgan. I know you're an important man with business of your own. But I ask you again to help me find Maria. My sister right now may be the victim of a vicious scheme that kidnaps pretty young girls and sells them into sexual slavery. Right now some disgusting man could be violating her while her captors pocket the dirty money.

"Isn't that disgusting? Shouldn't something be done about it? Won't you help me track her down and bring these criminals to justice?"

"Miss, what's your name?"

"Oh, I'm Melinda Warnick, and I'm from Denver, same as you. Will you help us, Mr. Morgan? I don't know if Maria is dead or alive or being raped ten or twelve times a day in some filthy crib somewhere. But I'm determined to find out."

"How old are you, Melinda?"

"Me? I'm twenty-two."

"And from Denver?"

"Yes, I have my own seamstress shop there. I have some wealthy clients I make dresses for."

"Good. You should get off this ship at the next stop and go back to Denver. If your sister is in deep trouble, you won't be able to get her out of it, and you might be pulled into the same trap. Go home, Melinda. Now please leave my cabin. I need to get some sleep."

"Me, too. Can I sleep here tonight?" She undid the top two buttons of her white blouse.

"No. And don't start to undress. I've seen all kinds and sizes of naked women. Out."

"Will you check into what happened to Maria in Yankton if you have the time?"

"Melinda, out."

"You've got to help me. There's no one else who can."

"Melinda, out."

She sighed and fastened the top two buttons of

her blouse. "All right, I'll go. But I'll see you in Yankton and convince you to help Maria. Just think of her in some filthy crib where she's probably chained by one ankle to the bed. Where—"

Buckskin eased her out the cabin door and closed and locked it. He shook his head. She did have a point. However, until he found out what kind of a task he faced in Yankton, his total loyalty and time belonged to Harold Evans.

For a moment, he wondered if Dawn Evans had fallen into the white slavery trap that Melinda had mentioned. He rejected the idea at once. If such a threat was made to Dawn, he imagined that she would pay the man twice what he could have sold her for, or she would have cut cards with the unsuspecting white slaver, cheated and won the card cut with an ace.

No, his first job was to find Dawn Evans and convince her to go back to Denver.

Buckskin had just put the material on Dawn Evans back in the envelope and pulled off his boots when he heard two pistol shots. He blew out the lamp, drew his six-gun and eased the door open. Another shot flared in the dark. Buckskin saw the muzzle flash, aimed somewhat in his direction. He saw a figure break from the smokestack and run toward him.

The hidden gun toward the stern fired again. This time Buckskin returned the fire, slamming two rounds just to the left of the flash. He heard a scream and the revolver went silent.

Then the figure slammed into him and he saw in the moonlight that it was Melinda, the girl in white.

He pulled her into his open cabin door and slammed it shut. Then he lit the lamp and found Melinda shaken and trembling sitting on his bunk.

"Now I know I'm on the right track," she said between gasps and sobs. "Somebody saw me and called me Maria. I ran. Back home not even our good friends can tell us apart, we look so much alike. I'm sure somebody thought he saw my sister Maria. Then he shot at me and tried to kill me. Why, Mr. Morgan? Am I a threat to them?"

She gasped again and held her shoulder. He looked at her closer and saw blood seeping past her clenched fingers. He eased her hand away and found the gunshot wound. The bullet had nipped a quarter inch of flesh on her upper arm, creating a bloody furrow but did little damage.

"I'll have to clean and bandage that wound, Melinda. Are you wearing a cotton petticoat?"

She nodded, lifted her skirt and tore three long strips of the cotton cloth an inch wide from her skirt. From his carpetbag, he took a small jar of salve and spread it over the cleaned-out wound.

Using a towel and some water from a jug he cleaned off the blood and almost stopped the bleeding. Then he put on the salve and a pad of the petticoat on the wound before he wrapped the lengths of white bandage around her arm holding the pad in place.

She watched him and between winces of pain said, "You've done this sort of thing before."

He nodded as he finished the bandage by tearing the last strip in half down eight inches so he could tie the ends together around her arm. "Too many gunshot wounds I've tended to." He sat down beside her and inspected the wound. The bleeding had stopped. "What's your cabin number?"

"Twenty-six. They know my number. I can't go back there tonight."

"Then you stay here. I can sit in the chair." He eased her back on the bunk and pulled a blanket over her.

"Sleep in my clothes?"

"Yes. Both of us. If they know you're in here, we may have to leave suddenly."

"Oh," she said softly.

He went to the door and eased it open enough so he could see the deck. No one was in sight. Good. He closed the door, locked it and sat in the cabin's only chair. He might sleep on the floor before the night was over. Either way he would keep his Colt six-gun firmly in hand, just in case of any unannounced visitors.

"Good night, Mr. Morgan."

"Since we're sleeping together tonight, you might as well call me Buckskin."

"Thanks. And thank you for rescuing me. I'm sure that man with the gun was trying to kill me."

"I'll talk to some people tomorrow. Now get some sleep."

She did. He didn't as he stood guard all night.

Chapter Three

Buckskin nodded off around four A.M. but awoke when he heard someone walk past the cabin with a heavy tread. The sounds seemed to pause at his door, then continued on. That kept him alert for another two hours, and when he saw daylight creeping into the cabin, he unlocked the door and opened it just enough so he could look outside. No one was on the promenade deck.

He closed the door and went to the bunk to awaken Melinda. Her face was pretty even in complete repose. Soft blonde hair scattered over the pillow. He shook her shoulder and she awoke at once.

"Yes, oh, I'd forgotten. I'm still alive. Did anyone try—"

She stopped and he shook his head. "No trouble. I'm going out to see what I can discover. I'll lock the door behind me. You can unlock it from the inside by pushing this little lever, see it?"

She nodded.

"Stay here and stay quiet."

He left and locked the door with his key on the outside as usual, then stretched and wandered back in the direction he had shot at the gunman last night, toward the stern. Just behind the main cabin and over from the lifeboat he saw some reddish brown stains on the deck. Dried blood. So he had found flesh with his shots. Good. He circled the promenade and went down the bow steps to the main deck.

Two seamen working on the wood pile quieted their chatter when he approached. He went directly to the older of the two.

"Just wondered about something. I thought I heard some gunshots last night. Was there any trouble on board?"

The seamen picked up a three-foot piece of firewood eight inches thick and carried it to the open firebox door and threw it in. He clanged shut the door and stood with his gloved hands on his hips.

"Mister, I got troubles of my own. I don't look to take on anybody else's. As for me, I didn't hear no shots last night. No sir, no shots."

Buckskin's six-gun came out of leather in a fraction of a second and the cocked weapon pressed gently against the man's temple.

"I wouldn't want to make a mistake here, my friend. What was that about shots last night?"

The man's eyes went wide showing lots of white and his eyeballs rolled upward to try to see the gun barrel. "Well, come to think of it, I did hear some, along about nine o'clock or so. Must have been four of them."

"Anybody get shot? Maybe one of the crew?"

Again the eyes shifted toward the gun barrel. "No, sir, not that I know of. Whole crew looks intact this morning. Only eight of us. Nobody looked hurt to me."

Buckskin moved the Colt and holstered it. "How many stops did we make last night?"

"Only two. We got clouds so we waited at one little town for three hours."

"How many more stops before we come to Yankton?"

The man wrinkled his forehead, looked at the other crewman. "Three more, I think. Not sure. I mostly just stoke this here firebox."

Buckskin touched the brim of his hat. "Thank you kindly. It's been interesting talking to you men. Stay happy in your work."

He walked past the boiler and around the freight piled high on board. Nothing seemed out of the ordinary. A half dozen men and two couples slept against some freight on the lee side out of the wind. He leaned against a stack of boxes and watched the vessel. All seemed routine. Ahead he could see the banks of Iowa. The ship slanted toward the Iowa shore and a small town. Another stop. He wondered if anyone would get off. Buckskin moved so he could see the gangplank where it had been hauled up on the main deck.

Two deck hands moved a number of boxes and other freight to the center of the ship on the starboard side, preparing to stop at the small town.

Two of the main-deck passengers gathered their belongings and moved toward the gangplank ready to disembark. Buckskin looked carefully but could find no signs of bandages on either of them.

The crew tied up the ship, the gangplank swung down, and the two passengers scurried off in front of the hand trucks that moved stacks of boxes down the gangplank to the rickety dock.

Less than five minutes after tying up at the dock, the lines were loosened, the *Far West* blew its whistle, and smoke stacks blossomed with dark black smoke as the craft swung out into the deeper water toward the center of the Missouri.

Buckskin strolled back to his cabin. He saw no one watching him. He walked close to the cabins so no one in the wheelhouse directly above them could see him. He unlocked the door and went inside.

The girl was not lying on the bunk.

He looked around quickly, but there was noplace in the small cabin to hide. He saw some of the bloody bandages beside the bunk, but nothing else. He started for the door and heard a knock. The knob turned and Melinda stepped inside. She had changed her clothes and wore all brown and a sunbonnet that hid most of her face.

"Good, you're back," she said. "I want you to come to my cabin for the rest of the trip. There's no way to get any food on these boats. I checked. So I brought along plenty of food for two days. Come and share it with me. You must be starved."

"Did anyone see you leave or come here?"

"Not that I could tell. Now come on, before the deck is full of people." She caught at his arm, then stopped. "Oh, why don't you bring your gear with you? Then if we have to get away quickly you won't leave anything behind."

He gathered up his gear and clothes and put everything in his carpetbag, then nodded at the door.

"Keep it casual, like we're just out for a walk, but stay close to the side of the cabin. That way if anyone from the wheelhouse is interested in us, they won't see us."

She grinned and opened the door.

Two minutes later they were safely in her cabin four doors down. She sat on the bed and winced as she moved her arm.

"You'll need to see a doctor about that arm once we get to Yankton," Buckskin said. "Now, I made a walk around the boat. Saw nothing suspicious except some dried blood down where I shot at that gunman last night. Somebody on board has a bullet wound. It isn't any of the crewmen. None of the main-deck passengers looked like a shooting case, so it must be someone in one of the cabins."

"So how do we find them, and what do we do if we do figure out who they are?"

"Not 'we,' small lady. I'm the one who finds them. There should be a considerable stop at Yankton. It's the largest town in this section of the country. A lot of the passengers may be getting off there as well. We'll be the last ones off. You'll stay in the cabin until everyone is off, then I'll get you and we'll leave. I'll be watching for anyone with a bullet in him."

"I want to watch with you. I saw a flash of the man who shot at me in the light from a window. He had a full beard, a black one. That's about all I saw."

"He might not be the one who shot at you, but it's a good help. Yes, I think you might wait with me. Dressed that way and with the sunbonnet, whoever recognized you before would be hard put to pick you out now." He watched her a moment. "Could you wear a blouse that was a little less revealing, not quite so tight? Every man on board will take a second look."

She smiled. "If it upsets you—"

"No, not me. We want you to look as little like last night as possible."

She rummaged in her bag and took out a heavy sweater also in brown. "Will this do?"

"Much better. I'll turn my back."

"Why? You don't have to. I'm no blushing maiden." She unbuttoned her blouse and took it off, showing a chemise under it that covered her breasts.

Buckskin chuckled. "You're not blushing, that's a fact. I always enjoy watching a woman dress. It's a kind of dance, almost a ballet."

She ducked into the pullover sweater and then fluffed out her long blonde hair.

"If you think this was a dance, you should see me try to get into one of those damned whaleboned corsets."

They both laughed.

Heavy treads went past their door and both quieted. The steps kept going.

They shared the food she had brought, a picnic basket with bread and butter and strawberry jam, a pot of cold baked beans and a half dozen sandwiches with cheese or ham. There was half a fried chicken and a jar of peaches. She also had brought two quart fruit jars filled with lemonade.

"You thought of everything," Buckskin said.

"Everything but getting shot. Do you suppose that the man who shot me had kidnapped my sister Maria and she escaped somehow and this man thought I was her?"

"Something like that. Maybe he didn't know that she got away but he figured she must have if she's here on the boat."

They ate more, then decided to save some for noontime.

He eyed the bed and lifted his brows. "Would you mind if I had a nap? I didn't get a lot of sleep last night."

"I'll sit in the chair. I guess I shouldn't go outside and let them have another shot at me. You have a nap, I'll stand guard. I do know how to use a six-gun. I hold it with both hands—"

Buckskin held up a hand, stopping her. "I'll keep the Colt. Anything that happens, I'll be awake in half a second and ready to shoot."

She grinned. "Yes, Mr. Buckskin Lee Morgan, I truly believe that you would be."

The previous night in Yankton, Dakota Territory, five men dressed all in black and wearing black hoods over their heads with holes cut out for their eyes, sat on black horses outside a shanty a quarter mile upstream from the town. The hovel had been made from pieces of tin sheeting, boards stolen from other buildings, a lot of cardboard boxes opened up and nailed to cross pieces, and other bits and pieces of anything that would keep out the rain and the cold. It was a hovel that no God-fearing white man would live in.

"Hey, you inside," one of the men bellowed. "Get your yellow tail out here. We got some talking to do."

It was after midnight and there was no light in the shack. A moment later a match flared, a candle wick caught, and a thin hand carried the light past the blanket that formed the hovel's door.

The man who emerged was an inch over five feet tall, had a long black braid down his back and wore a black sack like garment. He rubbed his eyes, then held the candle high so he could see better.

"You, Chinaman. We don't want you in our town. Get your woman and your spawn and get out of here. You understand?"

The man frowned in the pale candlelight. "Home. Chang's home. Build self. Do wash for lady in town. All legal and fine."

"Not so fine, Chink bastard. We don't want you in our town. You're too damn close. Don't want your kind here. This ain't no fucking China. Go back to where you come from."

Lee Chang frowned. "You unhappy? No understand. Have good the English. Learn hard. Do good wash for missies in town. Work hard. Have wife and baby. Work hard. Man said me work hard do fine in new country."

Another voice spoke up. It was softer, kinder. "We know all that, Chang. Hell, we're Americans. You ain't. We want your yellow hide out of our town. I've got ten dollars for you. Enough to get the three of you passage down to Omaha. We want you on the first downstream steamer tomorrow morning. Understand?"

Chang shook his head. "No understand. Work hard. Man said if Chang work hard, America fine place."

Another voice came in. It was higher with a nasal twang that sounded strange coming through the hood. "Yeah, a fine place for us, Chang, not your kind. We don't want your kind in our town, savvy? Now get your woman and brat out of there. We're gonna burn your shack down. Then you got to leave tomorrow."

One of the men stepped down from his horse and opened a gallon can of kerosene. He sloshed it around the outside of the mostly cardboard side of the shack.

Chang ran at him. "No, no hurt house."

The man swung the half-full can, hitting Chang in the side, and the slender man fell down. He got up and clawed at the man with the can. The black-hooded man adjusted his hood so he could see better through the holes, then clubbed the Chinaman to the ground with the butt of his six-gun.

"Damned yellow bastard, keep away from me."

"Get the woman and brat out of there," the tallest man on the horse said. Two of the mounted men got down and hurried into the shack. They lit matches and a minute later carried a protesting

Chinese woman and a baby out of the shack.

"Light it," said the rider who led the group. One man scratched a match, bent and lit the kerosene-soaked cardboard. It caught fire at once. A moment later some vaporized coal oil whooshed into flames and the entire shack boiled with fire. In ten minutes the fire had changed the cardboard and few boards into a shimmering pile of coals and two skeletal two-by-fours pointing at the sky.

Lee Chang came back to consciousness slowly. When he saw his house burning he screamed at the men and threw himself at them. They laughed and pushed him away. He found his wife and baby and held the child in his arms, screeching at the men in Chinese so they wouldn't understand the evil things he called them.

The tall man on the horse rode up to Chang and touched a rifle muzzle to his shoulder.

"Chang, listen to me. Chang!" The threatening tone of the man's voice made the Chinaman turn slowly and stare up at the dark figure.

"Chang, we're giving you a chance. Take the ten dollars and your wife and child and be on that boat tomorrow morning. Will you do that?"

Chang turned to his wife, gave her the baby, then looked back at the mounted man. He shook his head.

"Chang stay here. Chang work hard. Chang stay Yankton."

"Damnit, you foreign bastard. You don't understand. We don't want you here, we won't let you stay here. If you're still here tomorrow afternoon, we'll come back and kill you. Now do you understand?"

Chang screamed and lunged at the man on the horse. His hand came from his robe with a six-inch dagger and he stabbed it hard into the rider's thigh, then he twisted it and slashed it outward. The rider brayed in surprise and pain, kicking hard with his foot until it failed to obey his orders. The night rider still mounted charged up on his horse and fired his six-gun, putting a .45 caliber slug into Chang's chest before he could swing the knife again.

Chang plunged backwards, hit the ground and rolled over and tried to stand. Three six-guns fired almost at once and the Chinaman went down dead as he jolted to the ground.

The wounded rider bellowed in pain.

"That bastard cut me. Tie up my leg before I bleed to death. Come on, you helpless assholes!"

Two men came up quickly and pushed kerchiefs over the wound and bound it with more kerchiefs.

"We better get you right down to Doc Sims," one of the men said. "That's a damn bad cut."

"First the other two yellow heathen," the leader said. "Shoot them now and throw them into the fire."

There was a moment's hesitation, then one man swore, lifted his six-gun and fired twice. They threw all three bodies into the searing coals of the burned-out shack, then rode quickly for town.

Later that night, only one of the riders went into the office that was attached to the doctor's house. He wore a black suit and hobbled on one leg. Doc Sims scowled at the ugly wound, warned the man to be more careful with his knives and patched him up. Doc Sims didn't ask any questions. He'd found out long ago in this town that it was best not to get inquisitive when it came to stabbings and gunshot wounds and other violence. He patched them up, whoever came, no questions asked.

He didn't ask questions but he was good at putting facts together. A man comes in with a gunshot wound and the next day another man is found dead of gunshot wounds in an alley. Another time a man is cut badly, comes in at night, and the next day a house has burned to the ground and the man and his wife who lived there died in the flames. Now he dealt with a badly stabbed and cut leg on a man in a black suit who came in after midnight. The doctor would keep it all to himself, but he had a mental list of the men hurt at night and the series of vigilante actions the same night. If anyone asked, he could name the five men who were known in Yankton as the Five Angels of Death.

But so far, he wasn't talking.

Chapter Four

When the *Far West* docked at the rickety wharf at Yankton, Buckskin Morgan and Melinda Warnick watched closely as the cabin passengers left the boat. He could detect no one limping, no one with a bandaged hand, arm or shoulder, and no signs of any dressings at all. There were a dozen or so—several single men, four couples and an assortment of children and mothers.

No one bothered Buckskin and Melinda as they left at the end of the passenger line. He had his hand near his Colt, but no one made a try to capture or harm Melinda. He frowned. Why would they be so intent on killing her last night, but now in daylight not make a move toward her? They might have decided they were mistaken, or maybe that they would find her later.

The crewmen waited impatiently behind them to start unloading the small orders of freight in wooden and cardboard boxes and sacks that did not have to be lowered to the wharf by the forward loading derricks.

Buckskin kept his right hand free and close to his holster as they walked down the plank and to the dock, then across it and to the dirt street that stretched out a dozen blocks ahead. Nobody paid any attention to them.

Buckskin evaluated the small town as they walked. A hotel down a block seemed to be the closest one. Yankton had been described as twice as bad as the lawless railhead towns that rose up whenever another railroad pushed out into the west.

He saw saloon after saloon, gambling parlors, and dozens of painted women waving at him out of second-story windows. He saw no one with a star on his shirt. Everyone wore guns, even some of the women whom he figured were fancy ladies out for a stroll or for some shopping. A girl couldn't be too careful.

They registered at the Dakota Arms Hotel in separate rooms but both on the second floor. He asked for room 22 and got it. It was a tradition of sorts with him. Buckskin always got room 22 in any hotel he stayed at if at all possible.

He walked her to her room 28 door.

"Good luck on your search for your sister."

Melinda looked up with troubled eyes. "I thought sure that you would help me. I mean after last night when you were shot at and all."

"As I remember it, the gunman was shooting at you."

"Oh, true. But you did help me feel safe. I just thought—"

"As I told you, Melinda, I already have a job, and I better get busy trying to find the lady I'm hunting or I'll be out of a job. Again, good luck and take care of yourself. Last night these men seemed determined and were not afraid to use their guns. Today they didn't show up at all. Maybe they've changed their minds about harming you."

He tipped his hat, turned and walked down to his room. It was about normal for 1881 in the wild west. A single bed, a dresser with a mirror that had more distortions than a reflection pond on a windy day. One straight-backed chair sat against the wall, and the window opened to the street. He pushed back the thin white curtains and looked down.

He saw three men talking and then looking up straight at his window. Company? So soon? It had to be from the missing Warnick girl, Maria. Nobody else knew he was in town. Damn. He didn't need any complications. He eased back from the window, picked up his carpetbag and went down the hall to room 26. His key opened the door. Most of these door locks were jokes. There were three basic types of skeleton keys to fit the locks. If you had all three you could get into 90 percent of the rooms in most hotels.

He slipped inside and locked the door behind him. Two of the same men he had seen staring at him stood in the street and watched the hotel. The third one was gone. Buckskin watched a moment, then checked his six-gun, put his carpetbag on the bed and unpacked. He might be staying awhile and the shirts could hang out their wrinkles. He found a dozen wire coat hangers in the small closet.

He changed clothes, putting on a black Stetson that had seen many a trail ride, black shirt and a leather vest. The small difference in attire might get the riverboat hustlers off his trail.

He started at one of the better-looking saloons, ordered a beer at the stand-up bar and leaned on the mahogany bar watching the drinkers and gamblers. Players sat at six poker games, while other gambling games drew the attention of more players. The barkeep looked up at him when he waved.

"I'm new in town. What's the word on the local sheriff?"

The barkeep was a big man, over six feet and wide as an ax handle, with a shaggy mane of brown hair, a broken nose, alert brown eyes and hands like ham hocks but that had a delicate touch with a glass. "Hell, he got elected again. Stays out of trouble. Why you asking?"

"In town on business. Like to know how the law is set up. If anybody is buying it and what the price is."

The barkeep grinned. "No need for that in this town. We got ourselves some gents who take care of the tough stuff. Some black-hooded night riders. We call them the Five Angels of Death."

"Night riders?"

"You bet your billy. Sheriff don't have much law work to do except the paper stuff, county taxes, things like that."

"Thanks. Good things to know getting settled in a new town."

He worked three more saloons, heard about the same thing at each one. The sheriff of Yankton County was Jared Van Dyke. He had jurisdiction over a large swatch of land extending more than a hundred miles to the north and fifty miles each side of the town of Yankton.

When the Dakota Territory was first organized every bit of the land had to be cut up into counties and officers elected. By making huge counties, it took less organizing and fewer elections. They could always split the counties later if the people living there wanted to.

Buckskin found a cafe between two low-class saloons and enjoyed a surprisingly good steak dinner. When he finished, a man came in, watched Buckskin a moment and then hurried toward him. The man stopped four feet away and cleared his throat. Buckskin looked at him. He was small and slender, maybe five feet five. He wore a derby hat and a suit. Maybe a merchant.

"Mister, I hear you're just off the sternwheeler from Denver and that you're a detective. We sure need one in town. Can I talk to you?"

Buckskin shook his head and rose from the table. "Sorry, you've got the wrong man. I've been in town for a month. You best look somewhere else."

"Goldangit! I was sure they said you was the one. With that gun tied so low and all. Well, if'n you say so." The man walked away, took another look at Buckskin and went out the door.

"Who was that?" Buckskin asked the barkeep. The man chuckled.

"That's a man who's gonna get his neck stretched one of these days. He claims to be the head of the committee to stamp out the vigilantes. First thing he knows, he'll get stamped out."

"These vigilantes that powerful in town?"

"Oh, hell, yes. Almost nobody says a word against the Five Angels of Death. Not anymore. They don't strike so often now, but when they do, it's serious. Just last night a Chinaman and his wife and baby got themselves killed when their shack upstream got itself burned to the ground. Nobody knows anything about it, of course. Just an accident. Nobody would have the nerve to look at the bodies for bullet holes."

"Yeah, we all got our troubles," Buckskin said. He decided not to show Dawn Evans' picture to anyone yet. He'd wander around town first and see what he could dig up.

He surveyed the ten biggest saloons in town that night. He learned nothing about a red-haired young woman in town only a few months who loved to play poker.

At the Lonely Trail Saloon he found a man who said they had a redheaded girl who sang there now and again. Usually on Friday and Saturday nights. The man had no idea how old the woman was but he thought considerably more than 25.

Buckskin checked every poker game in the ten saloons and found not a woman at any of them. About midnight he gave up and went back to the Dakota Arms Hotel. He went through the lobby quickly and up to room 22, then he grinned and continued on to room 26. He eased the key in the lock hoping the room hadn't been rented to someone else. Inside he lit the lamp and found no one there and his gear intact.

He heard the door open behind him and whirled, his .45 leaping from leather into his hand as his thumb cocked the hammer back so the gun was ready to fire.

Melinda Warnick stood there in the same brown outfit she had worn on the boat. She gave him a tired smile, closed the door and held out her hand for the key. He handed it to her. She turned it, locking it, then twisted the key halfway around so another key from the outside couldn't push it out.

"I've been waiting for hours in the lobby for you to come back. I tried your room, twenty-two, but you weren't there."

"Melinda—"

"I know, you're tired. You've been working your other job, and you want to get some sleep. I do, too. But first I want to try to persuade you to help me."

She unbuttoned the brown blouse and, before he could protest, finished the task and let the blouse slide off her shoulders. This time she wore no chemise and her breasts glowed soft white at him with large pink areolas and red nipples. Her breasts were large and even with nothing holding them showed a line of cleavage.

"Melinda, I told you . . ."

She walked across the room and reached up and kissed his lips hard, then opened her mouth and found his lips parting and jammed her tongue into his mouth. When she broke off the kiss she caught both his hands and brought them up to cover her breasts.

"Yes, that's better," she said. "Now, tell me that you're not even the slightest bit interested in undressing me the rest of the way."

Buckskin gave a tired little sigh, then bent and kissed her and his hands caressed her breasts until she began to pant through the kiss.

"Oh, damn," she whispered when he stopped the kiss. "Oh, damn." She pulled off his vest and unbuttoned his shirt and then played with his chest hair for a moment. She pulled the shirt out of his pants and threw it on the floor, then worked on his belt.

He took off his gunbelt, then opened his pants belt, and she undid the fly buttons and pulled down his trousers. He wore white underwear.

"My God, look at that bulge. You have a serious swelling down there, kind sir."

He growled at her and found the button at the side and dropped her skirt, then the three petticoats, and found she wore short bloomers. They sat on the bed and she rolled on top of him.

"I'm not nearly as tired as I was a few minutes ago," she said. Her hand found his erection through the thin underwear and she gripped it. "Oh, not nearly as tired."

He kissed her again and fondled her hanging breasts until she whimpered.

"Spank me," she whispered. "Not too hard, just hard enough."

He spanked her round bottom until it turned red

and she yelped and nodded. He pulled down her bloomers and then lifted his hips so she could take off his underwear and they came together on the bed again. This time he was on top.

She began to cry, silently. Huge tears spilled over her eyelids and rolled down her cheeks. She smiled through it and nodded. "It's all right. I always cry when I'm happy, and right now I'm so happy I could bust. Please, now."

He moved and adjusted her and then with one stroke drove into her lubricated sheath.

"Oh, God!" she yelped. Then she cried again and wiped the tears away and smiled up at him.

"You are delicious. Simply delicious and good enough to eat. And I may have some bites of you before morning." Her hips came up to meet him, jolting their pelvic bones together with a satisfying thump, and then he started a slow stroke that she kept up with.

"Some women talk when they're getting laid, did you know that? Some really like to talk. I don't, usually I'm quiet, trying to find out what the man is feeling. Right now I don't care what you feel. I'm so pleased and getting fucked so good that I don't give a fig about anything but my own little pussy getting poked and poked and poked.

"Oh, no, it's almost here!" Then her eyes went wide and she stiffened and her whole body shook like a leaf in a windstorm. She rattled and spasmed again and again until he thought she would tear herself apart.

Suddenly it was over. She grinned at him,

reached up and kissed him, then fell down and began humping at him.

"Come on, I'm one ahead of you. Time to make your old cock do his business."

Buckskin laughed and stroked and built up a rhythm and power and slammed into her faster and faster. Then it was time. He moaned and growled and then he felt his muscles tighten and his hands grip the mattress as he crashed through a brick wall in a driving steam engine, blasting bricks a block down the street and racing ahead off the tracks until the engine gave one last puff and died right there in the middle of Union Station.

He thrust once more and lowered himself on her slender form, watching her breasts flatten with his weight on them.

She sighed. He gasped for air like the steam engine he had just left, struggling to get enough air back in his lungs to replace the oxygen when he didn't dare breathe. His panting slowed and stopped, and she laughed softly.

"Oh, it takes you a time to get there but then you are fantastic. That was beautiful. Now, I'm ready to talk business. I can't pay you much. In fact I can't pay you anything, but you can use my hotel bedroom and my willing body whenever you want to. All I ask is that as you're poking around town, be on the lookout for my sister.

"She's my size, has long blonde hair, or at least she did, and has my build. Actually my titties are a little bigger than hers but don't tell her I said so. You can do that much, can't you? It won't take away from your time on your other case."

She reached up and kissed his lips, then his nose, then both his eyes and his lips again.

"Please help me. There's no one else. So far I haven't been able to find anyone who even saw Maria. I can't go into those saloons, but I bet they'd remember her when she sang there. I don't know which one she sang at."

He put a finger over her lips.

"All right, I'll ask some questions and keep my eyes and ears open. I can't guarantee anything."

"Good, good, good. Great!" She rolled him off her and they came apart and she sat up. "I can guarantee to take care of your many needs once or twice a day, whatever it is you want. Just crook your finger and I'll be here or in my room. Maybe even that big couch in the lobby if it's late enough at night." She saw his surprised expression.

"I'm just kidding. I wish I'd thought to bring some cheese and crackers, or some beer or something. We're bound to get hungry before the night is over. If I read you right, Buckskin Lee Morgan, big-time detective from Denver, you are not a man to be satisfied with one roll in the old bed. You'll need three or four at least."

Buckskin sat up beside her and nodded. "Four or five at least, depending how long both of us can stay awake."

It was three times. Shortly after two A.M. they fell asleep in each other's arms.

That same night in the upstairs rooms of the Criterion Saloon where Nate Hill had his quarters, Nate sat on the side of a big double bed with feather mattress beside Sherry Crawford. His hand fondled her bare breasts and he bent and kissed both of them.

"You are so good at what you do, sweetheart."

"What's that, playing poker or getting poked?"

"Both, as a matter of fact. Yes, both. I've never seen anyone bluff the way you can. And when you lean forward and let the sucker have a good long look at your tits, you almost never lose a hand. I remember a couple of guys were talking about that before the game started, and they swore that they wouldn't look no matter if you were naked from the waist up.

"Yeah, that's what they said. Both looked plenty and both wound up losing their cash."

"You sure nobody saw me come up here?" Sherry asked.

"Damn sure. I sent everybody home and told them I'd lock up. We've got to protect your reputation. It's besmirched enough with you consorting with gamblers in a saloon. I'm sure a lot of the hoity-toity society ladies wouldn't even speak to you."

Sherry giggled. "You don't have any society ladies in town, unless you mean the Women's Society of the Baptist Church."

"You are a wicked woman, Sherry Crawford."

"Probably. How much time do I still owe you?"

"Ten months after tomorrow."

"How much money do I have that you've saved for me from twenty-five percent of my poker winnings?"

"You asked me yesterday."

"I'm asking again. I want to see the bank book

with my name on it. Show me."

He moved to a small office and came back with a small blue book with "Yankton Territorial Bank" printed on the front. She opened it and looked at the last figure.

"Three thousand, two hundred and forty-five dollars. Wow, I'm rich. Just like I was in Denver. Did I tell you I used to go out in an afternoon and spend two hundred dollars on clothes and jewelry?"

"You told me. But all that spending still didn't make you happy."

"What really didn't make me happy was that limp prick my so-called husband had. It would take me a half hour of coaxing to get it hard, then once inside he'd pump twice and go soft again. I got so wild crazy for a good fuck I jumped the gardener one day in the tool shed. Damn, but he was good. I think he was about twenty-five or so."

Nate bent and kissed her breasts again. She reached for his crotch and began to play with his limp tool.

"One more?" she asked.

"You're trying to wear me out so I'll have palpitations of my heart and die. You'd do anything to get out of an honest bet."

"It was in the heat of battle. You shouldn't have held me to it."

"Hey, a bet is a bet. No welcher gets to play poker in Yankton. All the saloon owners made a pact. A welcher gets thrown out of town on the next sternwheeler."

"But if I could have kept all of my winning, I'd have over twelve thousand dollars by now."

"Not so, Sherry, my dear. You wouldn't have had me in there shilling for you and driving up the size of the pot and then folding with no bellow of rage."

She grinned. "Yeah, true. You're a good help. But ten more months? Hey, every time you poke me you should take off a week."

"Not a chance. I won you fair and square. The minute you bet your ass and jumped up on the table and sat your pussy down on the pot to cover that last four hundred dollars I bet more than you had, you sold the whole package."

She shrugged. "Yeah. What the hell. It's just a year, no ten more months. Then I can always go back to Denver and play the rich society bitch again. Or maybe I'll go to Alaska. Up there I could sell my pussy nights and play poker all day. Yeah, might think about doing that."

"You'd become a whore?"

"What the hell you think I am right now?"

Nate Hill sat back from her and shook his head. "Hey, baby. You're no fucking whore. Told you I'd marry you a dozen times. Get some judge to give you a divorce, send the papers to Denver, and you'd be free and clear to marry me. Then we could really clean up at poker in this town. There's more money around here than you can shake your tits at."

Sherry shook her head, sending her short black hair swirling around her head. "No, not a chance. Old Hal Evans is my ace in the hole. He's my life ring if all else fails. I can wire him that I need money and he'd have a thousand or two thousand for me in the time it takes the key to click out the message. But that's just in an emergency in case everything else fails."

"That ain't never gonna happen, baby. Not with me around," Nate Hill said.

She looked at him curiously for a second, then removed his hands from her breasts and reached for a frilly, lace-trimmed nightgown.

"Now, just what would I get if I married you that I'm not getting now? If you're getting serviced by the bull, why buy him?"

"You'd get security, a wild, wild, wild time in bed or on the kitchen table or on the craps table downstairs whenever you want it. You can get poked five or six times a night anytime you want to. What more could a girl want?"

"Want? Want?" She stood and planted her fists on bare hips and spread her feet, her face angry and thoughtful at the same time.

"I'll tell you what I want. I went the wrong way on the Missouri. I should be in New Orleans right now where they know how to spend money on a lady, where they know how to gamble. Where a lady's bottom on a poker table means for the night, not fifty-two fucking, goddamn fucking weeks. That's what I want. I want you to sell this shitty little game room you've got here and take me to New Orleans where we can open a huge gambling hall and make ourselves a ton of money."

"New Orleans . . . damn. That's the big time. You need fifty thousand dollars just to buy a building down there. Then another hundred thousand to set it up and hire help. I don't have that kind of money. This place is worth maybe twenty thousand if I found somebody crazy enough to buy into this place. Them damn night riders gonna be the death of this little territorial village yet."

"So find yourself a new pussy. You don't get me in your bed anymore. As soon as that ten months is up, I'm on my way to Louisiana and New Orleans where the gentlemen know how to treat a fucking lady the way she deserves."

Nate Hill sat there naked and scowling. "You made a bet and you'll by damn live up to it. Your ass in my bed whenever I want it, that was the way you said it. That's the way it's gonna be. Hell, I thought you were happy here. You don't have to worry if you hit a losing streak. I'll take over the winning. Shit, Sherry, you've got the best possible deal here teaming up with me. You can't beat it anywhere on the river."

"Some of the locals know what's going on with you shilling for me and upping the ante," she said.

"Yeah, but most of our big-money players are just passing through, or in town to make a killing somewhere else. No worry there."

Sherry sighed and sat down next to him. She reached over and picked up his limp penis and began to stroke it, watching it start to respond.

"Oh, hell. Maybe you're right. I'll hold on a while longer here, but you start treating me nicer, you hear? A little romance sometimes, not just 'I need a fuck, baby, spread your legs.' A woman needs more tenderness than that. Like now. Pretend I'm your first and you can't wait and you want me, but it's my first time too. So you have to seduce me nice and gentle and slow. Got to take you more than an hour to get my clothes off. Come on, it'll be fun. Let's both get dressed and then have a fun little game of pretend."

He looked over at her and bent and kissed her breasts, then looked up. "You really want to do this."

"Yes, really. Come on, it'll be exciting. We can go slow and build until we're crazy and then do all sorts of wild, outrageous things."

Hill shrugged. "Hell, why not? Anything to keep you happy, at least for a while yet. Get your naked little ass dressed, I'm gonna peel you like a banana before we're done."

Chapter Five

The next morning, Buckskin Lee Morgan worked the saloons. The three biggest ones were open when he checked them a little after ten o'clock. He went into the Criterion, the nicest looking of the three. It had swinging doors, a solid floor, stand-up bar and room for a dozen or more poker tables and other games of chance. A stairway toward the back led upward and, he assumed, to the cribs.

There were no girls in sight and only one poker game going with a ten-cent limit on bets. He asked the barkeep if he had any coffee but the apron shook his head.

"You want coffee, they got it at that cafe across the street."

Buckskin had a beer instead and talked to the barkeep. First the weather, then the high level of the river and the story about the little town upriver that grew and prospered for ten years, then one spring the high water came and when the current settled down to normal two months later, the permanent channel of the river had shifted a mile and a half to the west.

"That little town died like an overripe melon in a dry summer," the apron said.

"There any good poker games around town?" Buckskin asked.

"You talking about good poker or high-stakes poker?" the barman asked as he preened a handlebar moustache that curled up on each end. "Them's two different kind of games most of the time. Don't often see good poker when the money in the pot gets too high. It gets to be too emotional."

"Agreed. So where is the big-money game in town?"

"We got one right here. Most of them are at night. But the one where the most money changes hands is on Friday night. Got to have two hundred and fifty dollar in chips to get in the back door. Big Wally stands guard. No lookers back there."

"Sounds like I might get to lose some of my daddy's money yet," Buckskin said. "He sends me up here like an errand boy to look for property to buy. Why does he want land up here, anyway? Hell, the river might change course again and Yankton could be a mile away from deep water."

"True, true. But you can't count on the Missouri to do anything. Now, if you still want a big-money game, you come Friday and bring lots of your daddy's money."

Buckskin finished his beer, waved at the apron and went out the front door. He asked about big-money games at the Beer Bucket Saloon. It was fancied up inside, had a small eatery along one side and the bar and poker tables down the other. Lots of different gambling games for the men's choice. Buckskin didn't see a stairway but it could be in back somewhere. He figured a place this fancy would also have easy women.

A poker game was in progress in the middle of the room and he pulled up a chair and watched. Five men played, the bet limit evidently was a dollar. On a seven-card stud game he saw the pot build into a respectable pile of greenbacks. No chips were used here.

When the hand finished, Buckskin stood and waved at the group.

"Gents, are there any big-money poker games around town? I'm new here, won't be here long and got a hankering to shed a little of my pappy's hard-earned money."

"How big?" a small man with a lisp who had just won the pot asked. "You can join our little game. Just for you we'll lift the bet limit to two dollars."

"I was hoping for something a little stronger than that."

"You want big money you get here on a Thursday night. They play it in the back room and I ain't never been there. Got to have two hundred cash money to get past the guard at the door."

"Two hundred is a start. Hey, they ever have any women play in this game? I hear there's a red-headed woman on the river somewhere who is the best at playing poker in a thousand-mile stretch."

"Ain't here then. We got us a woman player who usually is over at one of the other saloons, but she's got short black hair. So it couldn't be her."

Could be, Buckskin figured. He watched the next hand, then sauntered out of the place. A woman player at one of the saloons. Interesting. Did she play every night or just on the big-money game nights? He'd have to find out.

The third saloon had a sign up that said River Rat Saloon, and there were more men in it now that it was almost noon. Three men at the bar, four poker tables working, and some 21 games and lots of action at the faro and three-card monte tables.

A seat opened in a six-man card game and Buckskin asked if he could join them.

"You got twenty bucks for a fifty-cent limit game, you're in," a man with a full beard and spectacles said. His voice came out as a grunt and the others nodded. One man held a box of chips and took Buckskin's two ten-dollar greenbacks and gave him stacks of red, white and blue chips.

He played for half an hour and lost about ten dollars' worth of his stack. When it was his turn to deal, he looked around the table.

"Any big-money games in this town? I'm new here and I'm trying to lose my old man's money."

One of the men laughed. "Just stay right here, sonny, and we'll make it a five-dollar a bet limit, you want to play heavy."

"I was thinking more like no limit on bets."

The men frowned and looked at one another.

"That'd be the Wednesday night game in the back

room," the man with the beard said. His eyes showed more life now. "Can't say as I've ever been there, but I hear that some of them pots got a thousand dollars in them."

"Sucker bets," another player said. "Bunch of cheating bastards who try to outcheat each other without getting caught. Man who cheats the best wins the most."

"Hear there's a redheaded woman playing in town. She come to this Wednesday night game?"

A thin man with a slight hunch to his back blew his nose in a linen handkerchief and shook his head. "No such. We do got one woman who plays back there now and again. But, she's got black hair and it's short. They do got a hundred-dollar minimum stakes game going back there most every night. Don't know if no women play, but you could ask."

"Must be the wrong woman," Buckskin said. He concentrated on his poker then, always dealing five-card draw, and in ten minutes won his ten dollars back and bowed out of the game. He was a one-dollar winner when he cashed in. He chuckled and tossed the winning dollar chip into the pot for the next game.

He had just stepped outside when one of the men from the poker game came out behind him. He hadn't said much at the table, but now looked concerned in the noontime sunshine. He nodded at Buckskin and waved a hand. "You was talking about big-money poker. Knew a man who tried to get in that back room. Claimed he was a good poker player. Guess he was, but he played two weeks, and the third Wednesday night somebody put a knife between his ribs and we buried him the next day. The game here ain't one of the kindest."

Buckskin nodded. He wondered what this man's purpose was in following him outside. Surely not just to warn him about the dangers of playing high-stakes poker.

"So I'll watch my back. Was there anything else?"

"Well . . . yes, there is. Can we walk away from here? This place makes me nervous."

Buckskin shrugged and they walked down the street. The man beside him was a head shorter, wore a proper suit with a vest and a town hat with the brim snapped down. He cleared his throat twice before he started talking.

"A friend of mine asked me to talk to you. He's sure you're the man we sent to Omaha for. Didn't you get a letter from somebody here in town asking you to come and help us overcome a problem with vigilantes?"

"That again. Like I told your friend, I'm not the gent you wrote to. I'm here on other business. I hope this clears up any misunderstanding."

"Oh, yes, I'm sure it will. It's just that with your gun tied so low and the way you walk, like you're stalking a tiger or something, we figured you were the gunfighter we sent for."

"Do the Angels of Death know you sent for somebody?"

The man shivered and looked over his shoulder, and a muscle under his eye twitched. "We're not sure. Nobody knows who those five men are all dressed in black. I hear they murdered the Chinese family who lived out of town a ways. Sounds like them."

"Good luck in your endeavor. You're the ones who should be watching your backs, if what I hear about these night riders is true."

The man nodded. "Oh, we know it. I have two firearms on me right now and I bet you didn't know. If they try for one of us, we're going to kill one of them. They only have five. We have a lot more than that."

The man sighed. "I know we have a big job. That's why we're looking for help."

"Sorry, I'm not your man. Your gent from Omaha probably will be on the next boat."

The man frowned. "Not all that sure. We only offered him two hundred dollars and his expenses. Not sure he'll come for that."

"So about all you can do is wait. Now I do have some other business. Sorry I can't help you." Buckskin walked into a cafe and looked at the bill of fare printed on a chalkboard. The offerings consisted mostly of sandwiches, soups and steak. He headed for a stool at the counter just as a delicate arm pushed through his and held on.

"Mr. Morgan. I was hoping I'd find you. I think I owe you a lunch, as they're calling the noon meal now in the east. May I take you to lunch here at the Sandwich Box Cafe?"

Melinda Warnick looked up at him from soft brown eyes and Buckskin grinned.

"Now that's the best offer I've had all morning. I'm warning you that I'm a big eater."

She smiled and her face became gently beautiful.

"Oh, I remember about that. You nearly ate up half my sandwiches on that sternwheeler where we were trapped together on the run up here from Omaha. Could we sit by the window? I do enjoy watching the people going past."

They found a small table next to the window and she frowned slightly, dampening her fine smile.

"Have you discovered anything yet about my sister?"

"I've been doing some talking around, but I haven't seen or heard anything yet. There is a vigilante group in town. Do you think they would have anything to do with her vanishing?"

"I can't think why they should. Maria was just trying to make a living singing. I do have a bad feeling about this."

A young girl came and took their order. Both had the roast beef sandwich with mustard and horseradish and big cups of coffee. He watched Melinda as she ate. She was more on the cute side than beautiful with a gamin-type face that made you want to take care of her. The rest of her was delicious and sexy—long blonde hair and a svelte, curvy body that showed more than it should in the dress that she wore. He'd have to warn her that this wasn't Omaha or Denver where women on the streets were a little safer.

After they ate, he paid the tab and ushered her outside.

"Oh, darn. I was going to buy you lunch."

"You have to be fast when the bill comes," Buckskin said. They paused on the street in an awkward moment. He wasn't sure what she had wanted when she saw him in the cafe. She looked at him and then away.

"Well, I guess you have things to do. I should be talking to the people at the other hotel I haven't been to yet. Maria must have stayed at the last one. She wasn't registered at any of the other ones."

"Good, do that. Might give you a lead. I'll write you a note in your box at the hotel if I find anything." She nodded, and he waved, turned and walked away. He wasn't sure what to do next. There would be a poker game that night, a hundred-dollar stakes game. He wondered if he should get in it. The money was no problem. He could lose dollars a night and not worry. Then again he might win. Did he have to get in the poker game to see if there was a redheaded woman player? He wasn't sure. Maybe get to the saloon early and watch the people who went inside the back room. Yes, that would be a good idea.

The rest of the afternoon he made inquiries at several stores and shops, then at cafes and restaurants, but nobody had seen a long-haired redheaded woman in the past month. She had to live somewhere, to buy food if she had a house, to eat out in a cafe if she lived in a hotel. Nothing meshed.

He saw the undertaker's parlor and went across the street and walked inside. A bell tinkled when he closed the door. A fat man wearing a white smock came out a curtained doorway and stared at Buckskin.

"Yes? How may I help you, sir?"

"Did you handle the three bodies from the fire up the river last night?"

"I did. I'm the only undertaker and funeral parlor in town."

"Congratulations. I'm going to ask you a question you might not want to answer. On the death certificates, what was named as the cause of death?"

"Accidental death by fire."

"You're sure?"

"Yes. I signed them in lieu of an attending physician."

"So what was the real cause of death?" Buckskin demanded, his tone serious, cold.

"I just told you—"

"I said the actual cause of death, not what the sheriff wanted you to put on the papers."

"I'm afraid I can't help you. The cause of death—"

"Yes, you said, fire. Did each of the bodies have one or more bullet holes in it?"

"Bullet holes? I really can't say. They were all badly burned."

"But not so badly that you couldn't find a bullet hole. Did you find any?"

"May I ask who you are?"

"Just a man in the town wondering why a fit Chinese man and his active wife would die in a fire along with their child in a small shack like I'm told they lived in."

The man mopped his forehead with a handkerchief. He looked at the door and motioned Buckskin into the back room. It held a dozen caskets of different sizes including one child's.

"So what killed the three Chinese?"

The man mopped his face again and looked

around. "Understand I have a family. Three boys and a little girl and a wife. I don't want nothing to happen to them. The sheriff tells me it was fire, I say it was fire."

"But it wasn't?"

The undertaker shook his head. His voice came softly, almost a whisper. "Gunshots. At least two in each body. May have been more. I covered the bullet holes so no one could tell later . . . if they dug up the bodies."

Buckskin nodded. "I understand. No one will know you told me. I'll go out the back way. Thanks."

He went through the side door into the alley and around the block. So the Five Angels of Death had done in the Chinese. Probably to "purify" the town of the heathen Chinese. It was good to know, but not really his problem. He got back to thinking how he could find a woman who didn't want to be found. She would have changed her appearance, and probably her name, first and last. Or maybe just her last name. Her looks? Could the woman poker player here with short dark hair be the redhead from Denver who had cut and dyed her hair? Could be. Might not be. First he'd have to find the woman. That started tonight.

He had a quick supper and went to the saloon where the big game was set for later that evening. The barkeep said it was always set to start at eight, but usually didn't open until about eight thirty.

Buckskin warmed up with some dime poker and won three pots in a row, then had a beer and took a table near the door that led into the back room. The barkeep had said that the minimum for tonight in the back room game was 100 dollars. He'd already sold three boxes of chips and the gents were waiting to play.

"No women playing tonight?"

"Damn few times we get a woman here. Oh, there's one in town now, but she usually don't play here. Said she tried us once and the stakes were too low and the beer worse than hog swill. Don't think she'll be back, but you can't tell."

It was nearly eight o'clock when Buckskin fished out five twenty-dollar bills and bought a box of chips from the barkeep. He showed them to the huge man at the door to the rear room who had suddenly appeared, and was granted entrance.

It was a musty, poorly lighted room not more than fifteen feet square. A table with green felt on it and eight sides sat in the middle of the space with two shaded lamps that cast an adequate if not outstanding light on the table. There were eight chairs around the table but only four of them were being used.

Buckskin dropped into an open chair, placed his chips on the table in front of him and looked at the competition. He picked out the house man, the one with the red checkered gambler's vest and a black cigar. The man nodded and then gave Buckskin a long stare.

"Mister, don't I know you from someplace?" the checkered vest man asked.

"Could be, I've been a few places. How many playing tonight?"

"Six, and you make seven if they all show. We got damn few house rules here. Straight poker, no weird games. Deal rotates. Any man caught cheating loses his stake and the pot and goes out the back door with a bloody face. Agreed?"

Buckskin nodded.

"No markers allowed unless you can prove you can pay it. Cash on your person is accepted if you run out of chips. No limit on bets, no continuing to play if you run out of chips and cash. No light pots."

"Good," Buckskin said. "Let's get started."

The checkered vest grunted, brought out a deck of cards and let the man next to him break the seal and take out the deck of cards wrapped in thin paper. The two jokers were torn into pieces and thrown on the floor, then the house man shuffled. He knew his cards and probably cheated when he knew he could get away with it.

A tall man with red hair and a red beard rushed into the room waving his box of chips.

"Damn it, Scurvy, wait for me. I told you I'd by-God be here. Damn current held us up a good half hour." The man slid into a chair, took off his jacket and rolled up his sleeves two folds and waited for his cards.

Buckskin watched the other players the first two games. Both were straight draw poker. He bet conservatively and dropped out early. By the third hand he had figured out two of the men and had his sights set on the third of the six men in the game. Buckskin won the third game, a pot with over twenty dollars in it. As usual, everyone bet a dollar on raises. It was the way most games started as the players felt out each other.

Buckskin had made a five-dollar raise on the

third pot, three men still in dropped out, and the fourth called him. He had aces and jacks to beat the other man's queens over sixes.

Each time Buckskin dealt the cards, the house man watched him with unabashed concentration. On Buckskin's fourth deal he was over a hundred dollars ahead and the man across from him kept lighting a hand-rolled cigarette, then pinching it out and lighting it again. He yelled in fury when he lost the next hand, and flared up at Buckskin even though he wasn't in the hand after the second raise.

On Buckskin's next deal the man with the much lighted cigarette dropped his cards and leaped to his feet. His hand streaked toward his six-gun on his hip. Buckskin eased upward and his right hand came up with his iron and drilled a slug through the edge of the table six inches from where the man stood still trying to get his gun cocked and aimed.

The sound of the .45 round exploding in the room caused four of the men to clamp their hands over their ears to shut out the bouncing thunder of the shot. The man with the hand gun out but not aimed at Buckskin slowly let the weapon swing down to the floor, then he dropped it and began to shake all over.

The house man picked up the six-gun and helped the man out of the room. He had only ten dollars left in his chip box. One of the other players pushed the ten dollars into the pot, and when the house man came back he nodded at Buckskin.

"I think it was your deal," the house man said staring at Buckskin. He nodded and began to deal for five-card draw. Two hands later, Buckskin picked up his chips and stood.

"That's it for me, gentlemen. Have a good game."

"You can't quit a big winner," one of the men whined.

"Big winner?" Buckskin asked. "I'm maybe forty dollars ahead. You call that a big winner?"

"Shut up, Harley," the house man said. Another man dropped out of the game and he and Buckskin both cashed in at the bar. The small man with a Vandyke beard had come up a twenty-dollar loser.

"Usually I lose more than that," the man said. He took the money and frowned at Buckskin. "You're new in town."

"How can you tell?"

"Haven't seen you around. Big man like you gets noticed. Especially one who carries his iron tied that low. We're not exactly a wild west town here."

"Plenty wild from the six-guns I see on the street. I'm looking for a woman poker player. Supposed to be the best on the river. Long red hair. You heard of her?"

The man lit a thin cheroot and blew out a cloud of blue smoke. "Can't say that I have. Of course, I don't play all the big games. One woman in town now and then. I think she works the sternwheelers and then heads on down the Mississippi. She doesn't show up often, but she has short dark hair."

"Must not be the one I want to play against. I love a good poker game, and up and down the river I hear about this beautiful redhead who is a wow at poker."

The man with the Vandyke beard frowned. "Don't know if I could keep my mind on the cards."

"Could be a problem." Buckskin waved. "Maybe we'll play again sometime."

The man held out his hand. "I'm Van Dalton, a businessman here in town."

Buckskin took the hand. "Buckskin Morgan. I'm scouting property my father may want to buy."

"You're good at poker. I enjoy good poker whether I win or lose. Thanks for an entertaining evening."

Buckskin grinned, waved and headed for his hotel. Time to be calling it a night and figure out what to do tomorrow.

He had been in room 26 at the Dakota Arms Hotel for over an hour when he heard the explosion. It rattled the window and door and boomed through the wooden building like a thunderclap. Buckskin pushed open his door and looked down the hall. He saw a door sagging on its hinges. By the time he ran down there, three other men had arrived to look into the room. He saw the number over the door, 22. His registered room.

Acrid smoke and fumes filled the end of the hall and the inside of the room. Slowly the fumes and smoke blew out the window.

The desk clerk bustled into the scene and scurried back when he smelled the smoke.

"Dynamite," Buckskin said when somebody asked what happened. A few minutes later the room had cleared of smoke and Buckskin and two others went inside.

"Damned strange," one of the men said. "Look at the roofing nails sticking into the walls and furniture. Damned strange."

It wasn't strange to Buckskin at all. He'd used the same kind of deadly bomb in desperate situations. It was made by taping large-headed inch-and-a-half-long roofing nails to a two- or three-stick dynamite bomb. Tape fifty of the nails to the dynamite and you had a deadly grenade-type bomb that would work like grapeshot, killing everyone within thirty feet.

He was the one registered in room 22. Who the hell had tried to kill him?

Chapter Six

The deputy sheriff arrived on the blast scene and Buckskin faded out of the room. He didn't want the desk clerk connecting him with room 22. What happened was obvious. The window glass had shattered inside the room.

That meant the bomb had been thrown into the room from the outside, or maybe swung down from the roof on a string and crashed through the window.

The big question was who had ordered the kill try on him? Who knew he was in town? The riverboat attackers knew, but he had seen no indications of them. The problem was he had no idea who the sternwheeler attackers were. That was one possibility.

The other one could be the man he had beaten to

the draw that evening. Not likely. The man felt he'd been cheated and tried to draw and was humiliated. Once he cooled off he'd be glad to be alive. Drawing a gun in a card game was a known quick way to die. The poker player would realize it and be grateful, not angry.

So who the hell did that leave? The vigilantes? How could they know so quickly that he'd been nosing around about the Chinese? Even if they had found out about his visit to the undertaker, a bomb through a window didn't seem like the style for vigilante hangmen. Many times these night riders began as God-fearing men who made righteous endeavors trying to rid a community of killers and outlaws who the local law didn't or couldn't control. Over time such groups would change and could degenerate into a self-serving band of killers. He wondered how long the group here had been organized.

All of this speculation left him with no more answers than he had before.

Who had tried to kill him?

Going back to his room, he saw the door to number 28 open and Melinda poked her head out.

"What happened?"

"Somebody threw a bomb in a room I'm registered in."

She reached out and grabbed him and pulled him into her room. She wore a sheer silk nightgown that he could see right through.

"Oh, my," he said.

She scowled at him. "Somebody just tried to kill you?"

"Way it looks. That's why I often change my hotel room. Don't worry, nobody's got the job done yet."

She threw her arms around him and hugged him tightly. "This is all my fault. I got you into it. It has to be the people from the sternwheeler. They saw you with me. They saw you get off here in Yankton with me. Now they want to kill you. I'm so sorry. There must be something I can do to make it up to you." A slow smile creased her face, then blossomed into perfection. Her brown eyes sparkled and she rubbed against him with her hips.

"Now that you're here, you might as well stay." She reached up and kissed him hard on the lips and caught one of his hands and pushed it over a breast. When she broke off the kiss she tugged him toward the bed.

"It's the least I can do since I got you into trouble. Besides, there's no sense wasting this night. You're upset and I'm scared, and I want you to comfort me and we can be together and both of us will be happy. Right?"

"You have a powerful way of persuading a man," Buckskin said. He looked at her standing there in the faint light of the one turned-low lamp. Her breasts were large for a girl of her size. He bent and kissed each through the soft silk and then picked her up and carried her the two steps to the bed.

"Might be a good idea to stay here. Soon enough they'll know I wasn't in that room. They must have waited in the lobby until they saw me go up the stairs." He shook his head. "Still, no light came on in that room." He sighed. "Oh, damn, I'll worry about it in the morning."

She stretched out on the bed and spread her legs and pulled him over on top of her.

"I just love it when you smash me into the mattress this way."

She loved it the rest of the night.

The next morning a special activities committee of the Yankton Merchants' Association met in the back-room office of the Ingraham General Store. Gideon Ingraham, owner of the store, was also the town mayor and had called the meeting.

He looked around at the other four members of the committee and paced the small office in frustration. The last man, Deputy Sheriff Zebadiah Clay, had just walked in the back door of the store and into the meeting.

"Glad you could make it on short notice, Zeb. We could have a problem here. What I want to know is, did any of you have anything to do with the bomb that was thrown through the window of the hotel last night?"

He looked at each man in turn. Zeb shook his head. "I was on duty so I went and looked over the room. Nobody got killed or even hurt. Roofing nails were used in the bomb, so it was a kill try for sure."

Stacey Trumble, the town's leather expert, cobbler, saddle maker and seller of anything leather, shook his head. "Don't know nothing about it. Who the hell threw the bomb, do we know?"

"That's what we're trying to find out, Stacey," Ingraham said. "What about you, Jordan?"

"Hell, I was sleeping. Had a tough day yesterday and didn't even hear about it until this morning. I got troubles enough running the livery without doing anything like that on my own."

Van Dalton held up his hands. "Don't look at me. I have a hard enough time keeping up with our planned activities. I heard about it last night, but there's no talk around town about who threw the bomb."

Ingraham nodded. "Yeah, about what I figured. But if it wasn't us, then who did it, and why?"

"Whose room was it?" Dalton asked.

The deputy sheriff spoke up. "Registered to a guy named Buckskin Morgan. Word around town is that he's from Omaha looking for land and property to buy for his father."

"But he wasn't in the room. So was it a scare or a real try to kill him?" Dalton asked.

"Oh, a real try," the deputy said. "I've heard of those roofing-nail bombs. They can kill fifteen or twenty people at a time in a crowd. Definitely a try to kill this Morgan."

"Zeb, try to find out more about this guy. See if he's what he says he is. Somebody was in the store yesterday asking about a redheaded woman with long hair. Might have been him. My clerk said he was a stranger. This guy might be more than he says he is.

"Outside of that, I reckon we have no new business. No problem with the incident up the river the other night. If any of you have any suggestions, bring them up at the next meeting and we'll discuss them like we always do.

"Yankton is the territorial capital and we sure as hell want to keep the place as clean and upstanding as possible. I know, I know, we're a wide-open river town and some things we can't change or we'd be cutting our own throats. But, like I always say, there are some vices that we can tolerate, and some that we don't have to allow. We'll be the judge of which is which. This is the eighties now, we've got to look to the future. Some talk of moving the capitol when we get statehood in a couple of years. We can't let that happen. Yankton's been good enough for our territorial capitol since eighteen and sixty-one. Twenty years. By damn, we're good enough for the state even if they split the territory into North Dakota and South Dakota."

"Get off your politician's platform, Gideon," Dalton said. "We know you're going to run for the U.S. Senate soon as we get statehood. Let's just think about our own problems here in town."

Ingraham grinned. "Yep, you're right. I do get carried away sometimes." He looked around. "So I guess that's all. Oh, if anyone asks about the Merchants' Association committee, we met but didn't decide on any special celebration for the Fourth of July next year, but we'll have one. Any questions?"

Porter Jordan shuffled his feet and scratched his crotch as he often did. "Yeah. This guy who they tried to blow up in the hotel. If somebody else is trying to blast his head off, should we be watching him?"

"Good point, Jordan, but I don't think so. At least not right now. We do have that group trying to do us some harm. We will do better to see what we can find out about them and start putting together a list of names."

They nodded and soon drifted out through the front of the store. It was a legitimate Merchants Association committee.

When the other four were gone, Gideon Ingraham sat in his swivel chair and stared at the wall. They had done a lot of good for the capitol, for Yankton. But there was always more to do. He figured there must be over 2,000 people in town now and more coming every year. Somebody had to be on guard. It had just happened to fall his lot. He grunted as he got up from the chair and went out to the front of the store.

He loved the retail business. What was most satisfying was when he could solve a problem a customer had about what to get to fix a stove or a lamp or something around the house or yard. He loved the hardware section the most.

A customer came down the aisle between the islands filled with merchandise and Gideon walked out to meet him.

"Yes, sir, what can I do for you today?"

Buckskin and Melinda had breakfast in the Dakota Arms Hotel dining room and found that the food was not the best in town. Hot cakes, eggs and coffee were passable, but nothing to write to the state fair committee about for entry.

"Young lady, I have work to do. You must, too. So we'll go our separate ways. You realize we can't make a habit of our exchange of philosophical ideas as we did last night."

She laughed and her smile was full and undeniable. "So that's what you call it. I've often wondered." She sobered. "But you're right. I did find a man at the last hotel who remembered seeing Maria. She moved out of her hotel room after six days but she didn't say where she was heading. So I have something to go on."

They left, and he charged the breakfast to his room and checked his watch. They had slept late, not up at his usual six a.m. It was a little after nine when he walked down the street and located the biggest and best whorehouse in town. It was what they called a "parlor" house, where the girls were still the main item on the menu but where a variety of food could also be ordered, as well as wine, spirits and beer.

"It's a complete entertainment package," the woman who ran the Serendipity Restaurant and Saloon said. She greeted Buckskin with a wide smile and a wild gleam in her eye and led him to her private office.

"Fay is the name," she said. She was six feet tall, had massive breasts and a waist that had expanded with her forty years, but her face still held the hint of youthful beauty. Her hair was henna red and dark at the roots mostly hidden in a bandanna.

"Now, what is a handsome young guy like you doing asking for an old war horse like me?"

"I'm looking for a girl, two girls really. I'm hoping that you haven't seen them."

Fay nodded and waved him to an upholstered chair while she sank into another behind her desk.

"Two girls and you hope they aren't working here. I understand. Hey, I haven't always been in this business. I was on the stage for years until my looks started to go and I found out I could make more money on my back than on my feet. Hell, yes, I understand. Who are the girls?"

He showed her a picture of Dawn Evans with the long red hair.

Fay looked at the picture for a minute, then shook her head. "I've got a good eye for faces and figures. I've never seen this one, but if she wants a job, she's got it any day of the week."

"The other girl has long blonde hair, about twenty-four, has been trying to make a living as a singer. Might be working some of the fancier saloons in town."

"We don't got no fancy saloons in this jerkwater place. But it's wide open and there's lots of money here. If the capitol moves when we get statehood, a lot of money is going to take a walk upstream to Pierre. I hear they got a lock on the new capitol. Get away from the bad influences of good old Yankton."

"Have there been any blonde singers in town during the past two months?"

"Sure, three singers that I can remember, and I don't get to see them, just hear from the guys. Like how they'd like to throw a fast poking into that new singer, and they get the hots for honey and come flying down here to my hive of honeys. Don't remember hearing about any singer last three or four weeks."

"Any white slavers on the Missouri, Fay?"

"Oh, hell, yes. All the time. You just have to catch them. At least my girls have the chance to quit if they want to. I know one of my girls got caught up and put in a cabin on a sternwheeler and landed a thousand miles downstream. They kept her on laudanum all the way and used her, of course. She told me she got sold somewhere in one of the bigger river towns. She couldn't remember which one because they never let her out of her room. After a month she bribed a guard with a fast fuck and he let her get away. She came back to warn me about this particular bunch.

"I hear most of them got arrested in Omaha for kidnapping girls off the street. So that bunch can't be any trouble for you or this blonde beauty." She paused and lit a cigarette, then went on. "Let me see that picture again."

Fay covered the girl's hair and stared at the photograph. "Damn, but she reminds me of somebody in town. Just can't remember who it could be. My guess is the girl is still around somewhere. About the blonde, you her husband or something?"

"No, just helping a friend who lost her sister."

"Figured maybe you was the law. Fact is now that I think on it more, I do remember that little blonde. A real looker. She sang at the Criterion Saloon for two weeks, then quit in a tiff about her pay and went to work down at the Lucky Lady Saloon. That's the last time I remember hearing about her."

He showed Fay the picture of Dawn Evans again. "Any last-minute recollections of this little lady?"

"The hair seems wrong, somehow. Maybe I'm imagining things. Thought I saw somebody in the store the other day who looked like this but I must have been wrong. Sorry."

"Thanks for your help. Next time I need a good dinner with all the trimmings, I'll stop by."

Fay laughed and shook her head. "Not a chance, big guy. Man like you is getting all he wants regular. You don't have to buy love. Five will get you a hundred if I'm not right."

"You gamble?"

"Sometimes. I used to be a good poker player, but I'm a little rusty." She turned and waved. "You be careful now. I hear them white slavers are about as ruthless as they get when it comes to their girls."

"I'll keep that in mind."

Buckskin's next stop was the Lucky Lady Saloon. It had just opened and there weren't many patrons. He got a beer and a deck of cards and worked at some solitaire at a back table. A half hour later, two men came by asking about some poker. He shrugged and they got a 25-cent-limit game going. It lasted for an hour and three more men joined.

In a lull in the talk, Buckskin tried his leading question. "What the hell ever happened to that sweet little blonde girl who used to sing here a month or so ago?"

Most of the men shrugged. One looked up and grinned.

"Oh, yeah, I remember her. Big tits, the kind a man can get lost in if'n he ain't careful. Course I didn't have the chance. She just didn't show up one night to sing and we never saw her again."

The last man to join the game closed his hand and tapped his cards on the table. "Trying to remember this guy. One gent came in every night as long as she sang. He threw quarters on the stage and made a big play for her. Once she came to his table, but she warn't no whore, a man could tell that. The guy said he was trying to marry the girl."

Buckskin frowned. "You happen to remember who this man was?"

"Not sure. Oh, yeah, now I remember. Guy by the name of Homer who works at the tinsmith shop. Never knew his last name."

Ten minutes later, Buckskin closed out, pocketed his stack of one- and five-dollar bills in front of him and pushed some change into the next pot.

"I've got to leave, gents. It was a pleasure." The others waved and he went out the front door as if he weren't in a hurry. He was.

Across the street and half a block down, he found the Yankton Tinware store. It specialized in buckets, coal scuttles, pitchers, long-handled dippers and a hundred other items that any well-stocked kitchen or farmstead should have. The outside of the building was covered with hung-up tinware, everything from a washtub to a small bell on a string.

Inside he found a young man at the counter. He looked about 25, maybe a year older, had blond hair with a touch of brown and an open, trusting face.

"Hi, are you Homer?"

"Right as rain in the springtime. Can I help you?"

"I'm looking for someone," Buckskin said. "I hope you can give me some information."

"Well, I hope so, too. I know a few folks around town but not everybody. Seems like we get in half a hundred with every upstream sternwheeler."

"Homer, I'm hunting Maria Warnick."

The young man jumped as if he'd been hit with

a club. His eyes widened and he leaned forward over the counter.

"Maria? You know where she is?"

"No. But I understand that you knew her here in town and were friendly with her."

"Oh, damn. I thought you'd found her. Yes, I knew Maria, as well as anyone in town. She kept to herself most of the time, except when she sang. She was quiet that way, but when she started to sing on that little stage, she was a knockout."

"Then one day she didn't come to work at the Lucky Lady?" Buckskin probed.

"Yes, yes, that's right. No goodbyes, no hug or even a handshake. We had made some plans. She just vanished."

"Did she say anything about being in trouble, or anyone threatening her?"

"No, not a word. Why would anyone do something like that?"

"We don't know. I'm going to have someone come see you. Her name is Melinda. She's here in town now and she's Maria's younger sister. Don't be startled. She says she looks a lot like her sister, about the same size, coloring, hair. She's trying to find Maria."

"Yes, yes. I'll be thrilled to talk to her. I can't figure out why Maria would suddenly leave that way. Some days there's a steamer going down the river every three or four hours. All she would have to do is buy a ticket and step on board."

"Did you think that she might not have left of her own free will? Someone might have forced her onto one of those sternwheelers."

"My God! I didn't think about that. We were

working out an act. I'm a fiddler, quite good if I say so, and I know all the songs she sings. We were going to have a duo act. Not many around now. We planned on saving up some money, then working our way down the Missouri to the Mississippi and try to get a job in the lounges of those big boats as a duo act. Playing and singing. We even practiced together."

"Now, Homer, think back. Was Maria afraid of anyone at the saloon?"

"Well, there was one thing. A big black man guarded the whores. He didn't let anybody upstairs without a pink slip of paper the guys bought from the madam. One day he asked Maria to take off her blouse and show him her breasts. She knew he was a little feeble-minded, but he'd never bothered her before. He asked the same thing every day for a week, and she complained to the manager. He talked with the guard, and that was all there was to it."

"She kept singing after that?"

"Oh, yes. Let's see, for about a week. She sang late Saturday night, then had Sunday off and I never saw her again after that Saturday night."

"You need to talk to Melinda. I'll find her and send her over here. It might be later today. If she doesn't come, you go to the Dakota Arms Hotel. She's in room twenty-eight on the second floor."

Buckskin left the tin shop, tried Melinda's room at the hotel, but she wasn't there. He'd never find her in a town this size. He headed back to the parlor house and the madam, Fay.

She looked up from her account books in her office and grinned.

"Hey, handsome, back already? Just couldn't stay away from my girls, right. Which one do you want?"

"The one with some answers. You ever hear of a girl vanishing in this town before?"

She sighed, making her bosom heave and then settle. "Yep, I remember two or three. Just plain vanished off the face. Nobody ever seen or heard from them again. But that was two years ago. Mothers get protective of their daughters of a loving age."

"What about your girls? Do you lose a fancy lady now and again?"

"Sure, who doesn't? They get tired of the routine, or find a man who wants to marry them, or just quit here and move downriver to greener pay days."

"Have any contented ones disappeared? Good-looking ones?"

Fay sighed and looked at him sharply. "Yes, damn it. I've lost two girls. I thought it was the Five Angels of Death. You think it could have been slavers?"

"Sounds reasonable. Who would their contact be here in town? Who knows the town, could get to the girls?"

"The bastards! I'll kill them with my six-gun persuader, so help me. I'll shoot their balls off first. I'll—"

"Who? You have any idea who might be behind a white slaver operation here?"

"Yeah, okay, okay. Let me think. Some real low-down skunks in this town could do that. Yeah. Give me a few hours. I'll do some thinking and ask some questions where I won't get hurt. Get back to me tonight."

Chapter Seven

Nate Hill leaned back in the chair in his apartment he had built over the saloon well away from the cribs and frowned at the pretty girl who sat across from him. They had just finished dinner brought in from the restaurant across the street, and he felt mellow.

Dawn Evans, who now called herself Sherry Crawford, rose and walked around the small living room.

"I feel like a caged bird," she said. "Why can't we go out to a play or a concert?" She stopped. "Oh, damn, I forgot where I was. Here I am in the capitol of the Territory of Dakota and there isn't a playhouse or a musical group within two hundred miles. How do you stand it here, Nate?"

"Huh? Just admiring the way your breasts surge

out that way when you get talking. Stand it, hell, I thrive here. I'm making money, I have a beautiful lady to sleep with, and the poker games in the back room have paid off like never before."

"Most of that is because of me, then, Mr. Hill?"

He grinned. "Damn right. You're good at poking and at poker. What more could a man ask for?"

"Maybe not much, but there's a hell of a lot a lady could ask for. We talked about it before. I want you to sell this little place and we'll ride down the Missouri and then the Mississippi and dock at New Orleans where they really know how to gamble. We'll take your profits here and buy a place and open our own gambling hall."

"You have any idea of how much that would cost?"

"No. I'm not smart about money. But my daddy is. I could always say I was kidnapped and make him pay you fifty thousand dollars. That should help with the scheme."

Hill snorted, poured a shot of whiskey and downed it in one gulp. "Christ, woman, you trying to get me hung? Kidnapping for ransom is a capital offense around here. I'd be stretching a hemp before you and I could get halfway to Omaha."

"Not if we did it right. Look, I cut off my long hair and dyed it black so nobody would recognize me. How they going to find us?"

"For blackmail you have to give the man a place and a time to deliver the money. He does, we're there, and he has fifty policemen and gunmen there to arrest us. Crazy, that idea is crazy, so just forget it."

"You're always so mean to me. I might not feel like playing poker tonight." She pouted and turned away from him.

Hill came out of his chair, the cigar burning on the plate forgotten.

"Sweetheart, you can't do that. I've lined up some big money men to play tonight. We could clean up lots of money."

She turned, her pout still in place. Sherry sighed, put her hands on her hips and walked back to him. She pushed her breasts hard against his chest and looked up pleadingly at him.

"I guess I could play tonight, if you tell me that you'll at least think about selling out here and moving on south. It's glorious in New Orleans. That's the real south, with stylish gentlemen and beautifully dressed ladies. It's a marvel. And there is lots of gambling. Maybe we wouldn't have to open our own place, just work the other games."

"Now there is an idea." He pushed her away and bent down and kissed her breasts through her lace-covered blouse. Sherry smiled and stroked his hair.

"You know I love it when you do that. We have time?"

"Not nearly enough. I want you horny as hell tonight, showing off your tits and knocking these rivermen dead at the table."

"You know I do best at the table just after a quick fuck. How about now against the wall?"

"Standing up?"

"Sure, we've done it that way before." She pushed back from him and reached under her skirts and pulled down her bloomers. She kicked them off on the floor and grinned at him. Then she reached for his crotch and massaged him until he moaned. She lifted her skirts, showing him her red-haired swatch of pubic hair, and he growled.

"You little bitch in heat. You really love it, don't you?"

"Almost as much as you do. Now come on, show me that you're a man and not just all talk."

She backed up against the wall and held her skirts up around her waist and waited for him. He worked at his fly until he had it open, then pulled out his erection and she gasped.

"Oh, yes, big dick, that's what I want."

He walked up in front of her and she put her hands around his neck, locking her fingers together. Then she jumped off the floor and threw her legs around his waist crossing her ankles to stay in place.

She leaned her back against the wall and watched him. Slowly he eased their bodies apart until he found the right angle, then he brought his erection forward and drove it up her well lubricated sheath until their bones ground together.

"Oh, damn, yes!" she shouted. Then he began a strange kind of stroke. She could help only a little so she tightened her inner muscles around him each time he thrust forward, bringing a cry of pleasure from him on each stroke.

The strange angle excited him quickly and she grew red in the face, then bellowed as she climaxed in one long series of spasms that shook her and distorted her face and tightened every muscle in her body.

Just as she finished, he cried out and drove hard into her again and again until his load was planted deep inside her. He panted and perspired and panted some more. She watched him, eager for one more climax, but he shook his head and eased away from her.

She unhooked her ankles so he could move back farther and they came unconnected, and he sighed again and led her to the bedroom where they both collapsed on the feather bed mattress, still panting and trying to recover.

They lay there for five minutes, then Sherry sat up and bent over him and softly kissed his lips. He moaned. She kissed him again and his eyes came open.

"I had this little dream about New Orleans and all the money we were making," he said. "Then they said I was cheating and they threw me in jail and these two huge Negro women came into my cell and raped me and made me service them whenever they wanted, two, three times a day. After a week I was so exhausted I couldn't get it hard anymore and they threw me out of jail into a swamp."

"All that in a minute or two?" she asked.

"Sure, I'm a fast fuck."

She hit his shoulder. "Seriously, you think about New Orleans. It will be great. Then I'll be sure that my dear old husband will never find me."

"You must be crazy not to want to go back. All his money that you can spend."

"That gets boring after a while."

"I bet he'd send you on a tour of Europe."

"Oh, yes, he offered to do that, but I'd have to take

along some stuffy old woman chaperone."

Nate laughed. "You could con her or buy her silence. Then you could spend lots of money and sightsee and fuck your way across Europe and the Greek islands."

"Hey, you trying to get rid of me?"

"No, but it's about time you put on your tit show-off blouse for the poker game. It starts in half an hour. I better check the saloon and see that all is going well down there. No shots fired so far at least."

He watched her take off her lace blouse. She flapped up her chemise so he could see her breasts, then she laughed and took off the chemise to give him a better view. She wouldn't wear a chemise tonight so her breasts would show better.

He went down the steps to the saloon, and the apron waved at him. Hill went behind the bar and they talked quietly.

"Been a gent in here asking about a redheaded poker-playing woman with long red hair. Figured you might want to know."

"You hear any kind of a name?"

"Morgan. Something Morgan. He comes in now and then."

"You know Lefty Grant?"

"Yeah, sure. The little guy with the bad right hand."

"Find him. I've got a job for him. Send somebody out so I can talk to him tonight before the game starts."

"Sure, boss."

Hill thought about it. Somebody looking for a

woman poker player with long red hair. That was how Sherry had worked up the river from town to town until she hit here and cut her hair and dyed it black. So did this gent just want a good poker game, or was he somebody from Denver who Sherry's husband had sent to find her? Hill had to know. If Lefty couldn't find out, he would dig up a man who could find the facts. Sherry was important to him now after only a month. She was his meal ticket, but she was more than that. Yeah, she was his fucking woman.

Lefty Grant was not pleasant to look at. He stood five three, had thinning brown hair which he combed to one side, and a shot-up right hand that prevented it from even holding a fork. That made him into a lefty out of necessity. His face was slightly lopsided with his right eye lower than his left, and both were half hooded, giving him a sinister look.

His big nose was often red from drinking and he had jug-handle ears. His ears were his fortune. He sold what he heard in bars and stores to those willing to pay. There was always someone willing to pay for almost everything that he learned.

Now he was looking for this man named Morgan. From the hotel register, he discovered that the man went by the first name of Buckskin and he'd been in town less than a week. He had played in one high-stakes poker game, used his six-gun impressively, and didn't kill the other man who drew first. He also won the poker game.

Lefty discovered in three hours that this Buckskin Morgan had been in the three best saloons that had high-stakes poker games and at each one he asked about a young woman poker player who had long red hair.

Lefty knew that Morgan wasn't a big drinker, that he played dime-limit poker sometimes, and that he was said to be in town as a land buyer for his rich father who lived in Omaha.

The descriptions he got from the barkeeps meshed neatly. He was six feet tall, lean at 185 pounds, with dark brown hair, clean-shaven with high cheekbones, a thin mouth and a squared-off chin. In town he had worn good trousers, open shirt with buckskin vest, and he carried a Colt-looking six-gun low on his right hip with the bottom of the holster tied down for a faster draw.

Lefty finished his work about ten•o'clock and went back to the Criterion. Abe, the apron tonight and the man who had summoned him, was at the bar and kept a tab on Lefty. Abe knew that his boss always partly paid off Lefty with a tab here and upstairs.

Lefty borrowed a dollar from Abe and got into a penny-ante poker game with two old-timers at a back table. They cheated outrageously, but Lefty didn't care. Easy come . . . He borrowed another dollar from Abe and lost it, then wandered upstairs. He'd give his report to Nate Hill when they took their ten-o'clock break for beer and sandwiches.

There was no madam upstairs at the Criterion. Big Betty had the crib at the head of the stairs and did what was needed to keep the records straight and watch for flakes and cowboys trying to slip past her for a free one.

She waved out her door at Lefty.

"Hey, little prick, you working for the boss tonight?"

"Yes indeed. Just waiting to report."

"He told me you get a free one as part of your pay. Who you want?"

"You, Betty."

She laughed. It was the same every time. "Now, Lefty, not true. You want some nice thin young thing who can give you a good ride. Try Emily. She's not busy, and is fresh and feisty. I don't know why."

Betty's robe slipped showing one large breast with a soft pink areola and a small, almost black nipple. She grinned. "That free tit show get your dick up, little man?"

"Oh, yes indeed. Sure you don't need a good poking?"

"Best see Emily. I told her you might be by. I think she likes you."

"Yeah, I bet she does." Lefty went down to the third door on the left and pushed it open. Emily sat on her bed cross-legged so her crotch hair showed. She was naked. Emily was blind in one eye and when she looked at him and grinned, the grin came from only half of her face. It hadn't affected her speech.

"Lefty, you old bastard. You haven't been in to see me for months. Bet you're working for the boss again, right? Hey, I don't care. I need the work. I've been planning on something special for you next time you came in. I read about it in this book with dirty pictures of Japanese fucking. Come on, I'll show you how it works."

She lay on her back and put her legs on his shoulders as he sat in front of her and entered her. It was a fantastic position, but he found it hard to get up any kind of a stroke and they had to move to the usual missionary position to reach his climax.

She made him wait and try another position.

"I'm not real busy tonight, help me try this," Emily pleaded. He shrugged.

"First, you lay on your back on the bed with your legs spread wide." He did it.

"Has it been long enough since we finished? I mean are you ready to go again?"

Lefty nodded, reached out and fondled her breasts. She pulled away.

"Now, I sit between your legs and ease your big poker up into my tight cunny this way." She did and he yelped at the strange angle. She pushed her legs forward until they slid under his shoulders.

She cried out in pleasure. "We did it. It works. I didn't think it would. Now I have to do all the poking work. I just lift up and let down, lift up and let down."

A knock sounded on the door and Big Betty's voice came through.

"Hey, you two. This wasn't an all-nighter. Mr. Hill wants to see Lefty right away. Get finished in there and dressed, and Lefty, you get downstairs as soon as you can."

Ten minutes later, Lefty told Nate Hill everything he had found out about Buckskin Morgan.

Nate listened. It was time he had some good news. The poker game wasn't going as well as it should. When the report was finished he gave Lefty five dollars.

"Tomorrow I want you to be at his hotel at six A.M. Pick him out as he comes from the hotel. You might want to be in the lobby in case he eats breakfast in the dining room. Follow him all day, but don't let him know you're there. Change clothes at least twice during the day. Leave your changes in here. Don't let him know you're following him. I want to know everything he does tomorrow. I'll pay you two dollars a day, if he doesn't spot you. Can you do it?"

Lefty nodded. "For two dollars a day I can follow the devil himself through Hades and never even get singed."

Nate Hill grinned at him and hurried back to the poker game. It had to go better. The sternwheeler captain and the mining engineer had proved to be tougher poker players than he figured. So far he and Sherry were only 200-dollar winners.

Chapter Eight

Buckskin Morgan came out of a saloon and scowled. The big poker game at the River Rat Saloon had not happened. Only two players showed up. They knew each other and were looking for some fresh money. Buckskin held on to his 100 dollars' worth of chips and waited around with the others, but no one else came.

They all gave up about ten o'clock. Buckskin got into a dollar-limit game in the main saloon and lost ten dollars by midnight. He was still ahead in his poker playing. He finished his beer and walked outside, stretching. What he needed now was a good night's sleep.

Half a block down the street he saw some riders going away from him. In the splash of light from a saloon he could tell there were five horses and they were all black. He turned that way and walked quickly. Five black horses. Could it be the Five Angels of Death, the vigilantes?

He broke into a trot, dropping into the street so his boots wouldn't make noise on the boardwalk. He came within 100 feet of them and the horsemen stopped. Now he could see that they all had black hoods over their heads and shoulders. It was them. He was close enough now to hear the men talking.

"Hey, you, nigger," one sharp voice called. "What the hell you doing running around downtown this way late at night?"

"Probably looking for my daughter to rape, you black bastard." The new voice was lower, with deadly overtone. "You got your place, you best stay put in it and mind your manners."

"I'as jes goin' home. Did some night fishing."

"Where's your fishing pole?"

"Don't use a pole, jes a hand line."

"Lying bastard."

Two horses moved onto the boardwalk, crowding the black man off it into the street.

"You just walk straight down the street, black bastard." It was the heavier voice again, the one filled with anger and danger. "We got a surprise for you."

Buckskin saw two men come out of a saloon, look up and see the five men in black hoods. They turned and ran back inside. Someone on the other side of the street hurried down the block and turned into an alley.

"I's got to get on home," the black man said. "Wife waiting me."

One of the horses edged forward and crowded the black man down the dirt street.

"Boy, you just walk down the street like a good little nigger and we might go easy on you. Move it!"

Buckskin frowned as he walked along well behind them. He had no idea what they were doing. A good beating for the black man? He had seen only two blacks in town. On the river there were quite a few people who had worked their way upstream from the south. But only the two blacks.

"Keep moving, you black, ugly excuse for a man, right down the street." It was a new voice, a younger one Buckskin hadn't heard before.

He moved along behind them, keeping his distance and watching to see what would happen. Probably some threats, a beating and then an ultimatum to get out of town on the morning boat. He'd seen it happen before.

They moved another block, then to the edge of town upstream where a tall cottonwood tree drank from the edge of the river. One limb twelve feet off the ground came out at a sharp angle from the trunk.

The riders stopped there and one man threw a rope over the cottonwood tree limb. Buckskin scowled and moved up closer until he was less than 30 feet from the figures. He lay in the grass and the dark that hid him and watched the scene play out.

"Lincoln, we told you four times to get out of town, isn't that right?" It was the deep angry voice again.

"Yes, sah. Right. I didn' go."

"You didn't. We pounded around on you twice

and still your black body is here."

Another voice came clear. It was the younger one. "Damn right, Lincoln. We warned you. Now it's fucking too late. We gonna hang your black ass by your neck until you're croaking dead, then swing you like a target and use you for shooting practice. A head shot counts ten. Then when the fun is over, we throw your worthless carcass in the Missouri and let it float you all the way to the Gulf of by damn Mexico."

The other mounted riders laughed.

One voice Buckskin hadn't heard before sounded out of patience and a little angry. "Stop torturing the man, damn it. I didn't like this one from the start. If we're going to do it, let's just get it done in a hurry and get out of here. Let's get on with it."

Lincoln surged to the side away from the river, running hard. One of the riders kicked his mount in the flank and raced after him, cutting him off as he would a running steer, and turned him back to the other four silent horsemen.

Two riders got down and caught Lincoln, tied his hands behind his back and boosted him on one of the horses so he sat backwards on it near the rump. Another rider came up with the noose.

That was enough for Buckskin. He pulled his Colt and sent two shots just over the head of the rider with the noose. His horse spooked, he dropped the noose, and the mount pranced away a dozen yards.

"What the hell?" the deep voice bellowed.

Buckskin put two rounds into the dirt near the three men still mounted. They milled around searching for the muzzle flash in the darkness.

Buckskin had rolled in the grass ten feet from where he fired first. One of the men drew his weapon and fired where Buckskin had been. Buckskin changed his tactics and fired twice at the gunman. His second shot jolted into the man's shoulder and he almost spun out of his saddle.

"I'm hit! Kill the fucking bastard," the rider screeched.

Buckskin rolled again, thumbed new rounds into the six-gun, six this time, and shot twice more over the men's heads.

"Find the shooter!" somebody screamed.

"You find him, I'm riding out of here," another voice came.

Buckskin put four more rounds over their heads and the five hooded figures scattered. The two men on the ground jerked Lincoln off the horse, then they mounted, and the five men rode in five different directions away from the river.

Buckskin had no way to follow them. He looked for the black man. Lincoln was on his knees, his hands still tied behind him, and praying. Buckskin walked up silently.

"Thank you, Lord. Praise God from whom all blessings flow. Thank you, God, for saving this scrawny old nigger's neck. Me and the missus we be moving out tomorrow. No sense fighting them anymo'. We go south a ways, I reckon. Thank you, Lord."

Buckskin waited for the prayer and talk with God to end. Then he spoke.

"Mr. Lincoln, looks like the bad guys have gone."

Lincoln jumped at the sound of his voice and cowered away from it.

"No, don't be afraid. I'm the one who shot at them. They ran like cowards, didn't they?"

Lincoln turned and squinted into the night and saw Buckskin, who had reloaded, then holstered his Colt.

"Praise God and thank you, whoever you are. I was a dead man, I was sure of that. You saved this scrawny old black neck. My wife will thank you. Why you do that?"

"They are wrong. Vigilantes are usually in the wrong. I just happened by and saw them driving you out of town. I didn't like that either. You moving on?"

"Pack what I own soon as I get home and be at the dock for the first boat downstream come dawn."

"Want me to see you safely on the boat?"

"No need. Cowards like them five hide during the day. They won't touch me in the daylight."

"I'll walk home with you."

"No need."

"Might be. One or two of them might be waiting for you. I don't have anything else to do."

Twenty minutes later Buckskin left the man at his shack near the upstream edge of town. No one challenged or attacked them. Lincoln shook Buckskin's hand and thanked him again.

"I jes don't have the words to thank a man who saved my life. You know I'd been a dead nigger in about five minutes. I thank you again, and may the Lord of Hosts smile on you in all that you do the rest of your life."

Buckskin smiled and shook the man's hand again, then walked back toward town. The area here was made up of cheaper houses and a few shacks, even one tipi, but probably nobody lived in it. A leftover from the Yankton people, one of the seven tribes of the Dakota Indian nation. For some reason he remembered that in 1812 the Yankton people had fought against the United States. The better houses and businesses were on the downstream side of town.

Buckskin had found out from Lincoln that there were two doctors in town, one on Main Street just across from the post office, the other one toward the upstream side of town in a house in back of the bank.

Buckskin chose the doctor behind the bank. No lights were on in the house with a sign that read "Bramer Faraday, M.D." Buckskin sat across the street and leaned against a small tree and waited. He figured the vigilante who was shot would try one of the doctors. Which one was a guess. This less expensive part of town might be his choice.

After waiting an hour, Buckskin gave up and walked back to his hotel. He checked the entrance, then the lobby and the hallway on the second floor. He could find no one waiting for him. In his room he didn't turn on the light. He stripped off his gun belt and dropped on the bed for a moment. Then he slid out of his boots and pants and lay down on top of the sheets. It was a warm night again. Too warm for October at 1,200 feet altitude. Probably be some tornadoes or thunderstorms tomorrow.

* * *

Porter Jordan had spurred his horse away from the cottonwood tree as soon as he had been hit once. Damned if he was going to get killed just to hang some bastard of a nigger. He didn't know how bad his shot shoulder was. He hoped that the bullet had missed the bone. It was somewhere below his shoulder in his upper arm and it hurt like hell.

He pulled off the black hood and folded it carefully as he let the horse walk. Then he stuffed the hood in his saddlebag and hurried on to the alley behind Dr. Sims' office. The bachelor doctor lived in back of his small surgery. It was the best medical facility in fifty miles.

It took a dozen hard kicks and poundings on the back door before Jordan saw a light. The living quarters were nearest the back door and offered the best way to wake up the doctor.

The medic appeared with a lamp, wearing pajama pants, no top, and a scowl.

"You know what time it is?" he asked.

"Yes," Jordan said. "You know how mad I am because I dropped my six-gun and it went off and shot me in the shoulder?"

The doctor sighed. He was 42, had a good practice going here, and wanted to get married but couldn't find the right woman. With each passing month he grew less selective. He waved Jordan inside.

"Dropped your gun, huh? Seems to me this happened to you twice before."

"Just do your job and don't get nosy, Doc."

"Yes, sir." They were in his surgery room. He lit three lamps with reflectors, hung one overhead that shone downward with double reflectors, and motioned to Jordan.

"It would help if you took off your shirt."

Ten minutes later the job was done.

"The bullet went through your arm but missed the bone. Your arm muscles are going to be sore as hell for three weeks to a month. Don't do any heavy work with that left arm or you'll hurt like fire."

"When do I come back and see you?"

"A week. Change the bandage once. If it starts to bleed, come back. That'll be three dollars."

"Three dollars?"

"This was surgery. I do my job, I get paid. You charge me when I rent a horse. I charge you."

Jordan swore softly, gave the doctor three dollars and started out the door.

"Like I said, Doc. I dropped my gun and it went off. We can leave it at that, can't we?"

"No sense reporting something like that to the sheriff the way I'm required to do by law. Don't want to clutter up his desk with useless accident reports." The medic paused. "Of course, if the sheriff were to ask me specifically about anyone with a gunshot wound, I'd have to tell him."

"Sure, and make him believe it was an accident. You know why, don't you, Doc?" Porter Jordan looked at the medic with a stern gaze, then went to the door. He reached for the door with his left hand, felt the pain shoot into his upper arm, and closed the door with his right hand.

He went from there to the back door of the Ingraham General Store. When he tried the door, it was unlocked. Inside he found the other four all with grim expressions.

"Figured you'd be a little late, Jordan," Gideon Ingraham said. "We've been booting around some ideas who the gunman might have been."

"Tell me and I'll kill the bastard in a minute," Jordan said.

"Might not be that simple," Ingraham said. "We hear that somebody in that damn committee sent to Omaha for a deputy U.S. Marshal to come up here. That might have been the one."

"Just what we need," Jordan said.

"What doctor did you use?" someone asked.

"Doc Sims."

"Yeah, he's the one," Ingraham said. "He won't say a word. You don't know it but I've got a file on him. Two pictures and sworn statements by two underage girls. He was fucking them right there in his office."

"He knows about your file?"

"I told him the other night when I got that knife in my leg. He knows and he won't say word one about any of us."

"So where does this leave us with our attacker?" Jordan asked.

"What about this Morgan?" Stacey Trumble, the leather merchant, asked. "Think he's the one who shot at us?"

"Could have been," Deputy Sheriff Zebadiah Clay said. "He wasn't trying to hit us, not until somebody pulled a six-gun and shot back."

"So he was trying to scare us," Van Dalton said. "Sounds like a lawman."

"Or just some civilian who happened by and didn't like what we were doing," Ingraham said. "Let's keep this on the right track here. We're not in a popularity contest. We do what's right and what's best for the town."

Somebody laughed softly.

"Oh, yeah, Gideon. That's the way we started out. I was there with you, remember." It was Van Dalton talking. "Hell, people talked well about us, back then. Remember? Are we a little bit off the track here?"

"Hell, no, we ain't off the goddamned track. Tonight for instance. We don't want no nigger town here in Yankton. We got two, then we get six nigger families, then they tell their relatives and we got twenty more black as spades families and we got a whole damn nigger town there upriver."

"Cut the shit here, you guys," Stacey Trumble said. "Hell, yes, we're on track. I still think what we have to do first is find that damn shooter. My bet is that it's this new guy, this Morgan. Let's set up a trap for him. I don't know how. I'll get Morgan to the trap if you guys figure out one."

Ingraham rubbed his face and nodded. "Yeah, I think you're right, Trumble. We're still on track, and this shooter could cause us no end of problems. Like Porter's shot-up arm. Let's plan a hanging tomorrow night, only it won't be a real hanging. We'll hang a dummy and lead this guy right into it. We need a spot where he can't get out. I'll do some thinking on this. Bring your rifles and six-guns and we'll blast this guy straight into hell."

"Now you're talking," Jordan said. He groaned as

he moved his arm. "Damn this arm. Be a month before it's back to normal. I got to get home or my old lady will skin me. See you guys tomorrow night about what, ten o'clock at the usual place?"

They all nodded. One by one they left the back room of the store. When the others had gone, Van Dalton looked up at Gideon Ingraham.

"I meant what I said about getting off the track. Are we really doing now what we did that first year? Or have we veered off into personal prejudices and petty peeves, and sometimes to line our own pockets with gold? Hell, Gideon, I don't know. But I had to ask the question."

Gideon watched as Van Dalton walked out the back door and waved.

The man was on the edge. It was a dangerous edge. In this business you had to be 100 percent committed or you couldn't function. Van Dalton had slipped too far over that edge. It had happened once before, two, three years ago. Guy by the name of Tom something.

Damn, but Gideon hated to do this. He pushed his six-gun in his belt and walked out the back door, locking it and then running to catch up with Van Dalton.

Van heard Gideon coming and stopped.

"Didn't know if you were leaving yet or not," Van said. He turned and saw the six-gun in Gideon's hand, and before he could even throw up one hand, the head of the Five Angels of Death fired.

The round slammed through Van Dalton's shirt and jolted into his chest, shredding one section of his heart and dumping him lifeless in seconds on the side of the alley.

Gideon wiped a bead of sweat off his forehead and pushed his weapon back in his belt. He picked up the smaller man and carried him down a block through the alley and dropped him behind some trash and boxes. He kicked more boxes over him and wiped his face with his handkerchief.

"Sorry, Van, but in this game you got to be one hundred percent or the game is all over," Gideon said softly, then turned and trotted toward his home in the downriver end of town.

Chapter Nine

Just before dark that night, two men stepped off the sternwheeler *Ramona's Promise* and headed for the nearest watering hole. From the way they walked it was easy to see that they had been in Yankton before and knew where they were going.

They pushed through the front door of the Wayfarer Saloon, waved at the barkeep and took a table in the rear where they both sat with their backs against the wall so they could see everyone in the saloon.

Without any signal or order, the apron brought over four cold bottles of beer and put them in front of the men. They nodded and waved him away. He didn't ask for any payment and scurried back to the bar.

One of the men stood six inches over six feet tall,

with a beam wide enough to be a sternwheeler himself. His shoulders looked like the wheelhouse, and big, meaty hands went flat on the table as he grinned at the cold bottles of beer.

The second man wore a proper brown suit, white shirt and tie, and a town hat with narrow brim. He had taken it off as soon as they came inside and now held the hat in his lap. He picked up a bottle and sipped at it. He pushed five feet five from the low side, was slender, and moved with a quick energy that was belied by soft brown eyes and a pale complexion.

The big man lifted a beer, drained it without putting it down, and smacked his lips before he wiped them with the sleeve of his plaid shirt.

"Damn good beer," he said.

The smaller man scowled. "Bull, this is the first trip we've made together and it will be the last." The words came out precisely formed, in a clipped accent that made them sound even harsher. "I will work with you only because you were the only other man available. When our friend gets here, I don't want you to say a single word, do you understand me, Bull?"

"Yeah, sure."

"You will do exactly what I tell you to do and nothing more. You will speak with no one unless I approve. We'll get this pickup made and be on the boat in the morning if all goes as it should."

"Yeah, sure."

"Quit saying that. *Yeah* is not a word. The proper word is *yes*. In this case, *yes sir* would be suggested."

"Yes, sir."

"Good. Now enjoy your beer, it's the last one you're getting until we dock two days from now downstream."

Newton Jay Kerr frowned at Bull over the glass he had used to pour the beer into. This was absolutely the last time he ever came on a trip like this with Bull. He was half animal, half ignorant clod. It hadn't been this way when they started the whole scheme two years ago. Then it was more like a gentlemen's club with certain privileges and responsibilities. It was getting too big, too impersonal. Kerr still liked the personal touch, to know the suppliers and the clientele better.

Kerr saw a man come in the door and look around, go to a poker table and watch for a minute, then move to the next one. Soon the man came toward their table and without asking pulled out a chair and sat down.

Bull came half out of his seat. Kerr put a hand on his arm.

"Take out a deck of cards," Kerr said to the newcomer. "Then we can have some friendly poker."

The man produced a deck of cards, broke the seal on them and dealt three hands for five-card draw.

"Figured you had to be the ones," the stranger said. "You Mr. Kerr?"

"Yes. Are you Pastorini?"

"Yes, Anthony Pastorini."

"So where can we meet that's private?"

"You leave soon and wait outside by the hardware store next door. I'll be along in two minutes and take you to my place. I've got some good news for you."

"It better be good news. That's what your letter said. Let's play the hand. I'll take two cards."

"Can't the big man talk?"

"Not unless I tell him to. That's not what he's best at."

They played two hands of poker, then Kerr and Bull got up and left the saloon.

Ten minutes later they sat around a table in a small house two blocks from the downtown area.

"No pictures of this one, but she's delicious. Elsie Belle Parker is the name. I'd guess she's about twenty, blonde with good tits and not too fat, just nice and pleasingly plump. Damned good tits, in fact. Biggest damn knockers I've seen in a long time. She has no family here. She works at the bank as a teller, so she's used to meeting people."

"Yes, yes. Where does she live?"

"Best part. She had been in a boardinghouse, but two weeks ago she got a house of her own. It's two blocks over and there's no lock on the back door. Nobody around here locks doors at night anyway."

"Sounds good so far," Kerr said. "You have the materials we need here?"

"Right, everything. Also a supply for you on the boat."

"What time is it?"

"A little after eight o'clock."

"Good," Kerr said. "Let's go now before she gets into bed. I hate to dress women."

Kerr took a deep breath and nodded to himself. Yes, this was looking like it would be an easy one. It should be after that last fiasco he went on down-river. Such a mess and he almost got shot in the process. He liked them simpler, cleaner, with no problems and no danger. He did not relish physical danger.

Fifteen minutes later, Kerr knocked on Elsie Belle's front door. She opened it and lifted her brows in surprise.

"Oh, hello. I don't get many callers."

"You should, you're Elsie Belle from the bank, right? I wanted to ask you about something on my draft account and it can't wait until morning. Could you help me?"

"Oh, dear, I don't know. Is it just a balancing of your account or something like that? I guess we could leave the door open. Propriety and all, you know."

"Yes, just the balance," Kerr said. He saw Bull coming up behind her. The back door had been open. Before she made up her mind about letting him inside, Bull's big hand came around her mouth cutting off any scream, his other arm circled her waist, and he picked her up like a sack of cotton balls and carried her backwards into the living room.

Kerr went in, closed the door, and grinned at the girl. She was perfect. At least 600, might go 800, even 1,000 if they could find the right man. Pastorini stayed in the background. He poured an inch of fluid from a small bottle into a glass and handed it to Kerr. Bull still held her mouth closed, but let her breathe. His hand around her waist had crept up so it now covered her breasts and he held her firmly.

Kerr stood in front of her and smiled. "Elsie

Belle, I have some medicine for you to take. I promise it won't hurt you. It tastes rather good, matter of fact. You have to promise that when Bull takes his hand away from your mouth you won't scream. Will you promise me that?"

She nodded, her eyes wide in panic.

"Look, there's nothing to be afraid of. We're friends here to help you. We want to offer you a job as a dancer down the river a ways. A respectable riverboat show. Now, promise me again that you won't scream when Bull moves his hand."

She nodded. Bull let his hand off her mouth gradually. When it was off, she screamed so loud Kerr was sure the neighbors would hear. Bull's hand slapped back over her mouth.

"Elsie Belle, I'm disappointed in you. We have all night to give you the medicine. The way Bull is holding your breasts, I'm sure he could figure out something else to do with you while we wait."

Her eyes flared in anger and terror.

"Now, do you want to promise me again that you won't scream and keep your promise this time?"

She nodded. As soon as Bull's hand came away, she screamed. Bull's hand darted back in place.

"Bedroom," Kerr said, and Bull carried her down a short hall into a bedroom where Pastorini had just taken the lamp. Bull sat down on the bed and held her legs with his massive legs, then began petting and caressing her breasts. Soon he ripped the buttons off her white blouse and had his hand under her clothes and fondling her bare breasts. She squealed in anger.

"Enough, Bull," Kerr said. Bull reluctantly moved

his hand and held her waist.

It took them two hours to get the first dose of laudanum down her throat. She coughed and sputtered. They held her nose and forced her mouth open. She got about half of the first dose, but it was enough to relax her so she didn't fight them anymore. At midnight they woke her and gave her the second dose. She drank it willingly, not sure what it was or who they were but not caring.

After she had the second dose, they left her house. Bull carried her in his arms the two blocks to Pastorini's place and they put her to sleep in the only bed in the house. Kerr stretched out beside her but had no sexual ideas. He just wanted to get some uninterrupted sleep.

The first downriver sternwheeler was to leave the dock at 6:10 A.M. They woke up Elsie Belle at five. She was pliable and cooperative. The morphine derivative, laudanum, had kept her sedated. She could walk and now and then she would start singing, but the snatches of songs didn't last long.

Kerr and Bull walked with her to the boat landing. They already had three tickets, and walked on board and up to their cabin on the top deck. They had brought a sunbonnet from Elsie Belle's house which almost entirely covered her face. That way there was little chance anyone would recognize her. Only six passengers got on and two loads of freight. Two of the passengers were a black man and his wife. They stayed below.

In the cabin they gave Elsie Belle another drink of her "medicine" and she went to sleep quickly on the bunk along the wall.

"Now, Bull, get out of here. I want some sleep myself. You go watch the shore and wave at the funny people. You've done fine so far, don't mess up now."

Bull nodded and slipped out the door. Kerr locked the door behind him and looked at the young woman on the bunk. Quickly he undid the buttons on her yellow blouse, opened it and lifted the white chemise that covered her breasts. Even lying down, Elsie Belle showed large breasts.

Kerr settled down beside her. "This damn job has some compensations," he said softly, stroking her breasts. Then he lifted her skirt, anxious to see what kind of underwear she had on. Bloomers. Good. He rubbed his crotch. Nothing like getting these girls broken in by a professional. At that job there was nobody on the river who could break in a young virgin half as well as he could.

He knew she was a virgin, just knew. He couldn't help thinking about his time with the grocer's daughter in the storeroom. She'd been as anxious as he, and he had her blouse and chemise off and she was playing with his stiff cock when her father walked in on them. He snorted. That was the end of his job at the grocery store, but he did manage to meet the girl a week later and they finished what they had started.

He sighed and shook his head. How times had changed. How he had changed. He stroked Elsie Belle's large breasts and then eased her bloomers down. He felt a surge of desire. She was perfect.

He was always gentle, and when they were knocked out on laudanum, they never even knew when they lost their virginity. Later on, when they were back at headquarters, he'd do the job again, only next time pretty Elsie Belle with the huge tits would be awake and know exactly what was happening and what would take place in the weeks and months to come.

Buckskin was up at six, had breakfast across the street at a working man's cafe, and prowled the town by the time the stores opened. He had been too late to see the riverboat stop, but the ticket salesman assured Buckskin that the black man and wife were on board.

He was back on Main Street when the word flashed around town from one person to another. One of the local merchants had been found dead of a gunshot wound to the chest. A drunk found Van Dalton, owner of the Last Chance Saloon, on Main Street.

Buckskin had never met the man. He'd been in the Last Chance now and then looking for poker games, but he didn't remember talking to the owner. Barkeeps were his main source. The townspeople seemed genuinely upset. Evidently Van Dalton was a long-time resident and owned several of the business buildings in town and was an officer and partner in the local bank.

Buckskin was more interested in finding a girl who might or might not now have long red hair, was married to a Denver man, and loved to play poker.

He did what had become a habit when he was stumped on something and needed to think. He found a captain's chair outside the general store and sat in it, tipped it back on its rear legs until it leaned against the side of the building, and relaxed.

He pulled his wide-brimmed, low-crowned Stetson down so it shaded his eyes and left a small slit to look out at the world. Now and again he shut his eyes, just to rest them, and kept working over what he knew about Dawn Evans. It wasn't much.

The eyewitness could have been mistaken when he thought he saw Dawn here in Yankton. Or she might have been here and then gone up or down the river on a sternwheeler. She might have long red hair and she might not. She loved to play poker and was good at it, but she might not be the woman poker player here in town.

He walked the town again watching the women, but nowhere did he find anyone who came close to Dawn's description. By ten o'clock, he stopped by at the best parlor house in town and found Big Betty in her office working on the books.

"Oh, damn, Morgan. I told you I'd try and figure out who could be a contact for those riverboat white slavers. I really didn't come up with a positive. The only guy in town who I think is dirty and low-down enough to do something like that would be Lefty Grant.

"Lefty is a snoop. He listens and he talks. He will sell anything he knows about anyone to anyone. Hard to tell if he's working both ends against the middle sometimes. Lefty is a little guy, not over five feet and three. He's a lefty because he got his right hand shot up and can't do much with it."

"He's funny-looking, face kind of lopsided. Some

of my girls won't service him. He usually hangs out at the saloons. Used to call one his 'office' but I don't remember which one it was."

"No idea where I can find Lefty?"

Big Betty shook her head. "Not the slightest. You might check the bigger saloons. He must work them regularly."

Buckskin gave a long sigh. "Damn. I've been in the saloons so much somebody must think I own one. Maybe one of your girls knows where he stays or such."

Big Betty frowned. "Wait a minute. One of my girls took over for me part of last night. I tell her to write down everything. Let me get the paper she gave me."

After some rustling around on her desk, Big Betty found the paper. She waved it and then read it through her spectacles.

"Oh, yes, I thought she said something about this. Lefty must have come into some cash. He paid for a home visit tomorrow night. Paid in advance for a two-hour go-round."

"He usually doesn't do that?"

"First time ever."

"So how will his lady friend find his house?"

Big Betty laughed and showed him the paper. "I can't tell you that, but if you can read, I can't stop you."

She pointed to the passage and Buckskin read it. "Second house beyond the house with the white picket fence on Second Street and Missouri Street."

"Might need to pay him a call one of these days." Buckskin thanked Big Betty and left the parlor house by the front door. He saw a small man across the street stand up in a hurry from where he'd been sitting down and leaning against a tree.

Buckskin frowned. Yes, he'd seen the same little man at breakfast, then again when he came out of one of the saloons. Three times was not a charm for Buckskin. He turned toward town, then changed directions and charged straight at the small man twenty yards away.

For a moment the man stood there with his mouth open. Then he turned and ran. Buckskin caught him in half a block and both of them were panting and wheezing.

Buckskin grabbed his arm and spun him around. The big .45 Colt was an inch from the man's nose.

"Lefty Grant, I'd bet," Buckskin said.

"Why the hell you chasing me?"

"Why the hell you following me? Who hired you to trail me all day today?"

"Don't know what you're talking about." The small man with the jug-handle ears looked away quickly and his chin quivered.

"Oh, damn. I swore I wasn't going to shoot anybody today. So much for good intentions." Buckskin cocked the .45 and the sound it made was like the creaking of a coffin lid.

The man jumped, his eyes went wide, and he shivered. "Hey, you can't be gonna do that. I just followed you. Didn't hurt you none. Man's got to make a living."

"Lefty Grant?"

"Yep."

"Lefty, you want your left hand to look just like

your right one with two slugs through the back of your hand, mashing up all those little bones in there?"

"Oh, God, no!"

"Good. What I figured. So, Lefty, who hired you to follow me?"

"I got to tell?"

"That or meet the undertaker, professionally. Lots more fun up here than six feet under the Dakota Territorial sod, I can guarantee you."

"Oh, damn. He's gonna be pissed and not pay me."

"Hard to get work all over the Territory, Lefty." Buckskin moved the muzzle of the .45 so it centered on the back of Lefty's left hand.

"Oh, damn . . . all right. It's Hill, Nate Hill. The guy who owns the Criterion Saloon."

"Haven't met the gent," Buckskin said. He moved the .45, let the hammer down easy with his thumb and grinned at Lefty. "So what have I been doing today?"

Lefty spouted the litany of what Buckskin did, where he had breakfast and what time, then where he went, what saloons he went to, where he had lunch, and that he was in Big Betty's place for about ten minutes.

"Why is Mr. Hill so interested in what I'm doing in town?" Buckskin asked.

"Didn't tell me. Just said do it, so I'm doing it."

"I'll have to make the poker game at his place tonight. Not the highest stakes, but I can play with the hoi polloi. I've got nothing against the common people."

Buckskin holstered his Colt. "So you get back in position and do what you do. I notice that you even changed clothes. That's a good trick. You report just whatever you want to Mr. Hill, except our little conversation here. Right?"

Lefty looked up and nodded vigorously. "Oh, yeah, right."

Buckskin laughed and walked toward Main Street. He couldn't remember if he'd had a noon meal or not. Then he recalled Lefty's report. He had eaten. He'd stopped at a small cafe on Main and had coffee and a piece of apple pie. It had just enough cinnamon on it and the slices of apple were cooked up enough yet still chewy. The crust must have had a pound of butter in it.

Hill. What was he worried about? He had a poker game. Maybe he knew Buckskin had won one big game. Did the owners keep track of big winners? He doubted it. They were in competition, not working together.

Hill could be one of the vigilantes. Yeah, that made more sense. The shoot-out at the black man's attempted hanging was going to be a real mean mess of greens for the vigilantes to chew down. They'd want to find out who it was. So far today he hadn't given them any cause to suspect him.

That young, red-haired wife was not in Yankton. Somebody would have remembered her long red hair. A pretty redhead could not stay in hiding for two or three months. Which left Buckskin with the conclusion that either Dawn Evans had left town or cut and probably dyed her hair. Yes. Now at last he was getting some facts down on his pad.

So he would quit looking for the redhead and concentrate on the poker-playing woman. A much easier task in this town. That meant playing poker every night and sleeping till noon. He could manage that for a few days. If no one bothered his sleep.

He felt a little guilty about not being able to help Melinda much, but she had come to him with her clothes off, not the other way around. Maybe he would run into something that would give him a clue. He still wondered about the white slavers, but that would be a different problem.

Buckskin checked his Waterbury: 3:15. Time for an afternoon nap and then he'd be ready for a poker game tonight. He felt the money belt around his waist. Still plenty of cash for a long poker game if it turned out that way. He wondered just how Hill would react when he sat in on their high- or low-stakes poker game. It would be interesting finding out.

Chapter Ten

Buckskin had his afternoon nap, ate supper and walked into the Criterion Saloon at 7:30 with a hundred-dollar bill in his hand and asked the barkeep if there was a game tonight. The apron nodded and pointed to a trim man in his thirties who stood at the end of the bar drinking what looked like a glass of milk. He looked lean but somehow soft to Buckskin. His blond hair had been neatly combed and stayed in place. His moustache was a little darker shade than his hair.

He looked up when Buckskin stepped up to the bar beside him.

"Understand there's a poker game tonight for invited guests only. Is it a no-limit game?"

Nate Hill stared at Buckskin for a minute. He nodded, his face remaining impassive.

"There's a game in a half hour if enough gents show up. It's a two-hundred-dollar buy to get in the game."

"I'm in. I'll have a beer while I wait."

"Go in the back room with the others if you want to. Show your money at the door. We have three so far. I'm the fourth. Won't play unless we get six."

"Suits me," Buckskin said. He took another hundred-dollar bill from his wallet and paired it with the first and walked to the heavyset man at the door. His nose had been flattened and one eye nearly closed. Buckskin figured bare-knuckled fist fighting in a ring. Buckskin held up the two bills.

The guard looked over the bills, gave them back to Buckskin and opened the door. The room was maybe twenty feet square. In the middle sat a poker table complete with green felt on top and fancy little cubbyholes in front of six chairs where each player could keep his chips or cash. Two uncapped bottles of beer sat in front of each chair on small paper pads.

Two men sat at the table smoking and talking. They looked at Buckskin, appraised him closely, then went back to their conversation. The man behind the small counter at the far side of the room wearing a green eyeshade took Buckskin's 200 dollars and gave him a small box stacked with chips.

"Count 'em if you want," the man said.

Buckskin turned away without comment and went to one of the free chairs across from the two men. He sat down, put his chips in the holder in front of him, and reached for one of the beers. It had a wire-loaded permanent cap that is opened by lifting the heavy wire, which pops up the cap made of ceramic with a hole through it for the wire and a rubber gasket to seal the bottle tightly. He'd seen them before.

He popped up the wire and realized the men watched him. "I've worked these wire caps before," Buckskin said. "Is the beer any good?"

"Best in town and it's free," the man closest to Buckskin said. He reached across the table with a hand that showed liver spots and several scars. "Ken Quentin. Reason I know this beer is the best in town is because I brew it."

"Buckskin Morgan," he said, shaking the hand. "Hope we have a nice friendly game.

The other man stood and reached across to Buckskin. "Fritz Larner. I don't slosh around beer bottles. I run a restaurant. Ken and I do one of these games every month. You hit us on our lucky night."

They worked at the beers.

"New in town?" Larner asked.

"Week or so," Buckskin said. "Looking for commercial property to invest in. Either of you gentlemen interested in selling?"

"Not a chance," Quentin said. "Yankton is just starting to grow. I'm going to be here when this town hits a hundred thousand in population."

"None of us will live that long," Larner said. "I keep telling this idiot that the big money is going to be in Sioux City downriver in the state of Iowa. It has a railroad, it has the river traffic, it has farm land, things that draw people."

"Yankton has the same things. We pushed our own railroad from here to Sioux City to join the main line back in seventy-three," Quentin argued. "Just in case you've had your head in a beer barrel over there at the brewery and wasn't noticing."

The door opened and two more men came in. They looked at the poker table and went right to the cashier, who sold them chips. A moment later, the man at the bar drinking milk came inside. He stopped, closed the door and put a two-by-four bar on the door to the saloon.

"Just so nobody we don't want in tries to bust through the door," he said.

"Come on, Hill, let's get the game going," Larner called. "We're damn near late already."

"Where's the pretty lady?" Quentin asked. "Ain't she playing tonight?"

Hill, who Buckskin figured was Nate Hill, owner of the place, brought his chips to the table and the three men sat down in available chairs.

"Fact is the lady is suffering from a cold tonight and sent word from her hotel that she couldn't play. She hopes to be ready by next week."

"She don't act like no lady when she's playing poker," Larner said. "She's damn tough. I hate to get in a one-on-one betting contest with her late in the evening."

Quentin laughed. "Yeah, but you enjoy the tit show she makes when she's got you bluffed out."

"She don't mind showing them, I don't mind looking at them," Lawler said. "Seen a woman or two naked in my time."

"I remember them," Quentin said. "The ones who ran out of your hotel room down in Omaha that time screaming."

A half hour later the poker had settled down. One of the men who came in with Hill had splurged and played terrible poker and wound up broke. He sat at his place grousing and complaining.

Hill glared at the man twice, then threw him out the back door.

The new hand was straight draw poker, jacks or better to open, ten-dollar ante. Quentin dealt. Buckskin drew a pair of sevens, a queen, a six and an eight. Three of a run of five. Not a chance. He heard Hill open for 30 dollars and saved the pair and the queen. Three of the five players drew two cards; Quentin, dealing, drew three.

Hill went back to an opening bet of ten dollars. Two players dropped out, obviously not able to beat Hill's opening pair of jacks or better.

That left Hill, Buckskin and Larner. When it came to Buckskin, he raised ten dollars, making it twenty to Larner to stay in and ten to Hill to call.

Larner stayed, Hill met the ten-dollar rise and raised it another 50. Larner dropped out and Buckskin looked at his cards. He did not get another seven; he had his queen, an ace and a six. Hill beat him with his openers, but Hill didn't know that.

"So it's fifty dollars to me to stay in?" Buckskin asked.

Hill nodded, his face frozen, lifeless, giving away nothing. Buckskin let a small grin crease his face, then he wiped it away.

"So I'll see the fifty and raise it fifty," Buckskin said softly. There was now 450 dollars in the pot in the center of the table. It was the largest pot so far that night. That was about what a clerk in a store or a working man earned in a year.

Buckskin had won two previous smaller pots. He figured he now had about 150 dollars' worth of chips in front of him.

Hill frowned for just a moment, folded his cards and tapped them on the table as he closed his eyes. He lifted the cards and looked at them again so he could see just one edge of each of the five cards.

Buckskin's cards lay stacked and face down on the table in front of him. Hill stared hard at Buckskin, then reached for his chips. Then slowly his hand dropped to the table and he dropped his cards face down on the table.

"I'm out," he said.

Buckskin nodded and scraped the chips in. He pushed the cards to the side for the next dealer. He was careful not to tip over any card to show a man's hand.

Buckskin wanted to smile. He was over 400 dollars ahead for the night and he had learned that Nate Hill could be bluffed. He'd put that down in his book on Yankton poker players. It could come in handy down the road somewhere.

They played two hours more. Gradually Buckskin realized that on every hand Hill dealt, he won. He was bottom dealing, the kind of cheating that was easiest to do and easiest to catch. Whenever Hill dealt after that, Buckskin threw in his hand. No matter how good his cards in the deal, Buckskin knew that Hill would have a better hand.

Two more times he watched Hill deal. He sat right beside the saloon owner so it was easy. The next time Hill dealt, Buckskin's hand darted out just as Hill drew a card off the deck to deal it to himself. Buckskin's hand caught Hill's hand with a card halfway off the bottom of the deck.

Two chairs tipped over as men on the far side of the table stood up quickly.

"Gawd, Hill," Larner roared. "You promised us you wouldn't do no bottom dealing no more."

Buckskin's hand held the dealer's hand pinned to the table with the incriminating card halfway slipped off the bottom.

"Everyone see what our host, Mr. Hill, has been doing?" Buckskin asked. The two men last in swore and one of them drew a six-gun.

"Don't," Buckskin spat, dropping Hill's hands and drawing his own six-gun so fast one of the men gasped. "Put your iron back in leather or you'll be going up against me. Is that clear, friend?"

The man growled. "He's a fucking cheater," the man roared. "A bottom dealer. No wonder he wins every hand he deals."

"Just goes to show he's a cheat, but not a smart cheat. Now holster that weapon and let's see what Mr. Hill is going to do about this life-and-death problem he has."

Hill let his hands drop to his sides. Buckskin brought the .45 around to center on Hill's chest.

"Be so good as to keep your hands on the table, Mr. Hill. Since you're still alive, I'd say it would be prudent of you to reimburse all those who lost money in your game tonight. Including the first man to drop out. Who lost money so far?"

Two men held up their hands. The third one had been kicked out the back door earlier.

"Impossible," Hill said. "I won't be held up in my own saloon."

"The hell you say, Hill," Quentin said. "You cheated me and I'll be damned if I'm going to let you get away with it. Now fork over the money so I can get out of here. You can be damn sure I'll never play poker again with you."

Buckskin watched as Hill paid the men from the chips he had. He ran out of chips.

"I believe you know the cashier," Buckskin said. "Have him bring over a few trays of chips so you can settle up."

Hill made up the losses of the two men, then turned to Buckskin. "You won, why didn't you pay the men, too?"

"I didn't cheat. I enjoy watching a man who can cheat at cards without anyone seeing him do it. But you, you're so obvious I kept waiting for somebody else to challenge you." Buckskin reached over and took a hide-out two-shot derringer from Hill's inside jacket pocket.

"Hard place to draw a hide-out from if you need it, Hill. How in hell have you stayed alive so long?"

Buckskin took his chips and went to the cashier at the end of the room and cashed out. He was a little over 250 dollars ahead for the night.

The other players cashed out as well and Hill stood there glaring at them. He walked up to Buckskin and held out his hand for his firearm.

"This isn't the last of it, Morgan. I know who you are and where you live and I swear that the next time we meet you won't have a chance to get your six-gun in my face." The threat came softly so no one but Buckskin could hear it.

The detective grinned. "Hell, Mr. Hill, I've been threatened by a lot tougher and smarter men than you are. A few of them are still walking around. Most of them are six feet under.

"Oh, anytime you want to play poker one on one, I'll be glad to play," he continued. "A thousand-dollar buy-in, no limit, no IOU's. Just the two of us to see who's the best player. Only one condition. You try cheating on me in that game, and I'll kill you dead on the spot."

Buckskin turned around and walked out, presenting his back to the saloon owner who still held the derringer in his hand.

Nate Hill watched Buckskin Morgan walk out of the back room of his saloon. It was all he could do not to charge the man and shoot him twice. The four other men in the room had a lot to do with his inaction. He yelled at the other men to get out, that the game was over. The cashier took his box of chips and bag of money and left as well.

Hill stormed up the back steps to his apartment and found Sherry Crawford where he had left her, lounging in a housecoat on the big couch reading a book.

"Is reading all you ever do?" he barked.

Sherry grinned and put the book down. "Lost, huh? How much? No, don't tell me, it'll only make you madder."

"Damn him. The guy I had tailed today, Buckskin Morgan. He came in and played in the two-hundred-dollar buy-in game in the back room. That's the guy I told you I didn't want you to see.

He's the bastard who has been asking all over town about a woman poker player with long red hair."

Sherry rose from her seat and frowned. "Maybe it's time I moved on upstream . . . no, downstream. More people, more towns and more poker games downstream."

"You can't go anywhere. If he hears that you play poker and were here and suddenly left, he'd be on your trail like a bloodhound."

Sherry began pacing. "Well, just what do you suggest that I do, then? I can't very well stay here and get any playing in."

"Sure you can, just as soon as I have him killed. Nobody will be able to tie it to me. I'll get somebody good from out of town and have him take the boat out the same night. No problem. Yeah, I'll kill the bastard."

Sherry frowned and watched him. "I've only seen you this angry one time before. That was when that Mississippi riverboat gambler caught you cheating."

He looked at her sharply.

Sherry laughed. "So he did catch you cheating. I told you you were getting a little sloppy. You need practice."

"Shut up, Sherry, I'm thinking. I have to find just exactly the right man for this job. I can't make any mistakes on this one or I could be a dead man."

Buckskin went from the Criterion Saloon back to his hotel. He moved carefully, watching his back trail, moving away from alley mouths and careful when he crossed the street. He knew he had made an enemy tonight in Nate Hill. He just didn't know how skilled or resourceful the saloon owner was. He looked like the kind of man who would hire gun work rather than do the dirty work himself.

Buckskin frowned as he walked down the second-floor hallway of the Dakota Arms Hotel. He hesitated at room 26, the one he had moved to without benefit of hotel clerk after his other room had been bombed. He went on to room 28 and rapped gently on the door. It was a little after midnight. The lady should be in bed.

He heard a voice through the door. He knocked again and she edged the door open. "Buckskin," he whispered, and she opened the door and he slipped inside.

She wore only a blouse. The lamp was burning with the wick trimmed low. Melinda locked the door, turned the key halfway and then put her arms around his neck and kissed him hard and long.

"What a fine surprise to wake up to," she said. She began working on his shirt buttons. "Yes, you're staying the night, no excuses. I need you tonight. I found out absolutely nothing all day. I even went down and watched the boats come and go from the dock for a while. One man on board waved at me just as one boat left the dock. I'd never seen him before, but he evidently thought he knew me. Now tell me what you've been up to."

He told her about the cheating scene. "So I'd just as soon not sleep in my other room tonight. Somebody must know I moved down there. I'd just as soon not get blown up quite yet."

She had him undressed and his boots off and

pushed him down on the bed. Slowly she shucked out of the old blouse she wore as a nightshirt. Then she turned up the light and went on her hands and knees over him letting her big breasts swing down toward his face.

"See anything you'd like to chew on?" she asked.

"One or two things."

"Give them a try. You know they love it."

Buckskin tried to relax. He grinned at the girl and sucked one of her breasts into his mouth and chewed on it tenderly, then he switched.

"That feels so fine, so fine. It's been such a long time since you've been here. I want you so much. Are you ready yet? I want you right now with me up on top this way, right now."

It was two lovemakings later that they lay side by side on the bed holding each other.

"I've been thinking about going back to Denver," she said. "I don't think I'm doing any good here. Nobody remembers Maria except that one guy, and he doesn't know anything about what happened."

"Give it another week. Maybe I can find out something."

"That would be great. I'm getting a little short of money, but I can stay another week."

Buckskin was ready to offer her some of his poker winnings when he heard the unmistakable blast of a heavy shotgun. It sounded like it was in the room with them, but it wasn't, maybe a door or two down.

Before he could get out of bed, the shotgun boomed again, then he heard running boots on the hallway boards. By the time he got to the door and looked out, all he saw was a man in dark clothes racing down the far stairs.

He came back inside and put on his pants.

"What was that?" Melinda asked.

"Somebody just fired two rounds from a shotgun. I'm hoping they weren't next door in my room."

A few second later he saw that the shots had been fired into his room, 26. The door had evidently been opened by a key, since he hadn't heard it kicked open. He lit a lamp and looked around. One blast of double-ought buck chewed up the bed, the second blast shot the other side of the room including his carpetbag.

Two men carrying lamps crowded into the room. Then the room clerk came with a lamp of his own. He scowled at Buckskin, then put the lamp down. He shooed the strangers out of the room and closed the door.

"Mr. Morgan. This is twice we've had violent episodes in your room. I'm going to have to ask you to move to a different hotel tomorrow. You won't be charged for the damage, including the broken-out window. However, we will not compensate you for any personal loss." The clerk shook his head. "How come you're still alive?"

Buckskin shrugged. "Heard somebody unlock my door so I bunched the covers in the middle of the bed and slid off on the far side between the bed and the wall. I was on the floor safe as a baby in a crib."

The clerk scowled. "Even so, the owner said if anything else happened in your room, I was to ask you to leave. Check-out time is ten in the morning."

The clerk shook his head again, picked up his

lamp and marched out of the room and down the hall. When he had left, and the last of the curious had gone back to their rooms along the second floor, Buckskin tried the door of Melanie's room and found it open.

"Terrible, just terrible," she crooned, hugging him tightly. "I'm so glad you weren't in that room."

"I'd be dead," Buckskin said and grinned. "Tomorrow we move to a different hotel and register under different names."

"Rooms right next to each other?"

"Of course, and with a connecting door if they have one."

Buckskin took off his trousers and shirt and then they slid back into bed. She rolled half on top of him.

"Just one more to calm me down," he said. "Damn, but two shotgun blasts next door really gets me hotter than a whole whorehouse full of eager little twats. Come on, right now."

Chapter Eleven

Buckskin wasn't up at six the next morning as usual. He slept in until eight, satisfied a clinging and naked Melinda, then went down for breakfast with her. He overheard two men talking at the next table about Nate Hill.

"Yep, what I heard, some Jasper caught old Nate dealing off the bottom of the deck to himself. Made Nate pay back every man at the table who had lost money. I doubt if Nate will get his big-money games going again for a while, except for out-of-towners just off the boat."

That set Buckskin to thinking. Since the Criterion wouldn't be having big-money games, the other spots where large amounts of cash changed hands should be visited by the mysterious lady poker player. Now he'd get a chance to see her. He'd just check in at each game every night until he found her, then play and see if she looked anything like Dawn Evans.

Melinda hadn't been her usual nonstop talking machine at breakfast and now he looked over at her sipping her coffee and asked her why.

"Just don't feel like talking. I'm getting more and more upset about this whole thing with Maria. I thought I could come up here and find her right off, persuade her to come back home, and everything would be all right. Now all the other possibilities are starting to get on my nerves. Like I said last night, maybe I should just fold up my tent and go back to Denver."

"Probably would be best. You haven't been having any luck here in finding her. Wish I had more time to help you. I may at long last have some kind of a lead for locating my missing person."

"I'm glad for you. I think today I'll go down to the dock and find out how much a ticket is to Omaha in one of those little cabins."

They left together, and Buckskin made a mental check on the saloons that held no-limit poker games. Not many of them. The River Rat Saloon had a game every night with a 100-dollar buy-in. Then the Beer Bucket Saloon was said to have a big game. He wasn't sure about the Lucky Lady Saloon.

He headed that way when a young boy ran up to him. "Hey, are you Mr. Morgan, Buckskin Morgan?"

The kid looked about twelve. Buckskin nodded. " 'Pears to be I'm the one. Why you asking?"

"A man gave me a letter to give to you. I don't

know why and I never seen the man before, but he gave me a dime if I'd bring the letter to you."

"How did you know I was the right person?"

"Oh, he pointed you out to me. Said to wait until the lady left you, then bring you this letter." He held it out. Buckskin frowned. Why would someone send him a letter this way and take pains so he wouldn't know who did it? Not anything good could come from it. Then he thought of the vigilantes, the Five Angels of Death, and he decided the letter could be from the committee trying to fight them. He took the letter.

"Thanks, kid. What did this man look like who gave you the letter?"

"Can't say." The boy turned and raced down the boardwalk dodging between people and then across the street right in front of a team and wagon. Buckskin let him go.

The Denver detective leaned against a store front and opened the sealed envelope. Inside was a piece of white paper folded twice. He spread it open and saw the handwriting. He read it.

Dear Mr. Morgan,

We understand that you are interested in confronting the vigilantes now operating in Yankton. We are in sympathy with you and hope to help you. Our committee is compiling a file to show to the territorial attorney and hope you can contribute to the file.

We have evidence of the vigilantes' involvement in the deaths of three individuals along with witnesses and other evidence. We need more.

Last night we know that the vigilantes caught one of our Negro men on the street after dark and drove him out of town upriver where they must have been going to hang him. Someone disrupted the hanging and saved the black man. Some person or persons must have saved him since the Negro man and his wife were on the first downriver boat this morning. We need your help. Threats and attempted murder as in the hanging, will carry a lot of weight with the attorney general.

Could we meet you in some secret place today? We want to show our material to the attorney general tomorrow. There is an old house about two miles upriver and a quarter of mile back from the water. It's abandoned and used now and then by men on the move and bums.

If you would meet us there this afternoon about one o'clock we would appreciate it. Oh, yes, there will be two of us. We will put our horses around in back of the main house so no one will suspect we are there. If you would do the same it would help. If the vigilantes hear of this meeting, all three of us could be gunned down by rifle fire, so please be prudent. We hope to see you this afternoon at one o'clock two miles upriver.

The message was unsigned.

This is not my job, Buckskin told himself. He had a case of his own to work. One little attempted murder wouldn't sway a lawyer for the Territory. What the committee needed were more witnesses who had actually seen the Five Angels of Death hanging and shooting those men. He couldn't do it. Not a chance.

He walked down the boardwalk. Without realizing it, he took out his watch and checked the time. A little after 9:30. He'd have plenty of time to walk out there, or rent a horse at the livery and ride out.

What was he thinking of? Not a chance that he was going to go to some secret meeting of this committee. He'd met two of them. They didn't seem so secretive to him. Maybe the Five Angels of Death didn't take the men seriously. Maybe.

He looked in a store window and saw the reflection of a man ride past on a horse. Oh, damn. He was going to go out there. How did he get himself in these problem situations? The vigilantes were not his case. He just happened to stumble into that hang-try up on the river. But if he could help out the committee . . .

At 11:30 he finished an early lunch and walked down to the livery. He rented a horse, paying two dollars in advance for it for the rest of the day, and rode back into the main part of town. He stopped at a hardware store and bought a Remington repeating rifle that held eight rounds, and a box of shells to fit it, and slid the rifle into the boot on the saddle. Then he rode due east, away from the river. Anyone watching him would say only that he rode out of town east. Who would watch him? This was driving him crazy. He should be hunting Dawn Evans.

A half mile out of town, Buckskin turned north and galloped over to the river, then took the north road. It wasn't much of a road. A few wagons used it and some horses, but there weren't many settlers up north of town yet.

He saw the abandoned house as the letter had described. It had a barn in back of it and two other outbuildings. He pulled off the road and circled the place from half a mile off. He figured that no one in the place could see him because of a small creek that he followed with its brush and an occasional cottonwood tree.

When he was behind the barn, he moved up closer using the brush of the creek and a tributary as his concealment. A hundred yards from the barn the high brush petered out. He stepped down and tied his horse there, then, taking the rifle and his six-gun, he worked silently through the tall grass and small brush until he was within twenty feet of the barn.

No more concealment and no cover. He looked at the barn and saw a small man-sized door in the rear. He stood and jogged to the door expecting someone to call out to him at any time. Nothing happened.

He pressed against the weathered wood of the barn and waited. When nothing happened for two minutes, he eased away from the siding and slid over to the door. It had no knob or pull on it but stood an inch open. He reached in and lifted the door and eased it outward. One hinge gave a soft squeak of rusted metal on rusted metal. He stopped.

Nothing happened. He looked inside. Streams of sunlight bored through the place from holes in the roof or broken windows. He saw nothing but abandoned stalls, a place for hay and an old rusted farm machine that must have been pushed in a large door near the front. There was no loft or second story.

Buckskin slipped inside the opening and froze against the wall. He could hear nothing. A moment later someone coughed. The sound came from his right. To his left someone hissed for the man to be quiet.

Buckskin frowned. Two men in the barn? The letter said they would be in the abandoned house out front. What the hell was going on? The biggest possibility surfaced at once. An ambush. The letter could have come from anyone wanting to get rid of him. They used the Negro man as the bait. So who was trying to kill him? Maybe Nate Hill, the gambler from the Criterion Saloon. Maybe those sternwheeler guys who shot at him on the boat. Maybe even the vigilantes for his disrupting their hanging.

He was just a popular guy.

A moment later he heard a shell being chambered in a rifle. In the silence of the big building it sounded like a thunderclap. Again it came from the right. From the left came one word.

"Idiot!"

Then only silence.

Now Buckskin's eyes had adjusted to the low level of light inside the barn. He began to move soundlessly to the left, avoiding the shafts of bright sunshine, some no larger than a silver dollar that stabbed into the building and to the floor.

He estimated it took him fifteen minutes of slow moving and testing his footing before he came to where he could see the man on the left. He lay in front of a firing hole that had been kicked out of the front wall.

The man lay there on his stomach with his chin in his hands. Beside him lay a rifle and a six-gun. With his target in sight, Buckskin could move faster. He took an eighth-inch-square string of buckskin from his pocket and tied loops in each end. Then he moved forward with even more caution.

Five minutes later he heard the far man clear his throat. The nearby man swore softly. Buckskin was four feet behind him now. He left the rifle on the floor and lunged ahead with the strip of leather arcing out in front of his hands. The boot lace looped around the ambusher's head, and Buckskin crossed his hands at once and pulled, tightening the leather around the man's throat. He couldn't make a sound. Buckskin held both ends of the leather in one hand for a moment, then drew his six-gun and slammed it down across the man's head. He gave a soft groan and passed out.

From the other man came a "Shhhh," then all was quiet. Buckskin tied the man's wrists together in back of him, then his ankles, and used a kerchief to tie a gag through his mouth and behind his neck. He was breathing gently and evenly.

The other man swore. "When the hell's he coming?" the voice demanded. "I'm getting dirty and all cramped up laying here." A figure sat up directly in the path of one of the shafts of sunlight, this one from a roof board that had been lost.

Buckskin drew his Colt and cocked it. "Don't move or you're dead, hear me? Your friend here is not going to help you."

The man in the light screamed and dove away from the light, then fired twice at the voice he had heard. Buckskin returned two rounds, rolled to his left, and fired again at where the man had been. He heard no response. Cat and mouse? He stood, held the six-gun ready, and walked across the thirty feet of barn to the far side. A man lay there, his legs in a shaft of light, his torso twisted, and his eyes staring into the eternity of darkness.

"What the hell is going on in there?" a voice demanded from in front of the barn.

Buckskin was not able to identify the dead man. He hadn't seen any of the others. He ran back to where he had left his rifle and grabbed it, then went out the back door. He was almost to the heavy brush when a rifle slug drilled the air over his head. He dove to the ground and rolled in the grass, then worked through it without making the stalks overhead give away his position.

Half a dozen more rifle shots came his way, then he was in the tall brush and he ran up the tiny creek twenty yards and belly-crawled to the edge of the brush so he could see the barn but not be seen himself.

A man peered out from the far side of the barn. He lifted a rifle and fired into the brush. Buckskin levered a round into his rifle and fired twice, spinning chunks of the ancient barn's siding off on the corner near where the man's head had been.

Buckskin ran back the way he had come and heard four shots and hot lead cutting through the brush where he had been firing from. He caught his horse, mounted and rode under cover of the brush back to town, taking a round-about route so he came into Yankton from the south. He was back in town an hour later. He turned in the horse to the stable boy and walked away with his Remington and the rest of the rounds in his pocket.

His first stop was at the desk clerk of the Dakota Arms Hotel. He checked out, paid his bill, gathered what was left of his belongings, and moved to the Van Dalton Hotel a block down the street. He left word in Melinda's box where he was going and suggested she move down there as well.

The Van Dalton Hotel was better than where he had been. He got room 22 on the second floor and looked over his belongings. The shotgun the night before had shredded the top of the carpetbag. He'd have to buy a new one. A shirt on top of the bag had four holes in it and a pair of town trousers were ruined. He pitched them out. He'd been traveling with too many clothes anyway.

In the bottom of the carpetbag he found his spare Colt .45 in good condition. He had paid the clerk for a week's rent and registered in the name of Richard James. Make it that much harder for the assassins to find him.

He had a bath, shaved, put on clean clothes and went down and read the Omaha *Herald* in the lobby. An hour later Melinda came in with her bag and registered. He followed her up to the second floor and found she had room 28, the same as she had before. He let her go in her room, then when no one else was in the hall, he knocked and she opened the door at once.

He told her about his trip upriver and she scowled.

"It's time for you to get out of here, too. You can't spend any of the money you'll make on this case if you're dead." She prevented any response from him with a kiss on his lips.

"Now, I know the price of a ticket," she went on. "We can go together and enjoy the ride all the way downstream. There's something about making love on a boat that really makes me go wild."

"I can't go yet. You must know that. I have a job to do, and I've had people trying to kill me for the past fifteen years. Nobody has got the job done. Don't worry. Have you had supper yet?"

"No, its only four o'clock."

"Good, I'm starved. We won't have any trouble getting a table. Where would you like to go?"

After their supper, they went back to the hotel, and that was when they heard the news in the lobby. One of the sheriff's deputies had been shot dead that afternoon. A man at the desk nodded.

"That's right. Deputy Sheriff Zebadiah Clay is his name. Don't hear much about him. On night duty a lot, I guess. From what the sheriff said, Zeb was up north of town somewhere looking for a man on a wanted poster from Montana. Sheriff said he don't know for sure what happened.

"Some guy passing by on the road found the body near his horse that had been killed, too. Sheriff is putting out another wanted on that same killer."

The man shook his head. "Getting so it ain't safe to walk around the countryside these days. Next thing you know, we'll have to start locking our doors."

"Up north of town?" Melinda asked Buckskin as they walked up the stairs. "Wasn't that where you were?"

He chuckled. "You always want to tie things up in a neat little package. North of town could have been twenty miles, for all we know."

She shrugged, but it kept nagging at Buckskin. The man he killed in the ambush had to be one of the men trying to gun him down. Did that make the deputy sheriff one of the white slavers? Not likely. He wasn't free to work the riverboats. So was he working for Nate Hill and the Criterion Saloon? Again not logical. That meant that the deputy sheriff could have been one of the vigilantes. Only they would be the Four Angels of Death now instead of five. Interesting theory to ponder.

In Melinda's room, they sat on the bed and kissed and gently began undressing each other. They made tender, sweet love, and when both were satisfied they lay side by side naked watching the ceiling.

"I still want you to come back with me. If that deputy sheriff was one of the men trying to kill you . . ."

She didn't finish. Instead she pushed past him and sat on the edge of the bed. He sat up beside her.

"If he was, it's my problem," he said. "I don't want to get in your way of going back to Denver where you belong. This is no town for you. Do you realize that the whores wear derringers in their skirts when they walk the streets? They do. They don't want some familiar face to try to get some free poking in an alley somewhere. I hear they shot three men last year, killed one."

She sighed. "You're right. This isn't my kind of town."

By seven o'clock he had combed his hair, shaved again to be most presentable, and wandered into the River Rat Saloon. The barkeep said they didn't have a game set for that night, but if four showed up they would change their minds.

He went on to the Lucky Lady and found that there was to be a game tonight. Started at eight, and only six players were allowed. So far they had four.

"Is the lady poker player in town one of the four?" Buckskin asked. The apron lifted his brows.

"Don't know, ask the guard over on the door."

The guard said the lady was not among the four playing but she always came at the last minute when she did play. Buckskin waited until five minutes after eight and she hadn't shown up. The game had started. He said he'd find another game.

At the next saloon down the street, he stopped in. He hadn't been there before. The barkeep said yep, they had a game that night, a fifty-dollar buy-in. Nothing bigger. Buckskin looked through the door and saw a woman at the table for six. There were two openings.

He flashed fifty dollars and walked in and bought his chips. He sat beside the woman. Both chairs were empty next to her. She looked at him briefly, nodded. Nobody said hello. Nobody waved or smiled or looked at him very long.

The woman had short hair, short and dark. He would try to get a look at the hair's roots. He'd seen dyed hair grow out and show more than one color.

He looked at her in profile and tried to remember exactly what Dawn Evans looked like. He couldn't visualize the picture.

The game started. The lady could play poker. It was a five-dollar bet limit. Within a half hour two of the men ran out of money and left the game. The players took a five-minute break. When they began again, Buckskin sat across from the woman. On the break he had figured she was about the same height as Dawn Evans.

He couldn't bring himself to call her Dawn. That would be a dead giveaway that he was looking for her, if this was Dawn Evans. She looked something like the picture, but now he could see so much more of her face without the long red hair brushing both sides of her cheeks.

Could be, but he wasn't sure enough to ask her. He began to play poorly and blew his fifty-dollar stake. He wanted out of the game. Two players said he could buy more chips if he had money in his pocket. House rules. He declined, said fifty-dollars was all he could afford to loose.

He went outside and across the street and sat against a store front watching the saloon. He had to find out where the woman stayed, where she went from there.

He waited an hour. Then he stood and walked up and down, keeping the door to the saloon in sight. He had no thought that the woman might go out the alley door. He saw two of the poker players come out. The woman didn't leave. He scowled and walked back into the saloon. He noticed the name: Charley's Saloon. Inside he went to the door that led to the back room. It stood open, the room was empty of poker players. The cashier stood at his post evidently balancing his books.

"The lady? Yes sir, she left."

"I didn't see her come out the front door."

"Right. She always has an escort, a bodyguard. She always leaves by the back door. She likes it best that way."

Buckskin thanked the man and walked out the front door. He paused and looked both ways, then hurried up the street toward the new hotel. He went in the side door, up the back stairs and to his room. He saw no one on the way.

He started to unlock his door but saw that the door was slightly open and that there was a light on inside. He drew his Colt and pushed the door open hard so it slammed against the wall in case someone was hiding behind it.

He looked at the bed and saw a man sitting there, dressed in a proper suit and vest, tie and a black town hat. He blinked as he stared at the muzzle of Buckskin's six-gun.

"Who the hell are you and what are you doing in my room?" Buckskin demanded.

Chapter Twelve

The man sitting on Buckskin's bed rose slowly. He held his hands in plain sight.

"I am Dr. Sims. I'm not here to harm you in any way. I want you to kill a man for me."

"Dr. Sims, I'm not a gun for hire, and I don't murder people for money. Outside of that, is there anything else I can do for you?"

Dr. Sims sat down quickly on the bed.

"You were my last hope. A man here in town is blackmailing me, holding me hostage. He has a file of information about me and he says some pictures, but I doubt that."

"Sorry, murder is not my line of work. I'm a detective here on a case of my own. Is that why you approached me in this unusual way, because you thought I was a gunman?"

"I've seen your gun tied low, the way you move. You just look like a gunman. Sorry if I was wrong." Dr. Sims stood.

Buckskin motioned him back down. "Doctor, you've violated the privacy of my room. Breaking and entering, I think the law calls it. I could have you thrown in jail."

Buckskin watched the man. He didn't scare easily. He must have a much greater worry.

"Dr. Sims, have you treated a gunshot wound late at night the last day or two?"

The doctor looked up quickly. He frowned. Slowly he nodded. "Yes. He's the same man I want you to kill."

"Did he come to your clinic after midnight?"

"Yes."

"Is he one of the Five Angels of Death?"

"If I tell you, I could be the next one hung. Don't you see what a grip they have on this town. Only now there are only three of them instead of five." He looked around, then pointed to the door. "Would you check outside and be sure no one is listening, then lock it, please?"

Buckskin hesitated a moment. Panic grew in the face of the medical man. Buckskin checked the hall and locked the door. He had already holstered his six-gun. He sat on the foot of the bed and watched the doctor.

"Yes, I treated the man. I do quite a bit of work that way, late at night with no one knowing about it. Mostly I realized I was working on four, then five men who always cautioned me not to tell the sheriff about it. It took me a while to realize what was happening. Then I caught on that everytime I treated one of the five men at night, the next day I heard about some kind of a tragedy. A man had been hung, or shot, or a family burned out of its home, or some other act of violence.

"About the time I realized I had been treating the Five Angels of Death, one of them came to me with this file. It held a lot of innuendo and some ranting by an unhappy former assistant nurse of mine. Yes, and a bit of truth. Enough to make me listen to the man. He still has the file.

"You heard about Van Dalton being shot down in the street a few days ago. He was one of the five. I have no idea who killed him. He hadn't been robbed and no threats had been made on his life.

"Then today we hear that Deputy Sheriff Zebadiah Clay was killed while on a ride to catch a killer up north of town. He's dead all right, but I doubt if some wanted killer did him in. So the Five Angels of Death are down to three now, and I want to make it two, but I can't do murder. I hoped maybe you would."

Buckskin rose and went to the window, pushed aside the sheer curtain and stared down on the nearly dark town. "I've already helped you. I shot the man you repaired. They were about to hang a Negro man the other night."

"Good. Just wish you had hit something vital. I'm glad that old Ned got away. They've been hounding that black man for nearly a year now."

Buckskin rubbed his jaw. "I'm here on other business, but if I knew who these three are, I might find some way to discourage their activities."

"Discourage? Now, what would you be meaning by that?"

"Oh, might be any number of things. Ever have your chimney plug up just as supper was under way on the stove? Ever find your woodshed or detached stable on fire in the middle of the night? Ever slap the reins on a horse and have the animal stride forward right out of cut traces and leave you and the rig sitting there? Little things that don't add up to murder, but that are somehow downright discouraging."

Doc Sims grinned for the first time since Buckskin had arrived. "By Jove, young man, I think you and I have some of the same kind of feelings. You're telling me it wouldn't have to be murder. It might just be . . . discouragement."

"If I have the time. No promises."

"I don't need any signed agreement with you. Lands sakes, I thought I was the only one who has been so incensed these past two years because they are so vicious. Yes, there's that committee, but they haven't done anything now in almost three years. They're a joke and the Five, no, the Three Angels, know it."

"You and I, Dr. Sims, won't be a joke."

The doctor looked away, then frowned at Buckskin. "You realize that if they know that I told you, they'll kill me at once."

"I know. At least three men tried to kill me this afternoon up at that abandoned farm two miles north of town. They set me up with an ambush. Two in the barn, one or two in the house. I came in behind them in the barn. I shot one of them. It could have been the deputy sheriff. So I know what it means to be under threat of death. But they'll never know you told me. I'm on their list already."

Buckskin frowned, suddenly wary.

"How did you find me here?"

"I talked to the hotel clerk. I described you. Not hard to find you that way. This is a small town, strangers stand out like a smelly outhouse on Main Street."

Buckskin moved quickly, pushed all of his belongings into the tattered carpetbag. "Time I was changing rooms. Tell me who the men are. Then I'm taking another room without the aid of the room clerk. Who are the other three Angels of Death?"

"Gideon Ingraham is the leader, been with them from the start when they were dedicated, honest, and did a lot of good back six, eight years ago. He runs the general store and is the mayor. Then there's Porter Jordan who owns the livery stable. He was a former sheriff or marshal out west somewhere. Got into trouble there is my guess. Not the kind of man you'd invite to Sunday dinner.

"The last one left alive is Stacey Trumble, our shoemaker and saddle man. Runs the saddlery and leather shop. He seems to be in on it just for the thrill of killing."

By then Buckskin had his gear all in his bag. He picked up the bag and his rifle and opened the door. "As soon as you're down the back steps, I'll pick another room. Now get out of here and carry a gun at all times and watch your back. Go."

The doctor grinned. "A man of action, I like that.

Yes, I'll watch my back, and my front and sides as well." He walked out the door and didn't look back as he headed for the rear stairs. When he was out of sight, Buckskin looked for a new room. The first two he checked were occupied with sleepers. The next was vacant and he slipped inside, locked the door and struck a match to be sure no one had rented the room. It was empty.

He stretched out on the bed without lighting a lamp. No use letting the doctor know which room he had, either.

He lay there with his fingers laced behind his head. So, he knew the names of the other Angels of Death. What should he do about it? That depended on what they did. An eye for an eye might be a good balance, but that could take weeks. No, something quicker, more sudden, more drastic, something final. The men were killers all. Buckskin had a sour taste in his mouth just thinking about them.

He could burn out the merchant, but the store was butted up against other wooden structures that would burn along with the general store. The whole block could burn down. An idea came to him and he pondered it a minute. Then he grinned.

Ten minutes later, Buckskin found the lock on the back door of the Ingraham General Store easy to open with a skeleton key.

Inside he checked. There were no alarms or signals. He began trashing the store from front to back, working as quietly as he could. The first two islands that showed through the front windows he left alone, but the rest of the store was soon in heaps and piles on the floor.

Dishes were broken, displays ruined, merchandise tossed on the floor in an unending mess. Not a big cash loss, but a signal to Mr. Ingraham that his life would never be the same. When he left by the back door, he carefully locked it.

The next store was the much smaller leather man's saddlery and shoe repair and bootmaking shop. Getting inside from the rear was no problem. Buckskin looked around. What would give the leather man the most pain, cause him some anguish and regrets?

He looked over half the store before he found what he wanted. It was a strong acid used to etch leather. Full strength, it ate through leather like it was warm butter on a hot day.

He poured the acid on an almost finished fancy saddle on the bench. When the acid finished its work, the saddle maker would have to start over on that one. He did the same to three more saddles that looked finished and ready to deliver.

Then he trashed the shop as he had the store, to put a signature on the act and get the Three Angels of Death to thinking.

The livery posed some problems. Many townsmen stabled horses there rather than keep a small barn or shed themselves. It was convenient, and better for the horses, who had the freedom of a thirty-acre pasture.

Buckskin scouted the place. He found a lantern burning in the office and someone sleeping there on a bunk against the far wall. No one else seemed to be about. He slipped up on him quietly.

He recognized the stable boy he had turned his

horse in to yesterday. He brought the side of his six-gun down smartly across the young man's forehead. The victim groaned once, his eyes fluttered, then he passed out. Buckskin picked him up. He blew out the lantern and carried the stable boy out the big door to a spot fifty yards away and tied his hands and feet. Then he put an easy gag in his mouth so he couldn't yell but so it wouldn't hurt him.

Back at the livery, he opened the stalls and drove all of the horses out of the barn and well down in the pasture. Then he tossed matches into hay in the stalls and brought the lantern and smashed it against a wall. By the time he walked to the front of the livery barn it was burning brightly. He ran outside.

It was after two a.m. and all good people were fast asleep in their beds. No one gave an alarm. He watched for fifteen minutes until the entire structure and a small outbuilding were fully ablaze. Enough. He walked back to his hotel, went up the back steps and into room 20 right next to the stairs that he had appropriated as his own. He locked the door, turned the key in the lock so no one could get in with a key, and lay down on the bed with his clothes and boots on and his Colt six-gun beside his right hand.

Buckskin awoke the next morning refreshed and ready for the day. He wondered what the reaction of the Three Angels of Death would be when they saw their businesses this morning. He'd like to watch.

He heard a sternwheeler whistle at the dock and

walked down the half block to the river on Second Street. The 200-foot-long flat-bottomed sternwheeler was just pulling up to the dock. Two men half carried, half walked a woman along the street toward the wharf.

Buckskin frowned. The woman seemed to have the same dress on that Melinda Warnick had worn a time or two. Coincidence? He watched the big boat tie up and the gangplank come down. Then he saw the woman's sunbonnet blow off her head and hang down her back. Long blonde hair billowed out of the sunbonnet, and the woman's face turned toward him.

Impossible. The woman looked a little like Melinda. But it couldn't be she. Melinda would have told him before she took the boat. Also, why would she need two men to help her get to the boat? Melinda didn't drink that much.

He watched the crewmen unload the ship of freight. Then the last of the passengers boarded, the gangplank was hauled up, and black smoke gushed from both smokestacks. The *Nellie Peck* edged into the Missouri.

Something on the upper deck caught Buckskin's eye. A woman ran to the rail, blonde hair flying. She looked at the dock and screamed out his name.

"Buckskin, come and save me!" she hollered. She said it twice before the two men he had seen before took hold of her and carried her to one of the cabins.

He stood there a moment in shock. White slavers. That had been Melinda the men were taking to the boat. They had kidnapped her the same way they must have kidnapped her sister. He ran to the steamship office at the far end of the dock. The clerk there was positive.

"Next sternwheeler is due here at nine A.M. She's the *Key West*. She's older and slower than the one just left."

"How can I catch the one that just pulled out?" Buckskin asked.

"Well, she stops about an hour downstream at Caruthers' Bend. Usually she takes on wood there. Cheaper than it is here in town. You might grab a horse and try to beat her down there."

Buckskin took off running.

He had forgotten about the livery barn. Two men were picking through the remains. Four solid logs still stood pointing at the sky. The rest were flat on the ground. The heavy logs were blackened but still standing. Bits and scraps of leather goods had been laid out to one side.

Buckskin called to one of the men, "I need two saddled horses. Can you help me?"

"Going for a ride?"

"Yep, and I'm in a big hurry."

"Had a little problem here last night. I think I have a couple of old saddles in that outbuilding over there."

Five minutes later, Buckskin rode down the river road on one of the horses and led the other one. He had no idea how fast these boats went downstream this time of year. He figured that by riding one horse at a slow gallop and switching horses every half mile, he could make eight miles in an hour. If the steamer got there well before that, it could be gone and miles downstream before he arrived.

He rode hard, changed horses when he felt the one he was on begin to falter. He was close to the area of Caruthers' Bend when he heard a steamship whistle blowing.

Was the ship coming in to the landing or taking off?

He remembered that the ones he had seen sounded their whistle when they arrived to attract attention.

Buckskin rode a little harder and soon saw the bend in the river ahead and the glorious view of a flat-bottom sternwheeler tied to a small pier while men threw on board stacks of cordwood.

He rode down fast, jumped off the horse, and shouted to one of the wood loaders to take care of the mounts, saying he'd be back for them in three days. He ran for the rail and leaped on board just as the last of the wood was loaded.

"What the hell you doing, mate?" a muscled crewman called.

"Looking for passage downriver. This is the *Nellie Peck,* isn't it? Missed you at Yankton."

"Go up to the wheelhouse."

Buckskin paid for a trip halfway to Omaha, then tried to remember which cabin the two men had taken Melinda into. Second or third from the end? He wasn't sure. He was just ready to knock on the door of the second cabin when the same crewman waved at him.

"The pilot has one more question for you," the crewman said. He was as big as Buckskin, with an unhealed cut on one cheek and a bruise over his right eye. A brawler.

"What does the pilot want?" Buckskin asked.

"Didn't say. Said to bring you to see him or throw you overboard."

"I have a ticket."

"Ain't no good if the pilot says so."

"It's his ship. Which way?"

The crewman pointed up the steps to the top deck, then to the outside wooden steps that led up to the wheelhouse. Buckskin moved a few feet along the boat deck. This had to mean that the crew was in collusion with the slave traders. It would be impossible to work it any other way.

Buckskin stumbled on the deck, then turned and slugged the crewman behind him with a hard right to the jaw. The man shook his head and grabbed Buckskin in a bearhug that almost cut him in half.

"Anything more like that and you're over the side, mate," the crewman said, dropping Buckskin to the deck. He lifted the Colt from Buckskin's holster. Buckskin was too hurting to protest. He lay there a moment to get his breath. A kick to his legs brought him to his feet and moving ahead.

The pilot, the man in charge of these fragile craft, stared at Buckskin, then nodded. "Yep, figured as how. Saw you playing poker in Yankton. Why so anxious to get on board?"

"Poker, like you say. Big game downriver. Omaha if I can make it. Figured on playing some on board."

"No gambling of any kind permitted on my ship, my rule." The pilot sucked on his pipe, then waved it at Buckskin.

"They tell me you rode down here from Yankton."

"True. Missed you there so I came on horseback."

"One horse couldn't make that kind of time."

"Right, I rode two, trading them off when one got tired. Make good time that way, eight, nine miles an hour."

"We make twelve mile an hour sometimes if the current is right. Today we had a minor problem with a shifted sandbar or you never would have caught us. I'll put you in a cabin for the rest of the trip. Joe here will show you which one."

"Mighty neighborly of you," Buckskin said, trying to figure it out. Sweetness and light, for now.

Down the steps to the boat deck, the crewman led Buckskin to cabin 12 at the end of the row. Joe opened the door and waved Buckskin inside, then pushed him forward, slammed the door, and Buckskin could hear a heavy steel bar dropping into place. It was the brig, the jail he had heard about for unruly passengers. So it was a setup with the ship owners or pilots. He checked the window. Far too small to get through. The walls of the cabin were made of metal. No chance to get out that way. He'd heard the bar drop in place on the door. He sank down on the bunk and tried to think it through.

That had been Melinda the tall, heavy man and the shorter one in a suit had been taking on board the *Nellie Peck*. Now he was certain. He should have attacked them right then and he would have had a chance. Now it looked grim.

He would have a long day in the small cabin and no food. He could do without that. He just wondered what had happened to Melinda. How was she faring in that small cabin with the two men? They would not be gentle, he knew that. He had to get out of there.

After about two hours of his captivity he felt the ship slow and then veer to the left. They must be making another stop. That wouldn't help him. The crew would be busy unloading.

He heard the whistle, then the slowing and the sound of the wooden hull scraping against the wooden dock.

Just as the boat stopped, he heard something at the door. He looked down, and a piece of paper slid under the door into his cabin.

He grabbed it and read:

"I can help you. Pass $20 under the door now."

Buckskin opened his wallet, took out a twenty-dollar greenback and slid it under the door halfway. It vanished as someone grabbed it quickly.

There was almost no noise, but he heard enough to tell him that the steel bar had been lifted from its place across the door. He tried the door. It was not locked. He edged it outward and peered out. He saw no one. He thrust the door open, stepped out, closed the door and put the bar back in place silently. Then he hurried to the next door, which opened onto the main cabin. No one was inside. He found a small closet and slipped inside it.

The best thing he could do now was keep out of sight until dark. Then he could try for a rescue. But he had to deal with the crew and the two men in the cabin with Melinda. All that and he didn't have his six-gun. He grinned and remembered the .32

six-shot pistol in a small holster on his ankle. He'd taken to wearing it lately and was glad he had it on now. He lifted it out of leather. Five loads.

He tensed when he heard someone come into the main cabin. It was used mostly for parties and gatherings of the first-class passengers. Small slots for ventilation in the closet door let him see out. The pilot and another crewman settled down at a table and opened sacks of food evidently purchased at the last stop.

Buckskin relaxed against the wall. He had time to kill. He wasn't about to confront the two riverboat men.

A half hour later they left and Buckskin looked through the slots again. It was getting dark outside. Good. He wished he had his Colt, but the .32 would have to do.

He slipped out of the closet and went to the door and looked through a narrow crack. Dark enough. He went out of the main cabin as if he belonged there and turned back toward the passenger cabins. The cabin he had seen the men force Melinda into was on this side of the ship, the second or third cabin from the front.

He stepped up to the second cabin door when someone growled behind him. He turned and saw Joe, the big crewman.

"What the hell you doing out here?" Joe snarled.

Chapter Thirteen

Melinda had gone back to her hotel room that afternoon with her mind made up. She would stay with Buckskin Morgan tonight, have a lovely time, and tell him that she had decided to go back to Denver on an afternoon boat the next day.

She unlocked her door in the Van Dalton Hotel where she had moved on Buckskin's advice and stepped inside. Two men loomed over her. One pushed his hand over her mouth and the other one shut the door.

She kicked at the smaller man, landing her shoe squarely in his crotch and jolting him backward screeching in pain. He doubled over and leaned against the wall. Quickly the other man, the giant, had caught her around her waist, lifted her off the floor and slammed her down on the bed so hard one of the bed boards fell out and clattered to the floor. His hand clapped over her mouth before she could scream.

"Little bitch," Kerr said through his pain. "Kicked me in the balls." He slumped to the floor and brought his legs up into a fetal position to try to lessen the pain.

Bull grinned. "Yeah, hurts like hell. You won't be fucking this one on the trip downriver."

Bull held the girl down with his arm and fondled her breasts. He kept her mouth covered and carefully undid the buttons on her blouse, then threw back the sides and lifted the chemise.

"Damn fine tits this one's got," Bull said.

Kerr held his crotch tenderly and groaned. "Bull, you got to get me to a doctor. I think she broke my balls."

Melinda worked one arm free from where Bull had pinned it under her body and punched Bull in the face. He chuckled, caught her hand, pushed it back under her body and leaned on her harder.

"Don't do that, little lady. Not nice. I'm not going to hurt your fine little body. You do like Mr. Kerr tells you and you'll do fine."

"Bull, stop blubbering and go get a doctor."

"I been crotch kicked before. Just take it easy. You'll feel lots better in a couple of hours. We ain't in no rush."

Bull caressed her breasts again. Melinda hated it. There was nothing she could do. He was so big and heavy. Both her arms were under her now with his hand over her mouth. She hated it, but his touching her breasts that way made her nipples get hard and surge. She hated it.

Kerr rolled over and sat up against the wall. "Damn, I hurt, but I'm not wanting to die anymore. This bitch is going to pay for what she did. She'll pay dearly. Yes, no doctor. We'll get on with this in an hour or so. We have until five o'clock tomorrow morning. Yes, I'm feeling better."

Melinda didn't know what they meant. Five o'clock? They were going to stay here all night? What were they going to do to her? The answer came quickly: rape her, what else?

Then she felt the lump growing against her leg. It must be Bull's erection. For just a moment she wondered how big it would be on a large man like Bull. Then she pushed the thought out of her mind. She had to concentrate on getting away from them or talking them out of whatever they had planned.

Slowly the hard facts hit her one after another. She was caught, kidnapped. She was a woman. They said five o'clock in the morning. The boats came to the landing about six. Oh no . . . these two were white slavers and she was their new victim. It had to be. Why else two men? Not just a rape. It must be a kidnapping for the white slavers.

Tears formed in her eyes and ran down her cheeks.

Bull noticed. "Hey, pretty lady. No reason to cry. You'll have lots of nice things you've never had before. You might even wind up liking it and staying in the trade."

Melinda tensed. She felt her whole body tighten. She had to get away from these men. Maybe Buckskin would knock on her door and slip inside and make short work of both of them. Maybe, but not likely. He was getting so busy with his own case. She had to get away. She would not wind up as a love slave to some fat, sloppy, middle-aged man somewhere. She wouldn't!

Melinda trembled. She looked past Bull at the angriest man she had ever seen, the man she kicked in the crotch. So it really did work as a way for a woman to defend herself. The man's eyes were red and furious. His lips curved back in rage. His hands came toward her eyes, fingers stiff and ready to stab down.

"Mr. Kerr, she won't bring you fifty dollars blind," Bull said.

The hands shifted and slapped her face where Bull wasn't holding her mouth closed.

"Bitch, whore, filthy cunt-sucking bastard!" His face came down within inches of hers, then so close she couldn't focus on it. She could smell his breath, which had a slight peppermint tinge.

"You hurt me, you little whore. If I could, right now I'd take out my pen knife and cut off your tits. But a titless whore isn't much in demand on today's market. Even so, I'm going to hurt you so bad you'll never forget this night."

He leaned away until she could see the fury on his face. "I'd like to take a sharp knife and slice you up into dog food. But I'm a better businessman than that. You're worth twelve hundred dollars to me just the way you are, and I won't harm the merchandise.

"But I'll play all sorts of wild games with your

mind. Oh, you won't go crazy. A crazy whore is not worth a rotten cent. But you'll have memories of this night, awful, terrible, horrible memories. First some medicine for you to take."

He produced a small bottle, poured some in a glass and held it up. "You have to promise not to scream if Bull takes his hand off your mouth. Will you do that?" Melinda nodded. Bull took his hand away slowly. She didn't scream.

Melinda swallowed several times and tried to say something, couldn't, then it came out. "I want to warn you that I have friends coming in about a half hour. One is a deputy sheriff and the other a deputy U.S. Marshal. They won't be happy with what you're doing here."

"Yes, and I'm the king of England," Kerr said. "Now drink this, it'll make you feel better."

"I feel perfectly fine."

"Drink it or you will hurt badly," Kerr said. He pushed the glass to her lips where she lay. Bull grabbed the sides of her jaw and squeezed, forcing her mouth open. Kerr dumped in the fluid, and a moment later Melinda sprayed it out of her mouth and coughed.

"I won't take anything that you give me. No sense trying."

Kerr frowned a moment, then nodded. "Bull, why don't you give her our introduction class in whoring? Poke yours into her a couple of times just for practice."

Bull grinned. "No fooling? Right now?"

"Right now. She won't take her medicine so we'll give her a special Bull injection. Go ahead."

Melinda nodded. "Oh, yes, I agree. Now, Bull is my idea of a big handsome chunk of a man. I felt your cock getting hard when you were playing with my titties. It seemed huge. Is it really as big as I think it is?"

"Bigger and it'll crack you apart when he rams it up you, Melinda."

Bull dropped his pants and kicked them off, then pulled down his underwear. His erection flipped out and Melinda squealed like a young girl.

"Oh, wow, look at the size of him. I've never seen a cock so big, so thick. I want him. I want him deep inside me right now. Come on, Bull, get up here on my bed. I'll pull down my bloomers so you can get him right inside my little cunnie. This is going to be so good I'll never forget it. Come on, Bull, I don't want to wait all night for the first time. Do we get to fuck as many times as we want to, Mr. Kerr?"

Kerr scowled. He looked at Melinda, then back at Bull. "Now, wait a minute. Might not be such a good idea, Bull. I mean, if she wants it, she don't get it. She has to wait. Yeah. That's it. Right after you take your medicine, then you and Bull can fuck all night if you want."

"But, Mr. Kerr," Bull began.

"Quiet, Bull. I know what's best here. Melinda, you ready to take your medicine now?"

"What kind of medicine is it? Is it one of those potions so I'll be sexier and enjoy sex more? I've heard of them."

"No, it isn't that. But you'll find it pleasing. I know. I take some of the medicine myself when things get too tense. It relaxes me. You ready, Melinda?"

"I don't think I want the medicine. I just want Bull's big cock slamming into my cunnie and blowing me into all kinds of pieces."

"Put your pants back on, Bull. No poking work tonight. She wants it too bad. She must have some kind of a plan. Instead we use the new technique for administering our medicine."

"The nose way?" Bull asked as he pulled on his pants and buttoned them up. He reached over and felt Melinda's breasts and shook his head. "Damn, but you must be a great fucker."

"Now, Bull, let's get it started."

Bull reached down and held Melinda's nose shut with one hand and both of her wrists in his other big hand. Melinda frowned, then had to open her mouth to breathe. The second time she did it, Kerr poured some of the fluid into her mouth and she swallowed it quickly so it wouldn't go down to her lungs.

Twice more he did the same thing, and then they let Melinda alone for a moment. She sat up screaming at the top of her strong voice. Bull grabbed her and covered her mouth. The three of them sat there waiting for some reaction.

None came.

Kerr chuckled. Then he winced as he stood. "Cover her up. I don't want to see another woman undressed for at least a month."

"You'll change your mind tomorrow," Bull said. "She get enough of the juice?"

"Should have. She won't say a word until morning." He groaned again as he moved. "You don't really think I need to go see a doctor about my balls?"

"No. If it had been a big man who kicked you, it could have busted your balls. She just rattled them good. You'll be back in top shape in two days."

Melinda heard them talking but she wasn't sure what they said. Her mind was struggling to stay alert. She had fooled them by pretending to want to have sex with Bull. What a laugh. But it had worked. But then that medicine.

She knew it wasn't medicine. Knew it would do something bad to her, maybe make her less aggressive, less willful. Then they could do anything they wanted . . .

She wouldn't think about it. Just hold on. Hold on until Buckskin came. He would come, she was sure. He had to come. Was this what had happened to her sister?

Sister? She had a sister? She wasn't sure. The room took on a strange rosy glow and she felt light as a piece of goose down and could float right out the window. Only the window kept moving, and then everything turned into a dull red, and then it grew darker and darker until it was replaced by a sunrise, and with the sunrise Melinda drifted off into a laudanum-induced sleep.

Bull had been watching her. "Do I get to take her now? She's passed out for good. Won't wake up until morning. Do I get her now, Mr. Kerr?"

"Certainly not. You know you don't get to fuck the new girls. They have to be treated carefully, brought along slowly."

"You always dick them when we get them off on laudanum, Mr. Kerr. I watched you last time. You sure do have a little prick even when it's hard."

"Shut up, Bull. Okay, go ahead and have her, just don't hurt her or ruin her or you owe me fifteen hundred dollars. I sure as hell don't want to watch. I'm going downstairs and get some supper. Take it easy on her."

When the door closed behind Kerr, Bull locked it from the inside the way he had been told to do, then went back and looked at the girl. Melinda. Even her name was pretty. He started to reach for her breasts and stopped. He could talk big, but he couldn't touch the girl, not when she was drugged out of her mind.

When she had looked at him before, all that talk she did was just a front. He knew it and she knew he knew it, but Kerr didn't know it, and that's what made it so much fun for Bull. He had almost cheered when Melinda kicked Kerr in the balls. What a fine sight to see him groveling in pain there on the cabin floor.

He covered Melinda's breasts with the chemise, then brought her blouse together and buttoned it all the way up.

Bull slid her over on the wide double bed and lay down beside her on his back. He'd been up most of the night trying to get her right name and hotel room number. Right now he could use some sleep.

Kerr wouldn't be back for an hour, maybe an hour and a half. He liked to take long, slow meals. He could afford to. Bull yawned, then drifted off to sleep.

He let Kerr in when he knocked an hour later.

"She's been out all the time. Not even a murmur, and she's still breathing deep and regular, so there's no trouble with too much laudanum."

Kerr nodded. "We might as well stay here tonight. I'll sleep beside her in case she wakes up." He frowned. "No, I don't want to be that close to a woman, not yet. My balls feel better, but no sudden movement or they hurt like fire. I'll go down and rent a room and meet you here at five A.M."

He stared hard at Bull. "I don't want you harming the goods, you understand? I want her able to walk in the morning, and no bruise or cuts or scrapes on her lovely body. Otherwise you pay me for damage."

"Yeah, yeah, I won't touch her again. Just sleep on the bed. Plenty of room for two."

"That sounds like you, Bull. I'll see you early tomorrow. Oh, if she comes out of it too soon, there's more laudanum in the bottle on the dresser." Kerr went out and closed the door. Bull locked it and took off his shoes and pants, then lay down beside the drugged girl and went to sleep.

The following morning, Kerr arrived promptly at five. They roused Melinda. She was in that cooperative stage of the laudanum experience where she could walk, her eyes were open, and she would do anything anyone told her.

They straightened her dress, put the sunbonnet on her to cover her face, and walked her down the back stairs at 5:30. They were just in time for the boat at six. They had three tickets and helped Melinda up the stairs to the first-class passenger compartments.

Just as they were opening the cabin door, Melinda broke free and ran to the rail.

"Buckskin, come and save me!" Melinda screamed. Bull and Kerr caught her at once and hustled her toward the second cabin from the front. Her feet hardly touched the deck as they hurried her inside the cabin.

Melinda cried then. "Damn you both! I know what you're trying to do with me, but I won't be one of your whores. I'll kill myself first, right here, now or later. You won't make a dime off me. You hear me, damn it!"

Kerr settled back and grinned. "It's too late now, girl. You're on the boat heading downriver to your training grounds, then to the auction block. I've high hopes for you, at least fifteen hundred dollars."

"I won't take any more of your medicine. I know what it is, laudanum, a drug. It took two of you and drugs to capture me. My, aren't you both big strong men."

"Doesn't matter if you use any more laudanum now or not. No one on board will help you. We made sure of that. There are only a few passengers, and the crew is ours."

"Did you kidnap my sister, too? Her name was Maria Warnick. She was blonde, like me, about my size. It's been nearly three months since I've heard from her."

Kerr shrugged. "I see so many pretty blonde girls it's hard to keep track."

Melinda sat up on the small bunk where they had

thrown her. Her head pounded for a moment. Then it cleared. How could she get away? She'd kick the short guy again if she could. But if the whole crew was on their side . . . she wasn't even a good swimmer. All that Missouri river water sent shivers up her spine.

She looked out the small window and saw the shoreline slipping by. She had no idea how long they would stay on the boat. Would it go past Omaha? she wondered.

"Bull, you stay with her. I'll get off at the next stop after the wood stop and get us something to eat. They have sandwiches all ready for the passengers to buy right there at the dock."

Bull locked the door after Kerr left.

"Might as well sit down, miss. It's a long ride."

"How far do we go?"

"We'll get off at Omaha and get a larger boat heading for the Mississippi. Then we have another long ride."

Outside on the top deck, Buckskin turned and saw Joe, the crewman he had tangled with before.

"You deaf? I asked you what the hell you're doing out of the brig? Come on, you're going back."

"Not a chance," Buckskin said. He moved toward the rail not with any plan, but not wanting to alert those in the cabin holding Melinda.

"You a Fancy Dan or something?" Joe rasped. "I'll break you in half." He moved toward Buckskin in a stalking move that would let him dart either way in an instant. Buckskin kept moving until he felt the three slats of the wooden rail behind him.

"Come get me, you poor excuse for a sailor," Buckskin taunted. "I don't think you've got the belly for a real fight. You only fight when the other person is smaller, much smaller. I'm not all that little. Come get me, you bastard."

Joe bellowed in rage and charged Buckskin. The detective knew instinctively what to do. He waited until the last moment, then dropped to one knee, ducked his head and hit Joe in the thighs with his shoulder.

There was too much mass to stop. Joe's big body lifted over Buckskin, who jolted upward at just the right moment and hurled the big man over the rail. The splash was drowned out by the churning sternwheel paddles, and the *Nellie Peck* kept sweeping down the Missouri with the current.

Buckskin looked around quickly. He saw no one on that deck. The wheelhouse was right above him, but the pilot and another man concentrated on a river snag ahead of them, steering the lumbering 200-footer around the hazard.

Buckskin went to cabin 3 and listened. He heard nothing. He tried the door and found it unlocked. He opened it an inch and saw no one inside. He moved to cabin 2 and listened at the door. He heard a woman's voice. He drew the pistol from his ankle holster and knocked on the door.

He heard a key in the lock and the door swung outward a foot. Buckskin slammed through the opening, his .32 caliber revolver ahead of him and covering Bull, who threw up his hands in surprise and shock.

Buckskin saw Melinda sitting on the bunk. She

sprang up beside him in an instant.

"I just knew you'd come."

"We're not off of this tub yet. Turn around, big man, and lay down on the bunk with your hands on your back." When he did, Buckskin pulled the laces from the man's boots and tied his wrists together, then his ankles. He put a gag in his mouth and then opened the door for a quick look outside.

"Melinda, are you all right?"

"Just some laudanum. It never has worked well on me."

"Can you swim?"

"Oh, dear. A little. I'm no champion. I'm good at floating."

Buckskin grinned. "The crew is with these guys. We'll have to dodge them as well as the little man. Do these guys have names?"

"Bull is tied up. Kerr is going to get some food at the next stop."

"We need to be off before then. There's a toilet at the stern, right next to the paddlewheel. I'll watch it and when it's not being used, I want you to walk down there and go inside. Lock the door until you hear one rap, a pause, then two raps from me. Got it?"

"Yes. Swim?"

"We'll wait until the ship swings in close to shore. I can carry you on my back if you get tired." He checked out the door. "All right, someone just left the toilet. A woman, and she's coming this way. Go now. Casual but a little rushed."

Melinda walked out of the cabin and headed for the toilet 100 feet away. She was halfway there when a man walked smartly toward the first-class cabins from the bow of the ship.

He was almost to cabin 3 when he saw Melinda and must have recognized her dress.

"Melinda!" he called. "How in hell did you get out of the cabin?"

Just before Kerr began running toward the stern, Buckskin Morgan surged out of the cabin and pointed the revolver at him.

"Mr. Kerr, I believe," Buckskin said.

Chapter Fourteen

Newton J. Kerr slowed and then stopped. His momentary surprise quickly was crowded out by caution tempered with a large helping of anger held in check.

"What are you doing out here, Mr. Morgan?"

"Slowing you down, Kerr. Walk over to the railing as if we're old friends. You won't see it, but my hogsleg is aimed right at your gut. You ever been gut shot, Kerr? Toughest way to go. Pain you can't begin to imagine."

"Now see here, you can't wave some little gun at me and expect me to do as you say. One word and I'll have six crewmen on you with clubs."

"Ask Joe about that, Kerr. He's now either swimming for shore or treading deep water. Over to the rail now. You have two choices. Stand there and be shot dead, or walk to the rail and hope for something better."

Kerr looked around with alarm. He realized that he was in serious waters.

"Now see here, Morgan. I'm a businessman. I know when to fold my hand and when to buy in. Right now I can offer you a bonus of a thousand dollars if you'll put away that gun and go along with what I tell you. There's lots of money to be made in this business. What do you say?"

"Another offer like that and your choices will be down to being shot dead. Move."

Kerr went to the rail slowly. No one appeared on the upper deck to help him. The pilot in the wheelhouse was maneuvering the big craft through some troubled waters and around a grounded snag almost in midstream.

"The rail, now."

Kerr went to the rail and held it with both hands. They were ten feet above the roiling waters of the Missouri.

"How are you at swimming, Kerr?"

"Not good. Fifty feet if I'm lucky."

"Good, I hoped you weren't a champion swimmer. Now you have two choices again. One .32 caliber slug right through your left eye and into brain. Second choice is a clean dive over the side and then heading for shore."

"Told you I'm not much of a swimmer."

"Strange what powers a man can summon up when his life depends on it. So which is it to be?"

Kerr looked at the water, brown and muddy with the runoff. He looked back at Buckskin and started to run along the rail. Buckskin blocked him against the rail after ten feet.

"Looks like you chose the swim," Buckskin said softly. He picked the smaller man up and dropped him over the side. The bow wave of the *Nellie Peck* swept the thrashing Kerr away from the paddle wheel. They were nearly in the middle of the river here, and it had widened out to 400 yards.

Buckskin watched Kerr splashing as the current carried him along but much slower than the stern-wheeler as it was powered forward by the paddle wheel and the current.

Buckskin turned and walked toward the toilet at the stern of the ship right in front of the paddle wheel. He tried the knob, found it locked and knocked once, paused and knocked twice.

"Should I come out?" Melinda's soft voice came through the door.

"No, let me in. Going to be a search made out here before long."

He tried the knob again, found it unlocked, and turned it and stepped inside. The toilet was larger than Buckskin had figured. A two-holer as they said on the ranch, with three feet of space between the seats and the front. A pitcher of water sat on a small corner table in a cradle designed to hold it secure in rough water. A built-in sink emptied out down a drain pipe through the floor.

"I heard Mr. Kerr shout at me. Where is he?"

"Taking a swim, but we're not sure for how long. I doubt that he makes it to shore, and I couldn't be happier about that situation. Our problem is to hope we're coming into a stop soon, so we can get out of here and jump overboard when we swing close to shore and before they tie up."

"I told you about my swimming."

"We'll get as close to shore as we can. You'll get wet through, we can be sure of that, and dirt and silt in your hair and nose."

"That I can stand gladly after last night. They drugged me. I wasn't completely out but close enough. Neither of them touched me. I kicked Kerr right in the balls when they grabbed me in my hotel room. How did they find me?"

Buckskin grinned. He could just see Kerr curled up on the floor in agony. It made the day a little better.

"I don't know how they found you. What we need to do now is find out when we swing in to the shore."

"We'll slow down, I remember that."

"When that happens I'll slip out and take a look. We have to jump off the shore side of the boat and out far enough so we don't get sucked in by the big paddle wheel."

"This is sounding more like suicide all the time."

"No, by the time we jump, the wheel should be turned off and we'll be coasting in to the dock."

Someone tried the locked door, then knocked.

"Just a minute," Buckskin said. "Hold your horses."

Melinda tried to keep from laughing. She clamped her hand over her mouth to stifle it.

"I'll have to go out in a minute," Buckskin said. "I'll tell whoever it is that my wife is still in here. Then I'll try to make myself invisible. I just hope they haven't noticed that one of the crewmen is missing."

The door banged again. Buckskin kept the .32 caliber revolver behind his hip, turned the door handle and stepped outside.

"Sir, my wife is still in there. She's having some problems. It could be a while."

The man was short and fat and would waddle if he walked. He scowled, rubbed his face, then turned without a word and walked up the deck. Buckskin saw no one else. He went to the port-side railing and watched the shore. They were still 100 yards from the green bank of trees and brush.

He looked ahead but could see no settlement. Evidently the channel simply came closer to the shore here. He wondered if he could make it the 100 yards to shore towing Melinda. He decided not to try it. Too far out yet and going too fast. He didn't like the way those big, wide paddles chopped into the water on every stroke. They would have to wait.

Five minutes later, he saw one of the crew come on the top deck and look everywhere; then he walked around the cabins and through the space forward and at last went down the steps to the lower deck. Was he hunting for Joe? If so, an alarm could be raised at any moment.

Buckskin had five shots in his little .32. Where had they put his six-gun? It must be in the cabin where he'd tied up Bull. That might be a safer place to stay now that Kerr was out of the way. Yes.

He went back to the toilet and knocked on the door. "Let's go. Time to move."

The door opened slowly. "Are we that close to shore?"

"No, we're going back to your cabin. Might be the safest place for us to stay."

They made it to the cabin with no trouble. Buckskin opened the door, and once inside they found Bull halfway free of his bindings. Buckskin ordered him down and retied them, making them tighter this time.

He found his six-gun the first place he looked: in a leather traveling case under the bunk. He also found three bottles of laudanum and a packet of twenty-dollar bills. He took the bills and pushed them in his pocket, then watched the shoreline. It seemed to move farther and farther away.

It was nearly dusk when he went outside to check. Just ahead he saw a settlement, and the big ship edged closer to shore. The crew was busy now, and Buckskin and Melinda went halfway to the stern and stood at the rail. Two other couples were there watching the approach to shore as well.

Buckskin thought of challenging the crew at the gangplank. But even with the six-gun, he would be outmanned. They would have five or six guns available and rifles as well. He'd take the gamble on not being seen jumping off the boat.

At once he changed his plans. The water looked shallow here and they were no more than thirty yards off shore. He and Melinda went to the other side, away from shore, so no one on the dock or the crew would see them. The crew was already busy getting ready for the landing. It was a fair-sized town, so there would be freight and passengers to deal with.

"Why over here?" Melinda asked. He told her. She nodded.

"If it's not too deep we can simply wade ashore and hide behind those trees and brush and no one will notice us."

Buckskin watched the dock coming closer. When they were fifty yards from it and about twenty yards from shore, He told Melinda to take a deep breath and jump. She couldn't. He picked her up, stepped over the railing and jumped feet first into the Missouri.

The water was over their heads and they went under, but his boots hit the bottom almost at once and he pushed off hard and broke the surface quickly. He had dropped Melinda when they hit but found her beside him. Holding Melinda by one arm, he pulled her with him as he swam and kicked. She was good at floating.

After a few strokes he tried his feet again, found bottom and waded to shore. Two small boys were fishing. They held up two fish they'd caught and stared at Melinda's breasts, outlined by her wet dress. She quickly unstuck the dress and made herself less of an attraction.

"Now what?" Melinda asked.

Buckskin grinned. "Now we get dried out a bit, comb our hair, walk into town and have a bite of lunch. Then we catch the next upstream sternwheeler, and hope that the crew hasn't found Bull yet. They should be well downstream from this little town before he can get free of his bindings."

"Do you know what they had planned for me?" Melinda asked as they sat near a tree in the bright sunshine getting dryer by the minute.

"I can guess."

"They were going to *sell me!* Kerr said I'd bring at least fifteen hundred dollars."

Buckskin reached over and kissed her lips. Then he nodded. "Yes, I think he's right. But you'd be a bargain at that price. I'd bid twice that much myself."

She stuck her tongue out at him. "Now stop that. Don't tease me. I was terrified. You've probably never been kidnapped." She frowned. "Well, you sort of were, I guess, when they captured you back there on the boat. But I mean kidnapped for . . . for sexual purposes."

Buckskin chuckled. "I'm afraid no woman has ever kidnapped me for that reason."

Finally they were dry enough. Buckskin had a comb in his back pocket that had survived the swim. He let her use it, and when she finished the comb-out, she looked almost as good as usual. Some silt spots still showed on their clothes, but this wasn't Denver society.

The rest of the day went well. They had lunch at a small cafe where no eyebrows were raised at the wet twenty-dollar bill Buckskin used to pay the tab. At the dock they found that the next boat upstream was due in half an hour. They were about four hours from Yankton and should arrive there just before dark.

They did.

Back in the hotel, Melinda grabbed Buckskin and

pointed to the end of the hall. "This place has the fanciest bathroom you've ever seen. A big steel tub all white and towels and soap. I'm going to have me a fine bath and hairwash."

"That tub big enough for two?" Buckskin asked.

"Plenty big enough. I'll order extra hot water. I'll let you know when the hot water is ready."

Buckskin nodded and checked his room. He was registered in room 22, but lived in room 20. Nothing had been touched. He kicked off his boots and pulled off his socks. Then he shaved in cold water and had just finished when a knock came on the door.

He opened it slowly with the barrel of his .45.

"Sir, your bath is ready," Melinda said. "Just oodles of hot water. The boy who brought the water also gave me three extra towels. I told him I needed a whole bunch."

Inside the bathroom, they double-locked the door and Buckskin poured three steaming buckets full of water into the tub. Then he added one bucket of cold and tried it. Too hot. He poured in another bucket of cold water and put his foot in. Just right.

Melinda had been working at his shirt buttons, then his fly, and had his pants and short underwear pulled down before he had a chance to help.

"Oh, what a poor sad worm," she said. "He usually isn't this way until afterwards."

"See what you can do to get him interested," Buckskin said.

Melinda began a strip tease, pulling off one garment at a time, showing him a bare breast and hiding it, then dropping her blouse and dropping to kiss his growing erection.

"Bath first?" Buckskin asked.

"Bath second. A quickie first." She pushed Buckskin down on the floor and lay on top of him, then they rolled over and Buckskin found her heartland and she wailed in delight as he jammed into her until they could come together no tighter.

"Oh, yes, darling Buckskin. So absolutely perfect. I was afraid last night. They were so matter-of-fact about it. I was just another heifer calf to them that they could sell."

She humped upward at him and smiled.

"Quickly, my love. Our water is getting cold."

They pounded together, faster and faster until she wailed in delight and Buckskin grunted a dozen times as he thrust harder and harder with each explosion as he climaxed as well.

Almost at once, Melinda pushed up on him. "The bathwater before it gets cold."

Their bath was as quick as their lovemaking. They washed each other's backs and fronts and bottoms and tops and middles. Then Melinda washed her hair and they used the last bucket of hot water to rinse, then stood there naked, soaking wet and with water dripping from their hair.

They laughed. Next they dried each other off, put on what clothes they had brought, and hurried back to their rooms. Somebody else could clean up the bathroom.

When Buckskin came into his room, he found a long white envelope that had been slid under the door. He picked it up and saw it was sealed. His name was written by a feminine hand on the outside. He tore it open:

Dear Mr. Morgan,

I understand that you play poker. I've been looking for a good game for weeks. A few personal friends of mine will be in a game tonight at the Presidential Suite in this hotel. The suite isn't that nice, but one president did sleep there once.

The game is a $500 buy-in, but any new money from on your person is acceptable after the game is underway. There will be six players. We hope to see you in the first-floor suite sometime around 9 p.m.

Oh, for your information, Nate Hill will not be in the game. Look forward to meeting you and to find out if you really can play poker or are only good at catching cheaters.

The note was signed Sherry Crawford.

He looked at it and read it again. She was a woman and a poker player. It could be. He'd been trying to get a game with some woman player for two weeks. Maybe this was the one. No matter what else he did, he couldn't let on that he was from Denver or why he really had come to town.

Good thing he'd just had a bath. It was after the dinner hour, but the kitchen found some roast beef left. He had his dinner, then checked his watch. He had time only to polish his boots and put on a new shirt and his best vest before he pocketed 500 dollars from his money belt and walked down the steps to find the Presidential Suite.

The clerk looked surprised when he asked about the suite.

"There's a private gathering there tonight," the clerk said.

"I know, I'm invited. Were you?"

"No. It's down to the end of the hall and to the right."

Buckskin was ten minutes early. He checked out the room, two rooms, one with a bathtub in an alcove. Two men sat at a poker table that had been placed in the middle of the room beneath a chandelier holding three kerosene lamps.

Buckskin reversed his gears and went out to the lobby to see who else had turned up. One man carrying a cane with a gold head asked the clerk about the suite and was escorted to it. The next people up the steps were a man and a woman. The woman wore an elegant long black skirt and a frilly pure white blouse buttoned to her throat and with long sleeves. The man caught the woman's shoulders just outside the door and it seemed as if they were arguing. At last the woman pushed away from him, opened the door and marched into the hotel.

She had to be Sherry Crawford. She had short dark hair, a fine sculptured nose and a slim figure. Buckskin guessed she was maybe 26 or 27. She didn't approach the clerk, simply walked past Buckskin without a second look and down the hallway toward the Presidential Suite.

She went inside, said hello to the three men at the poker table, and talked for a moment with a man who sat at another small table with stacks and boxes of chips in front of him. Then she went back to the table and chose a seat beside the man with the gold-headed cane. This lady knew money when she saw it.

Buckskin waited until the fifth poker player showed up. He was a small man with a dark suit, hat and vest. His black shoes were spit shined until you could see your face in them. He kissed the woman's hand, sat down beside her, and said something that made the others laugh.

Promptly at the stroke of nine o'clock, Buckskin walked into the room. Everyone looked at him. He tipped his low-crowned Stetson but left it in place.

"This must be the right place, and you must be Miss Crawford. I thank you kindly for the invitation to play in your game. I take it you're ready to start?"

"Just as soon as you sit down, Mr. Morgan, Harry will bring over the chips and trade them to each of us for five hundred dollars. Then the game can begin."

He tried to feature her with long red hair, but somehow it didn't jibe. He didn't know why. She was smooth, sleek, she could play poker and play the men against each other. He noticed that now she had unbuttoned the top fastener on her blouse when the first hand started.

By the third hand two buttons were open. Then it was her deal. She smiled, called out the game five-card stud, a killer game to gamble with. Buckskin watched her critically and saw at once that she wasn't bottom dealing. The tight black skirt offered no place to hide cards, neither did her white, almost transparent blouse sleeves.

It was the fourth hand. Buckskin was down about fifty dollars. The important part was that Sherry had lost the hand she dealt. That was always a good sign the dealer was not cheating.

Sherry played man's poker. She was not put off by a strong bluff. She caught Buckskin bluffing with a pair of openers and nothing else in five-card draw and he lost another fifty dollars. He concentrated then on his poker and won two hands in a row, partly from good cards and partly because he bluffed two other players who probably had better cards than he did but wouldn't back them up with cash.

"You play well, Mr. Morgan," Sherry said.

"You play extremely well yourself, Miss Crawford. It is *Miss* Crawford, is it not? I see no wedding band on your left hand."

She looked at him steadily for a moment, then nodded. "Yes, that's right, no wedding band."

They played two hours more. One of the men went broke and refused to buy any more chips. He left the room. A second man had lost about 300 dollars and quit before he lost more. By that time Buckskin was over 300 dollars ahead. Sherry was on a roll and had won the last three hands. She had dealt none of them. Her stack of chips was twice what it had been when they started.

In this one poker game, Sherry had won more money than most workingmen made by laboring all year as a clerk, farm hand or on a sternwheeler.

"Four-handed poker is not a sporting contest," Buckskin said. "I suggest we have another game soon. I'll be in town another week yet."

"What is your profession, Mr. Morgan. Gambler?" Sherry asked.

"Hardly. I'm in town for my father who is looking for businesses to buy. So far I haven't found much to recommend to him."

She fanned herself a moment, then slipped the third button on her blouse open, and when she moved, the blouse let show a short line of cleavage. "Then, Mr. Morgan, your father believes that Yankton is a growing town?"

"Oh, yes. He's been watching it for five years. He says it has all the requirements to be a great city. Yankton could be the hub for business and commerce over the coming states of North and South Dakota and the other states to the west."

She stood and the sudden movement made her breasts bounce under the tightness of her white blouse.

"Your father is wrong. Yankton is the underbelly of the world. It won't amount to a hill of red peppers. This is a dead-end country with no resources, no wealth, no minerals, no oil. It will never be more than a catch-up state if it ever gets enough people in here to become a state. I must go. Harry, will you cash me in, please?"

She left first and by the time Buckskin got his chips changed into U.S. Federal banknotes, she was gone. She wasn't in the lobby or on the steps. The man who had brought her did not seem to be lurking around.

Buckskin went up the steps to his room. Was she or wasn't she? Sherry Crawford was the right height. She was near enough the same age. Her body size was about right, maybe a little larger-busted than the pictures of Dawn Evans showed. The hair was the big negative. He couldn't imagine Sherry as a redhead. Her short, black hair showed no variations at the roots.

He had to figure out some way to jolt her or shock her. Then she might reveal herself if she was the estranged wife of Harold Evans. She might slip up during the heated battle of making love. That was the only idea he came up with to determine if Sherry was Dawn Evans. Somehow he had to give that theory a try.

He turned and spat out the window. He still had a little bit of Missouri River sand in his mouth.

Chapter Fifteen

Buckskin was up early the next morning, had breakfast and found a man who would ride the next sternwheeler down to the Caruthers' Bend woodstop to pick up the two horses he had left there. He gave the man ten dollars for the trip and five dollars for whoever had boarded the nags for the two days. The man would ride them back and deliver them to the burned-out livery in Yankton.

That taken care of, Buckskin moved to his favorite thinking chair in front of the hardware store and let the morning sun warm him as he plotted out his day.

He had to follow up on Sherry Crawford. First he'd find out where she lived. She wasn't a homebody, that was obvious, so she must live in one of the four hotels. It took him only an hour to check the sign-ins at the four. He went back two months in each registration book but could find no one by the name of Sherry Crawford. At the same time he watched for the name Dawn. He thought Dawn might have changed her last name but not her first, but he found no one with that name.

Why?

It must be because she used another name at the hotel, or she had a house of her own, or she lived with someone else.

He checked the two general stores that sold groceries, and then the meat market. None of them could remember the woman ever being in his store. One of them said he had seen her several times going and coming from poker games at various hotel rooms and saloons. She hadn't ever been in his store.

That left few possibilities; the most likely was that she was being kept by some man in town. Who would that be? Something stirred in the back of his mind, but it wouldn't come full blown.

He watched the sun move higher, and when the saloon across the street opened, he wandered in, had a beer at the stand-up bar and waved at the apron. Buckskin had talked to the man now and then in his queries.

"Say, I'm curious. I played poker with that dark-haired woman last night in the hotel. She's good. I'd like to get in touch with her but I don't know where she's staying. She plays here now and then, I understand. She scheduled to play tonight?"

"No game tonight."

"Oh. Do you know anything about some man in

town who is furnishing her breakfast and supper these days?"

"Might. You got one of them fancy greenback bills with a five on it?"

"I think I can find one if you can tell me a name and location."

Buckskin took a roll of bills from his pocket, peeled off a five and held it in his hand.

"Yeah, that looks about right. I can't say for sure, but folks see her most often around the Criterion Saloon. The one that Nate Hill owns. Folks tell me that at every high-stakes poker game over there, both she and Hill play."

Buckskin slid the bill onto the bar but kept hold of it.

"Are there living quarters for Hill in the top story of his saloon?"

"Aye, there sure are. Nice as most houses in town, I've been told, but I ain't ever been up there."

Buckskin let go of the bill and the apron made it disappear into his pocket.

"If you need any more information about folks around town, I probably can tell you."

"I'll remember that. You're Phil, right?"

The apron nodded. Buckskin finished his beer and angled away from the bar for the front door. Outside, he found a place to lean against the general store across from the Criterion and watched the saloon's front door. So the woman was inside. It wasn't open for business yet.

Would Sherry go out the back door if she wanted to go shopping or such? No, too many saloon back doors were where drunks and muggers spent a lot of time. No, she would wear a sunbonnet or a hat to hide her face and she could be any of the ladies of the evening from the saloon going out for a stroll or shopping.

He watched the rest of the morning. One woman came out with a big hat on, but she was too tall to be Sherry the poker player.

He gave up at noon, wandered into the Ingraham General Store and looked around. About half of the goods had not been put back on shelves or straightened out. The clerk and the owner were working at it when they had no customers.

Buckskin waited until Ingraham was free, then approached him.

"Looking for a good small jackknife. One with three blades if you have one."

Ingraham scowled. "Few days ago I could have shown you a dozen in a few seconds. Now I'm not sure. They're somewhere under this pile of merchandise here.

"Damn them, whoever they were. Somebody did this to me. Can you imagine that? I try to be of service to the community, stocking things that seldom sell because somebody says he wants it, and now I get treated like this."

"Yes, I heard. Someone told me that the wheel of life spins round and round and eventually everyone gets his just deserts. I never quite understood that. Well, why don't I come back another day when you have your store put back together? Oh, did they find out who did this to you, or why?"

"No, no, and I'll probably never know. Maybe an unhappy customer, but I can't remember one. Well,

I better get back to sorting and stacking."

Buckskin walked out of the store with a grim smile. Ingraham didn't look nearly so formidable without his black hood and black horse and rifle.

He toured the leather shop next. It was in better shape. Less to put back together. The owner, Stacey Trumble, sat at his bench working on a saddle. Buckskin stood just inside the door and took a deep breath. Trumble looked up and shook his head.

"You're the second person today who's done that. After a while I get so I can't even smell the tanning solutions. What can I do for you?"

"Oh, I need some new boot lacings, the long ones."

"Just cut some last night. Finally got everything put back in order here. Can't figure out who would do such a thing to my store. They knew what they were doing. That acid ruined four saddles. Have to tear them apart and start all over again."

Trumble pulled a pair of four-foot leather boot laces from a box on the floor. "These long enough?"

"Just right." Buckskin paid for them and looked over a new saddle and a pair of fancy boots, then waved and left the store. So the three Angels of Death were getting a little of their own treatment back and they didn't like it. That was good.

He went back to the hotel and found Melinda packed and ready to go. She was dressed on the shabby side and had a large hat that would cover much of her face and all her long blonde hair.

"Why the disguise?"

"On this trip, I don't want anyone to think I'm a good candidate for the white slave trade."

"You want me to come downriver with you to Omaha?"

"No, but I want you to help me buy a derringer and show me how to shoot it."

Buckskin grinned. "That I can do. When does your boat leave?"

"Not until two. I figured we could have lunch, buy the gun, and I could shoot it a few times into the river before the boat docked."

They did. It was a Remington two-shot, .32 caliber. Buckskin showed her how to load it and take out the empty cartridges and reload. Then he had her do it herself. They were beside the boat dock, and no stores were within half a block of them.

"Hold it with one hand and point it at the river and squeeze the trigger. Don't pull with your finger or you'll throw off your aim."

She tried. When it fired she jumped a half foot off the ground and nearly dropped the weapon.

Buckskin chuckled, had her fire the other shot, and saw that she didn't react quite so much.

"Now pull out the empties and put in new rounds," he said. "If you ever need to use the gun, pull it out, push it in the man's belly and pull the trigger. Don't try and hit something six feet away. You'll probably miss because these little guns aren't much on accuracy. Understand?"

"Yes." She put the pistol in her reticule slung over her shoulder.

"Now pretend someone is trying to kidnap you. Pull out the weapon, thrust it forward and shoot all in the same motion. Do it now just like you would for real."

The first try she couldn't get the gun out of her reticule.

"Your abductor would have taken it away from you by this time. Open your reticule and carry it that way in bad situations. Then you're ready. Try it again."

She did, and this time it went better. She pulled out the derringer, held it in both hands, extended her arms quickly and fired.

"Good."

He had her do it three times. Then they heard the sternwheeler whistle that it was coming in and they went up to the dock to wait.

He saw her off on the boat. He reminded her to get into her cabin with her food and stay there until they got to Omaha if she could. She kissed him goodbye, a long, lingering, hungry kiss.

"We had good times," Melinda said. "Maybe I'll see you in Denver."

Then she hurried through the small gate, up the plank and on board the *Missouri Mistress*. She didn't look back.

Buckskin walked back to town. His first stop was the Criterion Saloon. He knew that Nate Hill hated him with a vengeance for the way he had exposed his bottom dealing. There was no other way to try and find Sherry. If she lived above the saloon she must come down sometimes.

He had a beer, got into a dime-limit poker game and lost two dollars in two hours. No sign of Sherry. He was about to cash in and give up when two men eased up behind his chair and one of them grabbed Buckskin's six-gun before he knew they were there.

"Sloppy," one of them said.

"A gun sharp who lets a guy get behind him in a saloon?" the other man said. "Don't you read how them famous gunners got themselves killed?"

Buckskin left his hands on the table. His ankle .32 was too far away for him to reach it in time. Maybe later.

"My deal," Buckskin told the players, ignoring the men behind him. The players didn't say a word.

"Game's over for you, gun slick. Stand up real slow and don't get anybody hurt. Man wants to see you in the alley."

Buckskin rose slowly and turned. As he did he saw the six-gun aimed at his belly. No chance to jump the gunner. The man moved back a step, hit the chair of a poker player at the next table. The player swore and jolted to his feet. The man holding the gun on Buckskin turned toward the angry card-player.

Buckskin's first powered down on the gunman's wrist, smashing the gun out of it and bringing a bellow of pain. The detective turned to face the second man, who was trying to draw his weapon. Buckskin kicked hard, aiming his boot toe at the holster. It connected and jolted the six-gun out of leather and spun it two tables over, where it crashed into the floor but didn't fire.

Buckskin powered a hard right fist into the second man's belly, bending him over in pain. Then Buckskin rammed his right knee upward, connecting with the man's jaw and jolting his head back. The man screamed in pain, then pivoted backward and fell across a penny-ante poker game table and passed out.

"You broke my wrist!" the talkative gunman bellowed.

"Damn shame. Go see a doctor. Next time you come up behind me I'll break your neck and pay for your funeral. Now get out of here and tell Nate Hill his little attack on me didn't work."

Buckskin bent and picked up his own .45 that the gunner had dropped, held it loosely as he angled for the front door. He backed up most of the way, then turned and walked out the door into the afternoon sunshine.

It had to be Hill who sent the two gunners after him. He'd wondered what Hill would do after getting caught cheating the other night. This wouldn't be all. Right now Buckskin was more interested in getting upstairs of the Criterion Saloon. He wondered if there were outside stairs to the second floor. Many of these saloons with cribs had back steps to service the bashful clients.

He walked down the block to the first alley and went in behind the row of stores and saloons on Main Street. He picked his way past trash and garbage and around a few outhouses that the saloons provided for needful drinkers, until he came to the sixth door from the alley. That was the rear of the Criterion Saloon.

It had a door opening into the alley and a wooden staircase that went up to a small landing and a door into the second floor. There would probably be a guard or a lock on the door.

He took the steps two at time and at the top tried

the door knob. It turned and the door came open silently. This wasn't the busy time for a brothel. He saw no one. To the left a hallway opened and he counted six doors leading off it. Directly ahead was another door with a big silver star on it. Curious.

Just before he moved toward the door, it opened and a woman backed out. She wore only a housecoat tied loosely at the waist and carried a stack of books. When she turned and saw him she scowled.

"Hey, Buster. We ain't open yet. They forget to lock that back door again? Damn. Sorry, we ain't open for business until after six P.M. Us girls got to have some time to sleep and eat and that sort of thing. So you just go back down the steps there and wait until we're open. Go around front and have a beer and play some poker before your poking."

Her lopsided grin was supposed to be cute. It came out more of a smirk.

"Oh, I'm not looking for a girl. I was supposed to come up to talk to Sherry Crawford. She said someone would tell me where to go once I got up the steps."

The woman, about 40 he figured, with lots of makeup on and hair that showed at least three different colors, shrugged. "Hell, whyn't you say so? She's down this way." The woman stopped and stared at him. "Ain't I seen you somewhere before?"

"I've been somewhere, maybe that was it."

She shrugged and one large breast fell out of the robe. She pushed it back with no thought of being embarrassed. "Well, hell, I guess she knows what she's doing. Nate is one jealous son-of-a-bitch. Don't let him see you up here."

She pushed open a door he hadn't seen in the wall and pointed down a long hall. "Down there, the apartment. Set up like a small house."

"Yeah, thanks. Hill isn't back there, right?"

"Right. He's downstairs tending bar. His apron got sick."

Buckskin nodded and walked down the hallway. His boots made too much noise on the wooden floor so he stepped with a more gentle tread.

As he walked, he could see part of the living quarters. It looked like a living room in one of the houses in town. As he came closer, he heard music that could be coming from a phonograph.

At the end of the hall, he could see most of the apartment. No one was in the living room. He saw the phonograph and its cylinders that made the music.

Two open doors showed on the far wall. Through one door he saw what could be a kitchen. The other he figured was a bedroom.

He stopped and waited. Then he called, "Miss Crawford? Miss Crawford, are you here?"

"What in the world?" A voice came from the far door and a moment later a head came around the door jamb. It was Sherry.

"You, the poker player. What in the world are you doing here?"

"I need to talk with you."

"Why?"

"I wanted to meet you, get to know you better."

"I'm not looking for someone to come courting. You'd better leave, right now."

"I can't do that."

She edged around the door a little more and he saw that she was dressed. "And why can't you? Crippled?"

"No, I told you. I need to talk to you."

"I told you I can't talk to you. Now out. Out or I'll call for the bouncer in the saloon to throw you down the stairs."

"He might have a hard time doing that. When are you playing poker again?"

"I don't know. I play whenever I feel like it."

"You're living here, then?"

"Yes, I guess you could say that."

"Are you living here with Nate Hill?"

"Out! What a terrible thing to say. Out. Get out right now."

She came from behind the door, her face furious, eyes wide with anger, color high, fists akimbo on her narrow hips. "If I was a man I'd knock you down for saying such a thing."

"Why? Because it's true and that bothers you?"

She took two long strides forward and then stopped. "You, you are insufferable. You're insulting and terrible, and I'll never play poker with you again. If you join a game I'm in, I'll leave. Now, if you won't leave here, then I'll go down to the bar and bring back the bouncer."

"What will Nate Hill think about that when he hears of it?" Buckskin asked.

She scowled and flounced back into the room but came out at once. "All right, all right. I'll talk with you. What do you want to say?"

Buckskin put on his best grin. "Partly I just wanted to see you again. You're a beautiful woman and I enjoy watching you, talking to you. I wanted to congratulate you for winning that much cash the other night without cheating. Or if you did cheat you're a doubly refined expert, because I didn't spot you."

"I didn't cheat. I don't need to."

"Good. You plan on staying here or going to better poker pastures?"

"Better games? I don't know. I like to do other things besides play poker."

"Ever been to Europe? There are some fine tours for folks with a few dollars."

"Never thought much about it. No. I think I'll just stay here for a while. Now I really must ask you to leave. Just maybe I'll see you in another poker game. If you're there or come, I guess I won't leave. Now, satisfied?"

"For now. I'd like to take you to dinner tonight. Would that be possible?"

"Oh." She frowned. "I don't think that would be a good idea."

"Mr. Hill?"

"Well, yes. We have a kind of . . . agreement."

"Fine, I tried. Maybe we can play poker tonight. Are you playing anywhere?"

"Yes, at the Lucky Lady. They have a game there tonight at eight."

Buckskin grinned and tipped his hat. "Good. I'll see you there." He turned to leave. "Oh, will Mr. Hill be there?"

She frowned. "Oh, my, no. Mr. Hill is not playing poker except at his own game here. Your exposure of him flashed around town and he isn't welcome at the big games anymore."

"Sorry."

She smiled. "It was remarkable that you caught him. He's extremely good at it."

"Not that good."

Buckskin touched his hat again and walked quickly away down the long hall to the door and down the outside stairs to the alley.

He'd made progress, and he didn't want Hill to catch him there quite yet and blow the whole thing. Poker tonight. Good. He'd go make a reservation at the Lucky Lady Saloon so he'd be sure to get a seat.

When he came out of the Lucky Lady twenty minutes later, he sensed something different. The atmosphere had changed. He could feel tension in the air. He hadn't gone twenty feet down the boardwalk when a man in the middle of the street called to him.

"Morgan. Buckskin Morgan, you coward and murderer. I'm calling you out right now for killing my brother in Omaha."

Buckskin stopped and looked where the man stood. He had his feet apart, his right hand flexing over a well-used six-gun in leather on his hip. Buckskin couldn't remember ever seeing the man before. He was medium height, wore range clothes and a low-crowned brown Stetson. He was bearded, and his hands both flexed in anticipation.

"Morgan, you've got a hogleg there on your thigh. Let's see how good you are when it comes to facing a man instead of shooting him in the back!"

Buckskin Morgan stepped off the boardwalk and moved into the street twenty feet away from the big talker.

Chapter Sixteen

Buckskin spread his feet in the dust of Yankton's Main Street and let his hands fall to his sides. He stared at the man twenty feet away and shook his head.

"I have no idea who you are or what you're talking about. You have a chance right now to say you've made a mistake and apologize and walk away. Otherwise you stand a good chance of being carried down to the undertaker."

"Always talking, Morgan. You gunned Billy in the back and now you're going to pay for it."

"Who paid you to do this? Why are you risking your life for a hundred dollars?"

"Shut up and draw," the man sneered.

Buckskin was sure he'd never seen him before. He was a gun sharp somebody in town had hired to get rid of a problem: Buckskin. He had learned years ago that in a stand-down like this, the man who drew first had a split-second advantage. Often that was all it took even with a man faster on the draw.

"Look, there's no need for anybody to die here."

"If that happens, it won't be me," the stranger barked.

Buckskin drew. His hand darted upward to catch the grip of his Colt, lifting it out of leather. His first finger slid into the trigger guard and as the barrel cleared leather, his thumb snapped back the hammer cocking the weapon. The split second the barrel was clear, he pushed the weapon forward in an aim-and-shoot move and pulled the trigger. By the time the hammer fell on the round the weapon had centered on the stranger's chest.

The whole draw took only the smallest part of a second and when the big .45 slug slammed into the other man's chest, the barrel of his weapon hadn't cleared leather yet.

His eyes went wide in surprise and then shock, then his body jolted backward from the force of the round. He fell on his back and started to rise, then slumped back, the six-gun fell from his hand, and eyes that would never see again stared at the front of the dressmaker's shop.

"M'God, did you see that man draw?" a watcher on the boardwalk shrilled.

"Some kind of shooting, you can bet your biscuits on that," another man said.

Buckskin walked forward slowly. Two men ran

up and checked the challenger before Buckskin got to him.

"Deader than a rat in a trap," the first one said. The second man pinched the body's nostrils and got no reaction. He nodded.

"Sure enough, he's down there in hell shoveling coal already."

"Somebody go get the sheriff," Buckskin said.

"No need, I'm here. Saw the whole thing." Sheriff Jared Van Dyke said, stepping off the boardwalk. "He called you out. He asked for the fight. Matter of self-defense. No unlawful act has been committed here. Now, everyone just go on about your business. The show is all over for today."

He walked up and examined the body, then stood and turned to Buckskin.

"You know him?"

"No."

"Me either. Must be a stranger in town. You mentioned something about who hired him?"

"Two or three people in town wouldn't mind seeing me at the undertakers, Sheriff. Figured one of them sent for a fast gun to do the job they wouldn't do."

The sheriff nodded. "Could be. Looks as if this one's gun just wasn't fast enough." He looked down at Buckskin's holster.

"You're mighty fast with that one."

"I'm still alive."

"There's a paper I'll want you to write for me down at the office. Might as well do that now if'n you have the time."

"Sounds right."

The sheriff yelled at two men to carry the dead man to the undertaker. Just as Buckskin left with the sheriff, he saw the two load the body into a wheelbarrow from the hardware and wheel the dead man down the street.

The formality of writing out the death report and signing it took only a few minutes, then Buckskin went back to the street. He had a poker game that night. Maybe a hundred-dollar buy-in. He'd be ready. First he wanted to have supper.

He didn't think about killing the man. He had been a hired gun and knew he had put his life on the line for blood money. This time it was his blood, not money. Next time it might be Buckskin being dragged off to the undertaker. He didn't have time to worry about the men who fell under his gun, especially when they were criminals who needed to die, or hired guns who knew the odds.

Before supper, he went up the alley to Dr. Sims' place and knocked on the back door. A nurse let him in and said she'd tell the doctor he was here. A minute after she left, the doctor came in and closed the door behind him.

"Thanks for using the back way. No sense in advertising our association. I don't know how to start thanking you for giving the Angels of Death something to think about. The livery stable was the best. Could put him out of business. I hope so. Then maybe he'll move away."

The doctor grinned and shook Buckskin's hand. "Ingraham's store was a beauty. I went over there the next morning and it was absolute chaos. Are you wounded?"

"No, I'm fine. Just want to check. Did all three of these Angels participate in hangings or shootings that resulted in death here in town?"

"Oh, absolutely. Going back four years, which is when I came here, I'd say the Angels have killed at least fifteen men and a few women."

"Just wanted to be sure in case I get into a showdown with one or more of them."

"No problem. If they fight and get killed, they deserved it. Oh, I heard about that guy in the street. Was he a hired man out to kill you?"

"Looked that way. The Angels may be striking back at me."

"From what I hear, you're the fastest draw anybody in this town has ever seen."

"I'm still alive." Buckskin moved to the door. "Thanks, Doc. I may figure out some more discouragement for our three friends."

After supper, Buckskin put on a fresh shirt, shaved closely, and used some bay rum and rose water on his face, then adjusted his brown hat with the red diamonds on the headband, and went to play some poker.

After he bought in for 100 dollars worth of chips, he found Sherry Crawford already at the table and a vacant seat beside her. Tonight she wore a white blouse with a scoop neckline, and even when she sat up straight a half inch of cleavage showed between her breasts. He wondered if she would be using every woman's two secret weapons in the game.

"Good evening, Miss Crawford. Nice to see you again."

"Good evening to you, Mr. Morgan. I hope you brought lots of money to lose."

"Then it's not table stakes at the start of the game?"

Three other men at the table laughed.

"In this game you can bet your house or your wife if you have a deed on either one," a big bearded man across the table said. "Any cash in your pockets or on your body can also be used, so feel free to lose a lot. All cash, no IOU's."

"Or maybe win a lot," Buckskin said.

The first two hands in any game were feeling-out ones for Buckskin. He wanted to learn something about the players. That's what he figured he would do, but instead he found himself concentrating on the lady to his right. She was young, attractive, social, and did much more talking during the game than the other players liked. She also occasionally reached out with a bet and the neckline of her blouse obeyed the laws of gravity and fell forward, revealing two lovely unencumbered breasts.

From his position beside her Buckskin had a better view down her blouse than the others, and she didn't seem to care who looked. He lost the first hand by looking too much and not playing poker. Then he quit looking at her at all and won the next two hands, one on good cards, which he had to show, and the next on a bluff where he didn't have to show his cards.

At the break, Buckskin realized he was down to 26 dollars in chips and he bought another hundred. Sherry had the most chips, and he figured she was about 300 dollars ahead. They talked briefly at the break as they sipped cold beers the management brought in.

"Been in town long?" she asked.

"Nope, just here on a business trip. How about you?"

"Two months or so. Looking for the best poker game around. For now, it's here."

"Sounds like you're going to get on a Mississippi riverboat and into some really big money games."

"Some steamship lines are limiting the games," she said. "I hear some even ban gambling. I'll stay here awhile."

"I've heard about some big games in Omaha, San Francisco, even Denver."

She looked up at him at the mention of Denver but didn't say anything. He noted her reaction, a sudden interest, recognition. It was another sign that she could be the girl he hunted.

When the game started again, Buckskin played his best poker, folding when he had nothing, bluffing when it seemed possible, and winning three hands out of five.

He lost the next hand on purpose, folding on the first draw, and watched Sherry work her magic and her neckline treatment on the two men across the table who were still betting. She rattled them, Buckskin could tell. She won the pot with more than a hundred dollars in it.

The next hand was good to him. He was dealt a pair of queens and a pair of treys, drew one and caught a queen. To make it look like he had been trying for a straight or a flush, he almost threw in his hand. Then he reconsidered in his best poker acting style and went along with a ten-dollar bet.

Two players dropped out. The third raised ten dollars, and Sherry raised another ten. When it came to Buckskin he raised it 15 dollars and saw the next-to-last player quit. Now it was just him and Sherry. She frowned, remembering his draw probably, and stared at the pot. It had more cash in it than any so far, well over 200 dollars.

"I think you're bluffing me, Mr. Morgan," she said softly and leaned toward him. He lifted his brows and looked across the table.

"Let your chips do your talking," Buckskin said.

She sucked in a quick breath, met his 15-dollar raise and raised another 25 dollars. Buckskin called her.

She laid out her hand with a flourish and a small smile on her lips. She had a full house, jacks and deuces.

"Sorry, Morgan, you didn't bluff me out this time." She reached for the pot.

Buckskin's hand closed around hers on the table. "I didn't have to bluff." He laid down his cards one at a time starting with the treys. When he laid down the last queen, Sherry laughed, a full-blown belly laugh that made everyone at the table grin.

When she finished, she wiped her eyes, leaned over and kissed Buckskin's cheek.

"You outdid me that time. But there will be another time. Right now I have to bow out of the game. I have a curfew. If I'm not in by midnight, I turn into a pumpkin." The men frowned. "You know, like in the fairy tale of Cinderella."

That broke up the game. Buckskin got to the

cashier first and waited for Sherry. She cashed her chips and hurried past him. He caught up with her before they left the saloon.

"I should escort you home this time of night."

She looked at him and shrugged.

"Can if you want to. I have my trusty derringer in case anyone gets frisky."

"Good game tonight," he said. She nodded. "I'm buying property for my father. This town doesn't look like much of a prospect. He's interested in Denver. Do you know anything about Denver?"

She stopped and frowned, then lifted her brows and shook her head, letting her short, dark hair swing from side to side.

"Denver? Absolutely nothing do I know about the place. I've never been there."

"Oh."

She was lying. She had reacted with surprise or guilt or something other than normal when he mentioned Denver. This was the second time.

"I enjoyed the game," Buckskin said. "Maybe we can play together again sometime."

"Maybe. Tomorrow night I'll be in a game at Nate Hill's place, but he won't let you play there. Maybe later."

At the front door of the Criterion Saloon, she shook his hand and asked him to stay outside, then she hurried in the door and vanished. Buckskin stood there a moment totally frustrated. He figured that this girl was Dawn Evans, but he had no proof. She looked like the picture, but with the hair so different it was impossible to be sure. She claimed she'd never been to Denver. Damn. She was lying.

He wanted to hit somebody. Why not hit the three remaining Angels of Death? How? He drifted down the street until he had passed the Ingraham General Store. Letting a skunk loose in the store tonight would give it a great atmosphere by morning. But he didn't have a skunk.

A couple of rattlers crawling around the store would be good, only the wrong person might be bitten. What about the Angel's house? Buckskin had seen Ingraham's house days before, a three-story place on a slight rise behind most of the town. It had a white picket fence around it. Ingraham had a wife and three kids. Buckskin took a walk to see what he could see.

The house was as he remembered it. What he hadn't noticed before were the two outbuildings. One was at least a two-holer privy, the other a modest-sized stable with a good-sized pasture behind it. He moved around to the back of the place and took another look. The stable had room for three horses. He saw them in the pasture.

Buckskin grinned and slipped through the gate and let the horses out. They nibbled on grass and wandered away a short distance. If they loved their oats they wouldn't stray far. He entered the stable and small barn and saw no other animals. He used some pocket matches and lit fires in four different places around the building, watched the fire grow, then sprinted away before it broke out a window or the roof. He was a quarter mile away and back into the heart of town before he saw the flames burst through the roof.

Now, to keep it all synchronized he needed to

visit the saddle maker and the livery. The livery would be easy—turn out a dozen horses or so and leave the gate down. He accomplished that in short order. Porter Jordan had built an 8-by-8 shack to do business from where the livery barn had burned down. Buckskin saw a low light in it and figured the same stablehand was in there sleeping. He wouldn't hear a thing.

The saddle shop was a different story. Buckskin had heard around town that both Ingraham and Jordan said they were going to sleep in their stores for a while to make sure nothing else happened.

Buckskin thought about it as he walked up Main Street, then he grinned when the idea developed. Back at the Van Dalton Hotel, he found the maintenance man's room. It was a little after one A.M. and no one but a sleepy room clerk was about. Buckskin slipped inside the storage room and found what he wanted. He carried a quart of red paint and two inch-wide brushes and went by the alley until he could come out near the saddle shop with only a short walk on Main.

In the alley, he pried the top off the can of red paint and stirred it up to mix the oil and pigment. Now he held the can and with an inch-wide brush began painting on the window and door of the saddle shop. He worked quickly, not proud of his penmanship, but the block letters could be read from across the street. He started with a "3" then printed "Angels of Death. Your own time is drawing near. Repent now!"

He had just finished when a man staggered up the boardwalk toward Buckskin. He was almost past, but fell sideways and Buckskin caught him, leaving a wide stripe of red paint across the man's shirt.

"Easy, easy," Buckskin said. He dropped the brush and led the man down the boardwalk away from the scene. Three doors down he left the drunk, ran back, grabbed the brushes and can of paint and ran the other way into the alley. He disposed of the paint can and brush in a burn barrel in back of a store and walked back to his hotel. He slipped into room 20 with no one noticing him and settled down to a short night's sleep, with his reloaded .45 Colt near his right hand.

The next morning just before noon, the three Angels of Death met in the back room at the general store. Ingraham's face was red, and he couldn't control his voice he was so angry. Jordan was exhausted after a three-hour roundup of twenty of his horses who had escaped through the open gate. Only Stacey Trumble looked halfway normal. He shook his head at the other two.

"Look, it's only a small problem we need to take care of, that's all. We know the man doing this."

"Your solution yesterday didn't work out, did it?" Ingraham snapped. "Your solution will be buried today. You have any more bright ideas for us?"

Trumble shook his head.

"I got one," Jordan said. "What we should have done two weeks ago when we found out about this gun slick. I'll gun him myself. Yeah, no worry, tenderfeet. I've killed a man or two in my time. So relax. It'll all be over within two days. I got to figure out any pattern he has, work out the best way and the best weapon. Then it's just a matter of pulling the trigger."

"You hope," Trumble said. "My man figured the same way, and now he's getting dug under this afternoon."

"That's why I plan the whole thing out. Plan and plan and work it over until nothing can go wrong."

"So how will you do it?" Ingraham asked.

"That's the point, I don't know yet. Give me some time. I'll work it out so I can't miss. More than likely I'll use a rifle."

"Good. Now, let's hope you get him before he does any more damage to our property."

"One more thing," Ingraham said. "He printed a three on your store, Trumble. How the hell would he know there are just three of us left?"

"Don't know, don't care," Trumble said. "It took me two hours of scrubbing and scraping to get that damn red paint off."

Jordan pushed his hat back and nodded. "Yeah, now that you mention it, only three of us got hit before, and only us three this time. How in hell could he know there are just three of us left out of the five?"

"Oh, yeah, I see," Trumble said. "How could he know?"

"Could be only one man who told the bastard," Ingraham said.

"Not him. You have too much evidence against him. He'd never tell anyone, let alone this Morgan son-of-a-bitch."

Ingraham snorted. "Why the hell not? It'd be his

chance to get rid of us and out from under my file of goods on him."

"Then why wouldn't he go for you first?" Jordan asked. Why kill Van Dalton first? We know how Zebadiah caught it. Why not the rest of us? I don't think it's the doc."

"I'll find out," Ingraham said. "My rheumatiz been acting up again. I'm going over to see the doc right now. Let you know how he reacts. If the file of goods doesn't keep his mouth shut, I'd guess that Doc Sims will have to go in a long swim in the Missouri."

"Let us know today," Jordan said. "I'll be busy setting up my target for some shooting practice."

Twenty minutes later, Gideon Ingraham looked up as Doc Sims came into a small room in the clinic.

"I've got a problem, Doc. You best shut the door. This is just between you and me." Dr. Sims nodded and closed the door. This happened often.

"What's the problem, Gideon?"

"You, Doc. You've been talking out of school."

"What do you mean?"

"I mean you don't have much respect for this file with those stories and signed statements by those three girls and the nurse who used to work for you before she got pregnant."

Doc Sims sagged into a chair in the examining room. "Look, I told you I'm afraid of that material in your file. Would I put all that in jeopardy by talking to someone about you? Absolutely not. What about the committee? They know a lot more about you than you think. Why do you think I talked to someone?"

"How else would someone know to print a 'three Angels of Death' on Stacey Trumble's window in red paint? Who but you knew about the two of us who died?"

"Hell, Gideon, you're losing your touch. Everyone in town knows about those two men dying. I'd say half the town has picked out their bet on who the five Angels are. People aren't as stupid as you think they are. Go out in the street and ask ten men who they think the Five Angels of Death are, and I'd bet that they come up with at least four names that are right.

"If you want some advice, I'd say now is a good time for you three to fold your tent and melt into the background here in Yankton. You've had your run. You probably think you've done the community some good by getting rid of some outlaws and bad guys. So why not retire while you're still ahead?"

"Thought about it. Then we get another wild-eye in town who messes things up and we need to take action."

"Need to? You really think you couldn't let the law handle some things, Gideon? We aren't a rough little settlement anymore. We're the territorial capitol, fer crize sakes."

"Hell, I don't know. As for you, Doc, remember I've got that file. We know where you live and that you have two sweet daughters and a sexy wife. Just remember that."

Ingraham frowned down at Dr. Sims, then

stalked out of the room and through the back door. Dr. Sims sat there a minute, then he wrote a note and hired a small boy to push it under room 20 at the Van Dalton Hotel. He had to see Buckskin Morgan just as soon as he could. His life and the lives of his family depended on it.

Chapter Seventeen

Buckskin Morgan slept until nearly eight o'clock that morning. He was groggy. Too much sleep was bad for a person. He shaved, had coffee instead of breakfast. He drank his brew at a different cafe that morning so no one could establish a pattern of his behavior. Made it harder for anyone to kill him that way.

He walked over to Main Street and watched Stacey Trumble scraping the red paint off his door and window. The man swore the entire hour he worked on it, and Buckskin stood on the other side of the street and grinned. He wondered how Ingraham took the loss of his barn and stable.

Then he pondered his own problem. He was thinking more and more that Sherry Crawford was the woman he hunted for Harold Evans. But how could he prove it and how could he talk her into coming back to Denver if she was the right one?

Nate Hill would be a huge roadblock. The gun slick in the street yesterday might have been paid by Hill. Or he might have been hired by the remaining vigilantes. Either way, both would undoubtedly try for his hide again. If he was smart, he'd probably make himself less public, stick to his room more and work the poker games at night. He wanted to make another call on Sherry in her apartment over the saloon, but the risk was far too great. At least for now.

There would be a showdown with Hill one of these days, Buckskin was sure. At least he didn't have to worry about the white slavers anymore. He had put a small hole in their operation but he was sure that's all he'd done. As long as there was a market for pretty young women, there would be men who would steal them.

He stopped at a gunsmith to look at some new six-guns that had come out, then went to a barbershop for a trim. He still wore his hair a little longer than most men and a little shaggy around the ears.

Then he stopped at Yankton Clothiers and bought two new shirts. When he took the shirts back to his hotel room, he found a note under his door.

Ten minutes later he made sure no one saw him, then went in the back door at Doc Sims' clinic. Dr. Sims saw him and finished wiping plaster of Paris off his hands.

"Johnson boy had a broken leg. Glad you came. I'm getting ready to leave town. I told my wife this noon so she should pack some things. There's a seven-thirty sternwheeler pulling in tonight and my family is going to be on board."

"Why? Did the Angels scare you?"

"Damn right. They figured I was the only one who could have told someone else that there were only three angels left. Ingraham was here. Said if he knew for sure I told you that I'd be a dead man before morning. He's watching me like an eagle looking for a mate."

"Hold on another day. I'll go have it out with Ingraham."

"No, Morgan. I know you're doing this as a favor to the town and to me, but I can't take it any longer. His threats were the last straw. I'll give you an address you can write to in Omaha. I have kin there we'll stay with for a week or so. You let me know if anything happens to change things."

"Looks like your mind is made up."

"I'd rather be running downstream than dead. He'd go for the girls first, I know he would. I won't let anything happen to my girls."

"Probably best. They might burn down your house. You want me to stay there and keep an eye on things?"

Dr. Sims blinked rapidly and wiped at his eyes. "I'd appreciate it. Hard telling what those killers might do. I just want to get out of town as fast as I can."

"I'll be there to cover your back at seven tonight. Oh, you best carry some kind of a weapon if you have one."

"I've got a .45 six-shooter. Right, I'll take it."

He waved and went on to see a patient. Buckskin faded out the back door and slipped away from the entrance as casually as he could. He headed back downtown.

Porter Jordan had been tracking Buckskin Morgan all day. He leaned heavily against the side of a store and watched the man go into a hardware store. What could he want in there? Jordan had established several things today.

He had firmed up the link between Dr. Sims and Morgan. Ingraham would be pleased to hear that. The town would probably have one fewer doctors by morning. He also discovered that Morgan didn't live in the room he had registered at in the Van Dalton Hotel. Interesting and damn clever. He was in room 20.

Jordan had been careful not to be seen. He had stayed well back, taken off his jacket once and carried it to change his appearance in case Morgan watched his back. He didn't seem to be.

Once, the bastard had reversed himself and walked right past Jordan. The livery man had stepped into a retail establishment and came out quickly when he realized it was a dressmaking shop.

Now Jordan edged around the wall of the building for another look at Morgan. He had been standing outside the hardware looking up the street only a moment before. Now he was gone.

Jordan darted out of the alley onto the boardwalk. He ran full force into Buckskin Morgan, who had been waiting for him.

"What the hell?" Jordan shouted. "Didn't see you. My damn horse is getting away down the street." Jordan bounced off Morgan, caught his balance and ran down the boardwalk thirty yards, then looked back.

Morgan walked toward him at a steady pace. What the hell was the guy doing? Jordan was supposed to be tailing Morgan, not the other way around. Jordan kept walking, stepped into an alley and ran flat out as hard as he could. He hadn't made it to the end of the alley and the safety of two stores on either side when he heard a shot.

A bullet slapped the air over his head and he saw Buckskin Morgan's gun smoking at the mouth of the alley.

He ran.

Buckskin knew who the man was. Why was he following him? He hadn't shown a weapon. The Denver detective picked up his sprint and made it to the end of the alley before Jordan turned the next corner. He was gaining on him.

Not another chase, Buckskin thought. He'd done too many of these. Jordan turned again and Buckskin saw that the man was headed toward his livery stable. Was he going for a rifle, six-gun or a horse?

Buckskin took a shortcut in back of some houses and gained half a block on the man, but he was still well out of handgun range.

The pace slowed, then both men were walking. The hard run had tired them. When they were less than 100 yards from the livery, the owner ran again and vanished inside the small building. He came out a moment later with a rifle and fired a shot at Buckskin.

Someone else came out, also with a rifle. Buckskin dove into a small ditch where runoff water from rains had dug a two-foot gully. He was safe for the moment. If they came close enough to shoot down into the ditch, they would be in handgun range. He waited, then peered over the top of the dirt.

One of the two had mounted a horse and spurred away downstream.

Buckskin rose up, only to hear a rifle slug sing through the air over his head. He worked along the ditch until he was as close as he could get to the shack. The other person, who he considered must be the stable boy, was now directly behind the small building watching where Buckskin had first dived into the ditch. Now and again a rifle shot sounded toward his former hiding spot.

He lifted up, drew his Colt, cocked it, then ran silently toward the shack. His luck held. The youth with the rifle fired again at the ditch, then before he could work the lever on the rifle to chamber a new round, Buckskin broke around the corner of the shack and tackled him. They both hit the ground and rolled.

Buckskin came out on top and smashed his fist into the kid's jaw, stopping any more fighting. Buckskin grabbed the rifle and made the kid lie face down on the ground.

"Where did Jordan go?" Buckskin demanded.

"Don't know, just said to hold you off while he rode downriver."

Another saddled horse stood at the edge of the old corral next to where the stables had been. Buckskin took the rifle and stepped into the saddle.

"Borrowing your horse for a while. Put me down as a rental. I'll bring her back."

Buckskin rode for the river and headed downstream. As he rode, he checked the rifle—six rounds left and no spares. He would be frugal.

Ahead along the shoreline, he could see no sign of the rider. Here there were considerable trees and brush along the shore. Jordan could be hidden in any of a dozen spots waiting for Buckskin to come along for an easy, close-in shot.

Buckskin angled out from the stream, keeping 200 yards between himself and the brush, making a much harder shot if the ambusher was there. He rode a half mile and saw no one. A few houses showed near the banks of the stream, but most were a quarter mile back so floods wouldn't sweep them away.

He kept riding, swinging in front of the first house and in back of the second one. As he approached the second house he saw a woman run from the back door toward the river. A man came to the back door, started out, saw Buckskin and slammed back inside and closed the door.

Had it been Jordan? Same dark hat and dark shirt. Buckskin turned his mount and rode toward a brushline from a small stream that came in from the left. He was only fifty yards away. He was almost there when a rifle snarled behind him and the round clipped some tree branches ahead of him, then he was into the concealment. One more rifle round sang through the trees but was again ahead of him. Buckskin slid off the horse and took the rifle.

He pushed up on his stomach to the edge of the brush so he could see the cabin. He saw the woman to the left rushing the last few yards toward the brush and trees along the river.

The rifle shots confirmed his guess. It was Jordan inside the house. He must have threatened the woman to make her rush out of her own home.

Buckskin waited. Jordan would make a move. He was the one running. He had fired the first shot. He might try the river. From this angle Buckskin could see about half the shoreline through the trees. At one end he saw a small dock built out into the water. He couldn't tell if there was a boat there. Even a rowboat would get Jordan downstream and away from Buckskin.

The detective crawled back from the edge of the brush and moved through it toward the Missouri. He was about 75 yards from the river. When he got there, he turned upstream and had a new view of the back of the house. A horse stood there with its head down tied to a porch post.

He moved silently through the brush until he spotted the woman hiding in front of him. He didn't want to scare her.

"Miss, don't be afraid, I'm the man chasing the man in your house. Are you all right?"

She looked up, then moved so she could see him through the brush.

"Me? Yes. But I have two children in there. I didn't know what to do. He said he'd kill me if I didn't do what he wanted me to."

She was young, maybe 24 or 25 with short brown hair, wide-set brown eyes and an ample figure.

"Who are you, a lawman?"

"I'm a detective, ma'am. Jordan in there is the bad guy. How old are your children?"

"Three and two. Just babies, really. My husband is in town getting some supplies. We run a few cattle down the way."

Now he saw the boat, a ten-foot rowboat, grounded on shore near the small dock with oars shipped and ready to go.

"Don't let him hurt my babies. Maybe I should go back inside and watch them."

"No. Then he'd have three hostages instead of two. Is the river easy to use here with the rowboat?"

"Looks that way, but there are some savage currents and a whirlpool just a little way down."

Buckskin considered how to get to the cabin. The right side he looked at was blind. No windows showed on that side. It was closest to the creek he had just come down. If he went back to the creek and up it to that point, he'd have maybe thirty yards to rush to the cabin on that blind side. Should work.

Five minutes later he rested against the side of the cabin with no windows. He still had the rifle. He carried it in his left hand now and the Colt in his right. He edged toward the back of the cabin and spotted one window built in low. This would be the bedroom.

He moved to it and rose up to look through sheer white curtains. A bedroom. Two small bodies slept on the big bed. The window was a swing-out and unlocked. Possible. He went to the far edge of the back of the cabin and looked around. Two windows up front, kitchen maybe.

He heard a door slam and a voice call out.

"Lady, if you want to see these babies of yours, you best get back up here to the house." It was Jordan. "You got nothing to fear from me."

There was no answer from the woman.

Buckskin went to the back of the cabin and swung the window out. It creaked, then was silent. He waited. The door he saw across the room stayed shut. Silently he put the rifle into the room, then rose up and bellied over the sill and went head first into the room. He lit on his hands and shoulders beside the bed and quickly got his feet under him and the rifle back in his left hand.

The older child stirred in his sleep, then settled down. Buckskin stepped cautiously toward the door on the new wood floors. They didn't squeak. At the door, he looked through the keyhole but could see no one.

He set the rifle by the wall side of the door and with his left hand turned the knob gently. It turned all the way, then he edged the door out an inch and looked through the crack.

Nothing but a wall.

He pushed the door a bit farther open and saw a large room that was kitchen and living room. Jordan stood at the kitchen window chewing on a piece of bread in one hand and holding his six-gun in the other.

"Where the hell is he?" Jordan said softly. "Where

the hell is that fucking Buckskin Morgan?"

Buckskin wanted to gun him down right then. To shoot the weapon out of his hand, tell him why he was dying, then shoot him full of holes before finally ending it. But he couldn't.

The babies.

The woman.

He waited. When the bread Jordan ate was gone, he picked up his rifle and bolted out the kitchen door. It came so suddenly that Buckskin wasn't ready for it. He reached for the rifle, knocked it down, woke up a baby who started crying, and when he got the rifle and headed for the door he was way behind.

Jordan must have seen the boat, too. He was almost to it before Buckskin got out the door. The woman stood up close to Jordan's path, ruining any chance of a rifle shot. She screeched at him and ran at him and pounded him with her fists as he stepped into the boat. Then he shoved off and Buckskin had a shot. He rushed it and missed. Then the boat was soon in the current and careened downstream.

The woman heard her child crying and rushed for the house.

Buckskin hefted the rifle and ran downstream looking for an open area through the brush.

About thirty yards down he found one. The boat had hit a slow place in the water near the shore, then suddenly it jolted ahead and nearly upset Jordan. He caught the oars and began working them, trying to bring the craft closer to shore.

Buckskin levered a round into the rifle and aimed

at the front of the boat just at the waterline. He fired. The round splintered the old wood an inch over the waterline, and he could see that water would flow inside the boat.

He aimed the second round at the center of the oar where it fit in the oarlock and made little movement even when being rowed. He fired. The round missed the oar but slammed into Jordan's knee and brought a scream of terror and agony. Buckskin saw one oar drop from his hand and, held in place by the oar lock, turn the craft toward shore.

Twice more Buckskin fired at the boat, hitting it near the waterline. Then the boat was downstream too far.

He raced along the shore again. Now with a second wind, he made good time and came to another opening fifty yards down. The boat edged closer to shore, but the current dictated the direction now. Ahead, Buckskin saw the roiling waters of the whirlpool.

There was no large flow of water into the Missouri right here. There was no reason for the whirlpool. It was one of the vagaries and mysteries of the mighty Missouri, which often did what it wanted to do.

The whirlpool was a hundred feet wide and a little higher than the usual water level on the sides where the circular swirling water threw up a water wall a foot high. The speed of the water increased as it dropped lower and lower in the whirlpool.

Porter Jordan looked into the throat of the funnel of crashing water and saw that it was ten feet below the level of the river.

Jordan screamed. He saw that the rowboat had been sucked into the outer edge of the whirling water. He dove out of the boat, surfaced and tried to swim away from the spinning water.

It was like a bug trying to crawl out from under a descending boot. The boat hit the swirling water first, spinning around and around until it was half full of water and then in one final swoop, vanished in the vortex of the surging water. By that time, Jordan had entered the second round of the whirl. He screamed and fought against it, and being a good swimmer he kept his head above the pull of the water.

On the third time around, he stopped screaming. He looked at Buckskin and shouted something, but the sound of the rushing waters drowned out the words.

Buckskin watched as the waters made quick work of Jordan on his final swirling round. Then his hand reached upward, and that was the last Buckskin saw of the livery stable owner as the mighty Missouri claimed another victim in its annual rite of human sacrifice.

Buckskin looked downstream but saw no parts of the rowboat or the oars. Both boat and Jordan could be carried a mile downstream deep in the bowels of the Missouri as it digested its latest victim before spewing the remains to the surface.

He walked back to the cabin. The woman stood on the rear step with a baby over her shoulder watching him.

"He make it?"

Buckskin shook his head. He reached in his

pocket and took out a twenty-dollar bill and gave it to the woman. Likely it was more cash money than she'd seen in six months.

"To pay for the boat, ma'am. He had no cause to steal it. You might just as well claim that horse, too. It don't seem to have a brand on it."

"Who are you, mister?"

"Buckskin Morgan, ma'am. I'm a detective working on a case in town. This Jordan thing kind of got in the way. You've heard of the Five Angels of Death?"

"Oh, my, yes."

"He was one of them. Now there are only two. I'll be finding my horse now and riding out."

At the shack, he called to the stable boy. Buckskin left the horse without a word of explanation and walked into town. He'd tell the sheriff what happened to Porter Jordan. No sense telling him the man was one of the Five Angels. No sense at all.

Buckskin had to hurry to get to the boat in time. He made it with ten minutes to spare. Just before the gangplank went up, Dr. Sims and his wife and two children scurried on board. They wore hats and disguises so no one could tell who they were.

Dr. Sims told Buckskin where his house was and that the back door was open.

"Take care of things. An address where you can reach me is on top of the grandfather clock in a small book, first page."

He hurried up the gangplank and didn't wave.

Buckskin went to find the house. It was just in back of the doctor's clinic, a two-story frame house that looked as if it had been freshly painted. It was dark by the time he went in the back door. He lit a lamp in the living room, checked out the pantry and left the light on low as he ate some crackers and cheese for his supper.

He ran over to the clinic and checked the front door. It had a hand-printed message: "Dr. Sims has been called to his ill mother in Chicago. Dr. Faraday will handle my patients. Stay well!"

He hurried back to the house, left the light on, lit another one in the kitchen, then went outside and found a soft spot to do his guard duty. If Ingraham was as angry as the doctor said, he'd see the ill mother in Chicago as an excuse for the doctor running away. The clinic and maybe the house could be arson targets. The house first, since that would hurt the town the least.

Buckskin sat and waited. At nine that evening he went in and turned out the light in the kitchen, then lit one in an upstairs bedroom and hurried back downstairs and out the back door. The house sat between two others, and he chose his guard position in the shadows of the house on the left since it was closest to town and offered some darkness from the bright moon.

He dozed, came awake and checked the star clock. A little after midnight. Time to stay alert. He chewed a stem of grass to keep awake and was amazed at how the motion of his jaw seemed to ward off any sense of slumber.

A half hour and four grass stems later, he heard someone coming. Two men walking. Something clanged a moment, a hushed comment, then they continued. They were in the alley behind the house.

Buckskin moved that way in the shadows and waited.

The shadows became men and materialized out of the darkness. They hurried to the back porch, where one man undid the lid of a can and began spreading some liquid on the porch. Buckskin had cocked his six-gun before, now he aimed and fired at the man with the can. He aimed low, hit him in one leg and drove him to the ground. The man bellowed in pain.

"Git running out of here or you're both dead men," Buckskin roared. Both men dropped their cans and ran on past the doctor's house and down the alley toward the main part of town. Buckskin retrieved the cans. Coal oil. Enough to start a fire that no one could put out. He drained the cans into the ground of the alley and threw them after the two men. They wouldn't be back tonight.

It would be a long night of waiting and watching, but it should be worth it.

Chapter Eighteen

The next morning when it began to get light, Buckskin went to sleep leaning against a tree outside of the Sims house. It should be safe now. He slept until eight o'clock and got up and limped for a dozen yards to get the cricks out of his back and legs. Then he walked with a purpose to the closest cafe. He found a seat at a small table near the back wall and settled in. He knew he was a mess, bearded, dirty, hair uncombed, and grumpy as an old she bear who'd lost her twin cubs.

He ordered the biggest breakfast they had and was almost through with the bacon and eggs, home-fried potatoes and three plate-sized hotcakes when two men walked into the cafe and looked around. They drifted to the back, and the next time Buckskin noticed them was when one of them knelt beside him and grabbed the handle of his .45 with one hand and pushed another weapon hard into Buckskin's side.

"Partner, we've got important business with you outside. Why don't you just get up slow and easy and move away from the table and we'll sidle out the back door over there."

Buckskin remained seated. "Don't see why I should do that. I ain't finished my coffee yet."

The revolver barrel in his side dug in harder. "This hogleg's all the reason you need, pilgrim. Just stand easy and don't make no sudden moves or you're dead meat right here in this eatery."

The second man had come in front of Buckskin and picked up the coffee cup he had been drinking from and poured it on Buckskin's crotch.

"Look there, the coffee's all gone," the second man said. He snorted. "Now, by God, stand up or die where you sit."

The whole conversation had been in hushed tones and no one else in the cafe was aware of the threat. Now Buckskin changed pitches and screamed at the men.

"These men are trying to rob me. Get the sheriff!" Buckskin's cry of rage caused two men who carried sidearms to rise and move toward the pair. The taller kidnapper drew and covered the two men. The first ambusher kept his six-gun on Buckskin.

Three more men moved toward the excitement. One of them pulled a six-gun. The man standing in front of Buckskin turned and fired, hitting the man in the shoulder. That gave Buckskin the opening he needed. He roared upward, exploding his right elbow out and up in a vicious blow that caught the kneeling gunman flush on the jaw and jolted him backward three feet, knocked him out and dumped the weapon from his hand.

By then half the people in the cafe had either ducked for cover or had crowded up to see what the trouble was.

The gunman standing grabbed a woman who got too close, his arm around her throat as he held her in front of his body for protection. He waved his six-gun.

"Anybody else try to draw a weapon and he's dead meat. Now, I want everybody to get down on the floor, lay down on the floor, right now."

To emphasize his point, he fired his weapon into the ceiling. Everyone dropped to the floor except Buckskin, who darted past the man and out the back door. Looking for some protection, he dropped behind a crate in back of a store. The gunman ran to the back door and looked out, couldn't see Buckskin, swore and dodged back inside.

Buckskin checked his six-gun. Still safely in his holster. The men inside had fifteen or twenty hostages. What would they do? It seemed obvious they had come in to capture and then probably try to kill him. Who had hired them? Still two good choices, Nate Hill the gambling saloon owner or the two Angels of Death. Right, just two of them left now.

The smart thing for the gunmen to do would be to revive the one on the floor and walk out the front door, holster their guns and try to get lost in the crowd. The sheriff was probably out fishing. Which meant Buckskin needed to get around to the front door. He ran down the alley up to Main when he wondered if the gunmen were smart enough to go out the front. Too late now. He charged ahead.

He found a stream of people leaving the eatery. He stopped one of them.

"The gunmen. They still inside?"

"Oh, hell, no. Right after you got away they ran out the front door fast as they could. Don't have any idea what direction they went even."

Buckskin thanked him and began to watch the people on the street. He walked two blocks, but saw no one who resembled the young-looking gunmen, who both seemed to be in their early twenties.

Damn lousy way to start the day, especially after not getting enough sleep. He checked his pocket watch. A little before nine.

So where would they try again? Or one of them at least. The one he knocked out wouldn't be worth much for a day or two.

Who, where and when, those were the questions right now. He wanted to sit in one of the chairs by the hardware, but passed them by. Too much of a pattern. The gunmen must have followed him into the cafe. How could they know where he had been?

Maybe the "who" was the two Angels of Death. They knew he was at the Sims house last night.

The "when" had to be anytime, all the time. He had to be on the alert every minute. He would never sleep in the same place twice. He had to prepare himself. He felt the hidden gun in the ankle holster. What else? He hated this. He should be closing in on Sherry Crawford, proving that she was Mrs. Dawn Evans and trying to convince her to come back to Denver. He had a whole treasure chest full of incentives for her.

He passed a saloon, avoided it and walked into the hardware. Hiding behind a counter, he watched the people on the street through the two big front windows. With the sun on the other side of the street, passersby could see little by looking in.

A man started past, then slowed, glanced at the door but kept going. Small black hat, gray shirt and black pants. Two other men stood across the street. One of them looked familiar and Buckskin stared hard. Yes, he was the second man, the tall one with the gun who had grabbed the woman.

So they were watching him again. Buckskin wished he had his rifle. He could get to the alley, shoot both of them before they knew he was there, and vanish down the alley and around the block, dumping the rifle in a burn barrel. How long would they hang out there? He ran to the back of the store, pushed through a rear door and hurried out to the alley. He went half a block to the next street, up to Main, crossed it and down the far side. The two men he had seen were no longer there. He frowned.

Had they caught on? He checked the other side of the street and saw the men come out of the hardware. One of the men had on a white hat, the other a brown one. They looked in both directions, then walked up the street toward the biggest hotel in town.

Halfway along, they picked up a third man who paced with them. He was shorter than the others, wore a black suit, white shirt and tie. Buckskin stared in surprise. The short man was Newton J.

Kerr, the white slaver he had dumped into the Missouri River several days ago. He had made it to shore after all. The liar. He said he couldn't swim.

Buckskin crossed the street behind them and moved closer. The little man had survived and come back for vengeance. Not smart of him. Buckskin wondered where the three were heading. Maybe he could give them a little more rope.

He followed them down Main, past most of the businesses and toward a small house at the edge of town half a block from the river. Nearby stood an old abandoned warehouse. Now the building sagged and weathered and had no windows or doors, and one end of the two-story structure had caved in.

The men headed for the house.

Time enough.

Buckskin slid a sixth cartridge into his Colt, then fired a round over the heads of the three men. He had closed to within fifty feet of them, so the round wasn't intended to harm.

"Hold it right there, Kerr. Not another step and don't turn around. I don't appreciate being hammered in a public place by two river rats. I want all three of you to lift your hands and lace your fingers on top of your heads. Do it!"

Kerr did it at once. One of the men did so slowly, then changed his mind, spun and dropped to one knee, drawing iron as he did. Buckskin had been walking forward since the first shot. He was now less than thirty feet from the men and he shot the kneeling man in the chest. He slammed backwards, bellowed in pain for a moment, then the six-gun dropped from his dead fingers.

"Any more takers?" Buckskin barked.

The second man lifted his hands to his head.

"Now, Kerr, I want you to turn slowly. I should kill you right now and throw your worthless carcass into the Missouri. Did you come back to town just to kill me?"

"Don't flatter yourself. You're only one small irritant that I'm about to eliminate. Now, Jones, now!" The last words were barked in command, and the man beside him darted one hand from his head to his chest and in one swift movement hurled something at Buckskin.

The Denver detective pulled the trigger twice and saw the man beside Kerr stagger backward and crumple into the dirt of the road. At the same time, Buckskin saw the missile coming toward him. Some kind of bomb? He dove to the ground and rolled into a ditch at the side of the road. The bomb fell short of Buckskin, but the roar of it shattered his ears as the explosion filled the air with deadly shrapnel singing through the air like a hive of angry bees.

A dust cloud smothered him in its choking density. He sat up pawing at his eyes and trying to get a good breath. The dust and smoke dissipated in the gentle breeze, and when he looked for Kerr he wasn't on the road. Both dead gunmen lay there. Then he sensed a movement to his right and saw a man entering the old warehouse.

Buckskin ran to the dead gunmen. He examined the first one to die and found what he thought he would: another small bomb. He stared at it in silent recognition. Two sticks of dynamite taped together, and twenty or thirty large-headed roofing nails tapped to the dynamite. It made for a highly effective bomb and produced a deadly handful of shrapnel.

He stared at the bomb. There was no fuse. How did it detonate? Then he saw a small vial taped to each end and one on the side. The vials must contain some highly explosive material, perhaps nitroglycerin. No wonder it exploded. The man who carried it was lucky that the round from Buckskin hadn't hit the explosive and detonated when he fell.

Buckskin carried the bomb as he jogged toward the warehouse. Then, remembering the sensitive nature of the nitro, he slowed to a walk with the bomb in his left hand and his reloaded six-gun in his right.

Buckskin paused at the door hole of the warehouse and listened. He heard footsteps deep inside. The detective went into the building in a short rush, then stopped in the shadows. He listened again but this time heard nothing. He waited. His living with Indians for a time had taught him patience. Now he breathed lightly and listened. The sounds of walking came again from the left. Was the sound from the second level?

He moved that way and paused again.

It took him five minutes to move without a sound to a wooden stairway that led straight up in one slant to a second floor. He listened again. Yes, the sounds came from up there.

He went up the steps slowly, careful not to make any noise. He heard sounds from above. Some boxes falling over, other sounds that he couldn't identify.

He smelled something and wasn't sure what it was. It had the sharp odor of kerosene but somehow stronger. What was Kerr doing? Buckskin moved a few feet from the top of the stairs and could see half the open space of the second floor. Evidently it had been some kind of packing plant at one time. The sharp smell came again, and he saw something move down the open room sixty or seventy feet. A shadowy figure slipping behind some wooden boxes.

Buckskin sat down next to a six-by-six beam that held up the ceiling. A moment later a figure jumped out from behind the boxes and threw something toward Buckskin. The detective stepped backward several paces even when it became obvious the item thrown wouldn't reach him.

Then the missile hit the wooden floor. It was a glass jar. As soon as it hit, the glass burst and a burning wick in the jar ignited the fluid and vapor in a small explosion as the burning liquid spread over a twenty-foot stretch.

That's when Buckskin realized what the fluid was. Gasoline. A further refining process from kerosene. Much more volatile. When it vaporized it exploded like dynamite. He stepped back from the heat of the burning liquid and realized that it had soaked into the wood and that the warehouse was on fire. He raced to the far side of the fire so he could see behind the boxes.

There he saw Kerr on his hands and knees filling another jar with gasoline from a gallon can.

"Give it up, Kerr, you're out of gasoline bombs."

Kerr started to stand, then grabbed another jar that was filled and pushed its gasoline-soaked fuse into a burning candle, and the fuse spurted with flame. In the same motion he lifted the jar to throw it, but it slipped out of his hand. It smashed into a wooden box and splashed burning gasoline over the area directly in front of him. He staggered back, then turned and ran for the stairway.

Buckskin still held the dynamite bomb. Now he threw it so it would land twenty feet in front of Kerr. Kerr ran faster than Buckskin had figured. The bomb hit less than six feet in front of the sprinting little man.

The explosion lifted him off his feet and threw him to the side. Half a dozen of the deadly roofing nails jolted into his body. When the smoke from the bomb blew away, Buckskin rushed to the small man with his Colt up and ready.

Kerr lay on his back where he had fallen. One of the roofing nails showed its half-inch-wide head closely against Kerr's forehead. The inch-and-a-half shaft of the nail imbedded deeply into Kerr's brain. Another nail had jolted into his throat sideways, slashing through his jugular vein.

Kerr was dead. Buckskin grabbed him and dragged him to the stairs, then carried him down the stairs and outside. Already half of the weathered-dry building was roaring flames. He heard the can of gasoline inside explode.

Half a dozen people ran up to watch the fire. Buckskin put Kerr in the grass at a safe distance and walked up to the people watching the blaze.

The whole building was burning by then. There was no danger to any other structures because none were nearby. The Yankton volunteer fire department didn't even turn out. They would clean up when the fire had burned itself out.

Sheriff Jared Van Dyke came when someone reported two dead men on the road near the warehouse. He scratched his head and had the bodies taken to the undertaker. The sheriff didn't notice Kerr until the fire was almost out. He shook his head at the way the man had died.

An hour later while Buckskin had coffee in another cafe, Sheriff Van Dyke slid into a chair across from him and took off his hat. He sipped a cup of java and waved one hand at Buckskin.

"Hear you had some trouble this morning early at a cafe down the street."

"Yep. Two gents wanted to riddle my body with lead."

"You got away, so did the two gents. I have two witnesses who swear the two who jumped you are the same two we found dead out by the old brewery building down on River Road."

"Interesting," Buckskin said.

"You gun them?"

"Somebody shoots at me, I usually shoot back, don't you, Sheriff?"

"Deed I do, but I got the badge to make it legal."

"Self-defense. You see the explosion marks on the road out there?"

"Did notice it. Dynamite and roofing nails. Seen it before. Damn deadly."

"They threw one bomb at me, but not quite far enough."

"Figured. What about the other one?"

"Name's Kerr, Newton Kerr. He was a white slaver working Yankton, kidnapping young girls out of town here and running them downriver to Omaha or St. Louis on the Mississippi. I tangled with him downriver a ways few days ago taking a young girl away from him."

"Another case of self-defense?"

"He threw gasoline bombs at me. Gasoline in a glass jar with a burning wick in it. Explodes in fire when the jar breaks."

The sheriff nodded. "You're out of Denver, I hear."

"True. Looking for a runaway wife. Haven't found her yet."

"Be obliged if you could find her right smart quick. This town has had too many corpses since you arrived."

"Soon as I find her I'll be gone, Sheriff. You can bet your badge on that."

The lawman finished his coffee, stared hard at Buckskin and put down his cup.

"I'll take that as a promise. Make it soon. I've got an election coming up in two or three months."

"Two or three days should be enough for me, Sheriff Van Dyke."

The lawman rose, nodded, settled his hat in place and walked out the door.

Buckskin smiled. It wasn't often that he found a sheriff who was so casual about a few corpses suddenly showing up in his county.

He stood, paid his tab and walked out to the boardwalk. He turned north toward his hotel. So it had been Kerr who had set him up that morning. Not anyone in town. That still left two potential problems.

He walked slowly and soon realized someone was beside him matching him stride for stride. He looked over and saw a woman taking big steps. She wore a soft blue dress and a sunbonnet so he couldn't see her face.

She turned toward him. Under the sunbonnet was the short black hair and face of Sherry Crawford. She smiled.

"Wonder if we could walk a bit . . . and talk?"

"Be my pleasure." He held out his arm and she tucked her hand through it and smiled.

"Now this is nice. Not fighting over cards and money. I hear you were busy this morning."

"Minor inconvenience."

"Three dead men is a minor inconvenience?"

"Goes with the job. They were white slavers. Usually kidnap girls here in town and take them downriver."

"That's terrible."

"They tried to kill me, so I had to kill them."

He felt Sherry shiver.

"Sorry, didn't mean to frighten you."

"Not that. I was just wondering what it would be like to know that someone was trying to kill me. Must be terrible."

"Not too bad. You learn to live with it . . . or you die. Quite simple, really."

They walked to the end of the boardwalk and

turned and started back the way they had come.

"When we talked before I said something about maybe moving. I'm not sure now. Might just stay here awhile."

"With Nate Hill?"

"He's good to me."

"He should be. You make money for him gambling and you warm his bed."

She looked at him quickly, the start of a blush showing.

"Sherry, we aren't children. I'm not condemning you for it. I'm just saying that Nate Hill has a mighty fine arrangement there going for himself."

She flashed him a smile. "Thank you."

Her arm slipped farther through his so his arm pressed against her side and her breast.

"He can be insufferable sometimes." She looked up at him. "I was just wondering . . ."

"Wondering can get people into big trouble."

She sighed. "I know. It's just that . . . Well, you're a better poker player than Nate. Just wondered how it would be teaming up with you to play in the big-stakes games downriver."

"Wouldn't that make Mr. Hill extremely unhappy?"

"Oh, yes. But by then we'd be half a day downstream and he wouldn't come after us. Besides, Nate Hill is a realist. He knows how good you are with your six-gun. He'd never go up against you."

"Maybe we could talk about it at another time."

"When we're alone?" she asked.

She turned and looked at him, and the invitation was there. He wasn't sure how to respond. It might be the only way to get her to admit who she was.

Buckskin grinned. "That sounds delightful. Tonight?"

She frowned. "No, we have a game. Tomorrow Nate has to go downriver to do some business. He'll be gone overnight."

"Your place would be too dangerous," Buckskin said. "We could find a hotel room somewhere?"

She hesitated for just a moment, then color rose in her cheeks and she smiled. "I would like that. I truly would like that. I'll meet you outside the hardware store tomorrow at seven-thirty. You might not recognize me, so I'll find you." She smiled. "I know this is naughty, but I just can't think of anything else to do to solve my problem with Nate."

She took her arm away from his. They were near the saloon. The fancy women came and went out the front door when they needed to. She nodded to him and turned into the saloon.

Buckskin smiled. Now maybe he would get somewhere. Now at least he would have all night to convince her to go back to her husband. Even if it was as wife in name only, Harold Evans would be thankful. She could play the role and have her heart's wildest dreams come through about travel, dance, whatever she wanted.

Buckskin nodded. It just might work.

Chapter Nineteen

Buckskin Morgan checked the sun as he watched Sherry Crawford walk into the Criterion Saloon. It was still morning. So far it had been an active day. He had been concentrating on the Angels of Death until Kerr popped up. Now he wasn't sure just what he should do. There were still two of the Angels. They should be dealt with. He knew why he went after them. Because they were there and they were evil and someone had to bring them to justice for their crimes.

The leather man, Stacey Trumble, was one of the two left. Buckskin had no set plan to deal with the man. It might be interesting to walk into his shop and accuse him of being one of the Angels of Death. There would be denial, denial, denial.

What the hell, he'd give it a try. He turned and

walked back down the block to the leather store and went in. Trumble stared at him in surprise for a second, then smiled.

"Yes sir, what can I do for you? Want that saddle you looked at before?"

"Not quite, Trumble. I just want to tell you that I'll be watching you. I have evidence that you're one of the vigilantes in this town called the Five Angels of Death. Of course you know there are only two of you Angels left. I don't quite have enough information to go to the district attorney with yet, but I will when I find two or three more witnesses.

"Trumble, you're rather distinctive even when you're wearing a black hood. Your fancy boots give you away. Who else in town has hand-tooled boots with a hundred dollars' worth of silver inlaid in them? Nobody. So I just wanted to give you fair warning."

Buckskin watched the surprise on Trumble's face turn into anger and then a touch of fear.

"I don't know what the hell you're talking about. Now get the hell out of my store. I don't have to stand here and be insulted by some damn drifter like you."

Buckskin grinned. "Remember, Angel, I'll be watching you. One more false step and you'll be stretching some county hemp down in front of the courthouse."

Buckskin turned and walked out of the building, showing his contempt for the man with his unprotected back.

Outside, Buckskin crossed the street, went down three doors and into a meat market. Amazing the kinds of meat the man had for sale. Even without the refrigeration some of the bigger towns were using, he had six or eight kinds of meat. Most of it wouldn't last more than half a day in this weather. Then he saw that the meat lay on a bed of crushed ice.

He left without buying anything and went up the street careful not to be walking alone. He went behind a couple or a group, or near another walker. That way he would be a much harder target to hit for a sniper with a rifle.

Buckskin knew that Trumble would make a play. With three of the five Angels dead, he had to be nervous. Now that he was challenged, he'd respond. Buckskin decided to make it easy for him. He went back to the hotel, slipped up to his unofficial room to get his rifle, and went down to what was left of the livery.

He'd heard that the bank had taken over the livery because of a loan, and they had two men handling the rebuilding and business. Buckskin rented a horse, pushed his rifle into the boot and rode out north along the river. He never looked behind him.

A half mile out of town he entered some brush near the Missouri River, and when he was shielded to the rear, he dropped off his horse and worked back so he could see through the brush but not be seen.

At first he spotted no one following him. Then a horse came out of brush along the river, galloped for a hundred yards and vanished back into the brush. Buckskin grinned. He couldn't tell who the rider was, but he was tracking Buckskin and didn't want to be seen.

Buckskin came out of the brush and galloped for a quarter mile, then slacked off the bay mare to a gentle walk. Again he didn't look behind. He wanted to appear only to be a man out for a ride, or maybe on a small hunting expedition.

Buckskin checked once more on the man behind him when the usual route took him into some trees. The same man with the black hat and tan shirt riding a gray was back there. He moved at a quicker pace now, as if he was trying to make up time.

So Buckskin had a fish on the line. Now what he had to do was plan how to reel him in and see who he was, or let the man make a play and then track him down. He had to be careful not to make himself too good a target. He would stay at least 500 yards ahead of the other man. That would put a crimp in the shooting accuracy of most of the riflemen in this Dakota country.

He hit another stretch of woods, broke through and galloped again hard for over a quarter mile until the high-rumped quarter horse began to wheeze. He checked down to a walk and let the bay get her wind. There should be a good interval between him and the tracker. Now for the trap.

It had to be a good one, or the man would cut and run.

He looked around for a place he could work the campfire trap. He selected a spot near the river where trees formed a half circle around a pleasant meadow. From the fringes of the brush and trees on the far side the tracker could see Buckskin's mount tied to a tree.

Just inside the trees he scraped to bare ground and built a fire from dry leaves and twigs and a few branches. It sent up a plume of good solid bluish smoke that should signal the start of a campfire.

Buckskin got more wood so the fire would last more than a few minutes, then took off his hat and jacket and put them on the remains of a blown-down cottonwood tree. The hat looked as if it were on a man's head, and the red and brown jacket bunched so it looked as if someone sat there leaning against the stump. It should be convincing enough to draw a bushwhacker's bullet.

Buckskin grabbed his rifle and slid deeper into the brush but made certain he had a good firing line toward the stump, the blaze and the edge of the brush beyond.

He settled in to wait. He heard his mount making horse talk with another animal, then all was silent again. A meadowlark sang just below where Buckskin had tied up his bay. Then suddenly it went silent and a crow that had been sitting in a tree near the half circle of brush lifted off its tree perch with a series of angry squawks.

Buckskin tensed and stared through the trees. He could see part of the opposite side of the brush around the clearing, but saw no movement. Where was the guy? Why wasn't he sneaking up on the innocent camper where the smoke was and the horse tied up? Maybe he was.

The Denver detective looked at the brush again, this time dividing it into quarters of the whole picture and working each quarter of the scene by itself. Nothing in the first quarter, or the second. In the third quarter he saw some grass move and a tree branch start quivering. He saw a man with a rifle climbing the tree.

The climber was on the far side of the arc of trees but only 100 yards or so from the fire. Buckskin waited. The man had to make the first move. Buckskin aimed his rifle at the man, eased off and watched the big picture again. He waited a minute, then saw the climber settle into the crotch of the big cottonwood and bring up his rifle for a shot.

Buckskin sighted in on the chest of the rifleman and waited. The instant he heard the bark of the other man's rifle, Buckskin squeezed the trigger. He opened both eyes and looked up as the gunner across the way jolted backwards out of the tree, smashed through some branches and fell into brush ten feet below.

Buckskin came to his feet and went around the arc, staying in concealment through the light brush and trees, to get a better view of the bushwhacker.

He saw him a minute later. The man sat on the ground next to the big tree, trying to stop the flow of blood from a splotch just under his clavicle but above his lung. Not a fatal shot. Buckskin fired a round into the air to get the man's attention, then he came in with the handgun covering the shooter.

Buckskin stopped ten feet from the man and stared at him. The man was not Stacey Trumble. "I don't even know who you are, why are you trying to kill me?"

"You killed my brother in Omaha."

"Not likely. I've only been through Omaha a few times, I've never worked there. You'll have to do better than that."

The man groaned and stabbed at the flowing blood. "Damn it, you shot me, ain't you going to help me stop the blood?"

"Why the hell should I? You shot at me first."

"Damn it, man, I could bleed to death sitting here."

"So who hired you to gun me down?"

"Didn't say anybody did."

"Didn't have to. It's happened before. Who was he?"

"Oh, damn. I tell you and then he kills me."

"You tell me and I might kill him before he can kill you. Especially if you get patched up and grab a sternwheeler tonight. You don't tell me and I'll kill you sure as rat poison right now."

"Oh, shit! Not much choice. I'll tell you. Trumble, Stacey Trumble who runs the saddle shop."

"Figures," Buckskin said. "Throw down your six-gun and I'll tie up that shoulder. If I'd aimed a mite lower I wouldn't have had to do this 'cause you'd be pushing up clover in boot hill cemetery."

"I guess, thanks."

Buckskin ripped half the man's shirt off and used the cloth to make a pressure pad over the front and back holes in the man's body and then tied them in place with strips from the shirt and two boot thongs. They would hold until he got to the other doctor in town.

"Now get on your horse and go to town and find a doctor. One is out of town and I don't where the other one has his office. After you get patched up you get on the next boat going either way or I'll eat your liver for supper. You understand me, rifleman?"

"Yes, sir."

"You better. I see you in Yankton again and I'll drill lead through your heart. Now git."

Buckskin watched the man struggle to mount, then ride off with one backward glance. Buckskin held the bushwhacker's rifle.

He rode back to town, left the horse and spare rifle at the livery, then stashed his own long gun in his room and ambled down the boardwalk toward the leather goods store. It was open. When Stacey Trumble looked up he ran behind the counter and charged through the back door into the alley.

Buckskin followed him, put a lead slug in the dust beside his boots and called for him to stop. To Buckskin's surprise, Trumble halted and held up his hands.

"Why the hell you running, Trumble? You got a guilty conscience or something? You better have."

"Look, I'll leave town. I'll sell the store to somebody and get on a sternwheeler and be gone."

"Not a chance. You've got an iron in your waistband. Do you want to draw it and take your chances with me, or go down to the courthouse and tell the sheriff about the murders you did?"

"Christ, he'd hang me." Trumble's eyes went wild and he looked at the gun in his belt. But he shook his head. "Hell, no. I'd rather take my chances with a jury. You'll have to convict me first."

"Won't be hard, because you're going to confess

that you shot the Chinese man, his wife and baby. You'll confess and write it down and swear to it. Otherwise you feel the sting of three forty-five-caliber slugs right into your belly, so you'll have at least an hour of agony before you finally die. Not even Dr. Sims could help you on wounds like that. So, Angel of Death, make up your mind."

Stacey Trumble turned and ran. Buckskin shot him twice, both times in the upper legs, and he went down in a billow of dust there in the alley.

Buckskin carried the tall, thin man over his shoulder to the other doctor's office, which now he remembered he'd seen on First Street in back of the bank. The doctor clucked at the bullet wounds, patched him up, and Buckskin borrowed a wheelbarrow and rolled the miscreant to the courthouse and the sheriff's office.

It took nearly an hour for Buckskin to get Trumble to write out his confession on the Chinese killings. He kept saying that there were four more in on it. Buckskin said all they wanted was what he had done at the death scene.

Sheriff Van Dyke sat by watching with a grin. When the paper was done and signed, the sheriff pushed Trumble into a jail cell, then said he was going to talk to the district attorney.

"Why didn't you just kill him in the alley?" the sheriff asked. "Would have been a lot less bother for everyone."

"Figured I owed you one, Sheriff. Then too, this way the town gets to know that the Five Angels of death are no more, except for the last one. I can't make any guarantees about the final one. He's the organizer and promoter of the whole thing."

Buckskin paused. "Don't mean to talk ill of the dead, but did you know that your deputy Zebadiah Clay was one of the Angels of Death?"

Sheriff Van Dyke lifted his brows. "Didn't know until now. Never quite bought some of the stories he told me, though. Especially that last one about him hunting a wanted man up north there in that abandoned ranch. I'd have known about that one." The sheriff shrugged. "At least he got his justice. Now we'll see about this one."

The sheriff thought a minute and looked back at Buckskin. "You said something about another one, the fifth Angel of Death. You know who he is?"

"Can't say, Sheriff. I brought you one of them. Can't promise anything about the last one."

"So you do know. Be damned glad if you told me."

"Can't. I best be going now. Have some more things to get done today." He walked out of the sheriff's office and hoped that no one followed him. No, the sheriff didn't have that many men, and probably no one who could do a good job of tailing someone.

At the boardwalk, he heard the whistle of a sternwheeler coming in to dock. He wished he could grab Sherry or Dawn or whatever she wanted to call herself and race down and get on the sternwheeler and take her back to Denver.

He'd just as soon let Yankton take care of the rest of its problems by itself. He sighed. Not the way it would happen. He went back to his hotel room and washed up, shaved closely and put on a clean shirt.

He'd have a civilized supper, then work out his strategy against Gideon Ingraham, the last and leader of the Five Angels of Death. How, when and where. That was all he needed.

Supper turned out to be beef stew, the country kind with six kinds of vegetables, big chunks of well-cooked beef and enough brown stew gravy to soak up all the potatoes he could mash from the steaming pot. It was fine eating. He used up two thick slices of white bread and a second cup of coffee before he pushed back.

Outside he stretched, belched and then became aware that someone was motioning to him. It was a woman with a sunbonnet that covered her face. He pointed to his chest and she nodded.

He walked over to her at the side of the cafe on the boardwalk and he saw she was Sherry Crawford. He smiled for the first time in hours.

"Miss Crawford, I believe," he said.

She took his arm and they moved up the street. "Not so loud, I'm not supposed to be here, remember? Now to the point. This afternoon, did I . . . I mean, did I indicate that I would come . . . come to a hotel room with you?"

"That's what I understood."

"Oh. I guess I'm not losing my mind after all. This must be one of the most foolish thing I've ever done, or that I'm about to do, or that I said I would do. I mean, I know absolutely nothing about you."

"That's true. I might be a white slaver for all you know. A hotel room, some laudanum, and I'd have you on the next boat south."

"No, no, I'm not worried about that. It's Nate.

He's been growling about you for two days. Telling me how you've ruined his game here in town and that it might be a year before the locals would play poker with him again."

"Easy to fix. Tell him to promise everyone that he'll play but that he won't deal. Hard to cheat if you don't get to deal."

She smiled. "I'll remember to tell him that. I just don't want to put you in any more danger. If he ever found out I even talked to you, let alone went to your hotel room . . . Oh, goodness, he might kill us both."

"I thought you said he'd back away from a fight."

"A fight with you, yes. But a sneak attack or a bushwhacking would be different."

They came to a closed store. It wasn't dark yet but the shadows were deepening after the sun went down. They went into a small alcove that led to the store's front door.

"I'd like a sample in advance. You may kiss me if you wish, Mr. Morgan."

He bent and kissed her half open lips and held the kiss longer than he had intended. Her hands gripped the back of his neck forcing his mouth against hers.

When he came away she nestled close against him. She frowned and looked up. "I'm not sure. Let's try that again."

This time her lips were open and so were his and their tongues dueled for a moment, then she let him plunge deeply into her open mouth. As she did she pressed her breasts hard against his chest.

As the kiss ended, she leaned back and his hand

settled over one of her breasts and he massaged it gently through the cloth. She sucked in a long breath and then nodded.

"Oh, yes, Mr. Morgan. I think that you and I will get along just fine tomorrow night."

"I'm hoping that you'll be staying for the whole night," he said.

"Can't. I'll have to be back in my bed by six a.m. That's when I usually let the swamper out the back door."

His hand moved to her other breast, and she sighed softly.

"I think I can have you safely to your alley door in time for that." He took his hand away and kissed her forehead. Even in the faint light he could see color creeping up her neck. She whirled away from him.

"Good. I better get back now before someone misses me. I can get to the Criterion from here with no problem."

He walked a dozen feet behind her as she crossed the dirt street and down half a block to the saloon. No one spoke to her or touched her. He felt better when she slipped into the Criterion.

Now all he had to do was convince her that he knew who she was and that it was time to return home to her husband, even if it was in name only, to preserve his standing in the community, and to let her spend hundreds of thousands of his dollars on good works, to start her dance school and take worldwide trips with a companion. He hoped it would work. It had to work.

Chapter Twenty

Buckskin spent a restless night. He dreamed. He awoke in a sweat when he saw that he was trapped by ten men in a box canyon with no way out and no more ammunition. He snorted when he woke up, threw off one of the covers and went back to sleep.

The morning came cloudy and cold with the threat of a thunderstorm. After breakfast, he wandered into the Ingraham General Store.

Ingraham himself came forward, then slowed when he saw who his customer was. His lips moved into a tight line and his eyes went hard.

"Those pocket knives, did you ever find them?" Buckskin asked.

Ingraham didn't say a word, just motioned to the

side and pointed to a selection of pen knives laid out on a white cloth.

Buckskin grinned and looked them over, picked out a two-bladed one that had a black bone handle. The blades folded, one coming out each end, and were about two inches long.

"I'll take this one," Buckskin said. Ingraham still hadn't uttered a word. He took the dollar bill and gave Buckskin twenty cents change.

"You're not talkative at all this morning," Buckskin said, pocketing the two dimes and the jackknife. "I guess you must have heard that Stacey Trumble was arrested for the murder of that Chinese family a week or so ago. I hear he's talking his head off down at the county jail."

Ingraham nodded, his lips tight, his hands at his sides and quivering.

"I figured you might want to hire a good lawyer for Stacey since you two were such good friends."

"Hardly knew the man," Ingraham said, his tone cold.

"Seems strange, Ingraham, you not knowing a man you rode with as one of the Five Angels of Death. Only two of you left now."

Ingraham surged toward Buckskin, but stopped three feet away. He backed off.

"If I had a gun, Morgan, I'd challenge you to a shootout right now."

"But you don't so you'll hire somebody else to gun me down from ambush preferably from the back, right? It hasn't worked the other times. Now, you're the only Angel of Death left. How does it feel to be naked and unarmed?"

Ingraham's face went white, he spun around and walked away. "I don't have to listen to talk like this."

Buckskin fired a shot into the ceiling and Ingraham stopped in mid stride.

"I'm afraid you do have to listen, unless you want to go down to the courthouse right now and confess to about a dozen murders, various assaults and beatings, and forcing citizens out of town by threat of death or bodily harm."

Ingraham turned slowly, shaking his head. "Told them you were a lawman at the very first. You had to be with no other reason for being in town. I knew you weren't scouting property for your pa in Omaha. Damn, I should have killed you that first day."

"Now, that is a shame. Right now I want you to go to the front door, hang up your closed sign and then come with me into the alley. You and I have a lot of talking to do."

"You'll kill me out there. I wouldn't have a chance."

"More chance than the Chinaman had or any of your hanging victims. Get a move on."

A six-gun blasted from somewhere back and above, and Buckskin felt the slug rip into his left arm and stagger him backward.

"Drop your gun and don't move," a voice called from above. "I've got a ten-gauge shotgun and it's loaded with double aught buck so it'll blow you in half. It's up here, see the muzzles?"

Buckskin followed a haze of blue smoke and found the twin black holes twenty feet from him and pushing out of an overhead storage area.

Slowly Buckskin let his Colt drop to the floor, then held up his hands.

"Good man, James. I told you we might have an armed visitor today trying to rob us. You did just fine. I'll get his six-gun, then you come on down and bring me the shotgun. I'm gonna enjoy this. Yes, the alley is a good idea, deadman Buckskin Morgan."

Ingraham moved up cautiously, pulled the Colt away from Buckskin with his foot, then picked it up and trained it on his enemy.

"Yes, James, come down now. I have the situation in hand. Thanks for being so alert. Good shooting, you hit him in the arm. Too bad it wasn't in his heart."

He grinned and Buckskin saw the gleam of killing in the man's eyes. Somewhere this man let murder take over his whole being.

"Just when did your vigilantism turn from honestly doing good for the community to doing whatever you wanted to do?"

"Never has. What I want is good for Yankton. Always has been, always will be."

A strapping youth of about twenty hurried up to the scene, a big Greener in his hands.

"Son, you know what this man here is?" Buckskin said. "He's the head honcho of the Five Angels of Death. He's killed fifteen to twenty men, women and children in this town."

"Gawan. He ain't neither. I worked for Mr. Ingraham for two years. He'd never do nothing like that."

"What do you think he's going to do to me?"

"Razz you a little. Maybe pound you around

some while I hold the shotgun on you."

"Wrong, James. He has murder in his eyes. Look at him good. He can't wait to gun me down with that double aught buck."

"Shut up, Morgan. You've done enough talking in this town. Let's go out to the alley right now. James, you put up the closed sign, then watch the store. I'll be back soon."

"You gonna mash him up some, huh? Make him think twicet before he comes back to our town. Yes, sir. I can carry him to the dock if you want me to so I can flang him on board the next boat."

"Won't be needed, James, thanks. Just get the door."

"James, he wants to kill me, can't you see that? He won't let you see because then you could testify against him in a trial. He's the killer in town, James."

It was almost enough to cause Ingraham to lose control and make a mistake, but not quite. He lunged at Buckskin with the shotgun, but stopped himself just in time.

"Outside, you damned troublemaker. Now!"

Ingraham waved James toward the front door and then motioned Buckskin toward the back one.

"I'm gonna have me a time with you, Morgan. Oh, lordy, but I am. You'll rue the day you ever came up the Missouri. Get out the damn back door and into the alley."

Buckskin walked ahead slowly, looking for any way out, anything that might help him. He saw nothing. He knew now that the .32 caliber six-gun in his right ankle holster was his last resort.

Somehow he had to get to it. Stumble or fall down, somehow he had to get his hands down to his right ankle.

"That's the way, deadman. Just keep walking straight ahead. You can't miss the back door. But then you've been here before, haven't you? You trashed my place and burned down the livery and destroyed those saddles over at Stacey's place. I've got a lot to settle up with you, you bastard."

"What about the fifteen people you murdered? Who is to settle for them?"

"Not murdered. Executed on orders of the Five. Legally, normal procedure in a citizen-run community."

"Murdered, you stinking bastard, Ingraham. You had no authority. You were never elected to any office. You were a terrorist, a damn outlaw, a baby-killing vigilante." He put so much emphasis on the last word that Ingraham looked up at him.

That was the soft break that Buckskin needed. He stumbled, hit the floor of the back room at the store, fumbled a minute getting up, and pulled the .32 revolver from leather and fired a quick shot from his back.

The round burned into Ingraham's right upper arm, ripping the shotgun from his hands. He dropped to the floor scrambling for it. James came through the back door with a handgun and fired at Buckskin, who scrambled up, sent one wild shot at James to back him off, then darted the last ten feet to the back door and lunged through it just as another round from the six-gun whistled past his head and struck the wooden door.

Outside he turned up the alley and ran. He had only the little .32 with a range of fifteen feet if he was lucky. They had all the weapons they wanted from the store. He ran again, sprinting hard for the end of the alley, hardly noticing the burning, raw fire in his left arm. Yes, he'd been shot. He raced on.

A rifle bullet ricocheted off a brick building to his left almost at the end of the alley and missed him. Then Buckskin was around the brick wall and charging toward his hotel a block away. There he had another Colt and the rifle. He would need them.

James was the fastest runner. He also had the rifle and took two more shots at Buckskin but missed. Inside the hotel, Buckskin hurriedly wrapped a bandage around his left arm, took his reserve six-gun and loaded in six rounds, then filled the magazine for the rifle and took a pocketful of loose shells. He was going to need them.

He eased open the door and looked out. They would know he was on the second floor from the registration but would get the wrong room number. He waited for them. They came up the far stairs and went to room 22. James kicked in the door and both rushed into the room.

Buckskin darted out of room 20 next to the stairs and charged down the steps. They heard him. Only one shot came at him as he dropped to the first floor and rushed out the back door into the side street.

He ran half a block and waited for the pair to come out the door. They didn't. Had they given up? He turned the other way and saw James slide around the other end of the hotel and lift the rifle.

Buckskin pulled up his long gun and fired by instinct and long practice. The round killed James before he smashed backwards into the dust of Main Street.

Now Buckskin was the hunter not the hunted. He raced to the corner and looked past it at Main. A dozen people were between him and the hotel, but he spotted Ingraham among them, walking quickly toward his store. Where else would he go? He didn't have the shotgun.

Buckskin ran after him, holding the rifle in front of him the way a soldier does as he charges with both hands on the weapon, bulling forward in a rush.

He got there just as Ingraham unlocked the door with a key and stepped inside.

Buckskin wondered if the man had locked it after him. It didn't matter. Two good kicks and the door would spring open. But that could bring a belly full of double aught buck rounds.

He ran to the edge of the store and looked through the window. He saw Ingraham putting on a gunbelt with six-shooter. Then he hefted a shotgun and took it with him as he headed for the back door. Where was he going? Two doors down there was a hole in the line of stores along Main Street. Buckskin ran to the opening and down alongside the building to the end of it and looked around in the alley.

By that time, Ingraham had brought a horse from a stable in back of the store and mounted. He turned toward Buckskin, then turned and rode down the alley the other way.

Where would he be going? Buckskin ran back to Main Street, saw a man riding in on a sturdy-looking mount and pulled a twenty-dollar bill from his pocket. He ran to the rider.

"Rent your horse for the day for twenty dollars cash money?" Buckskin asked. The young man grinned.

"Hell, yes. She ain't worth much more than that." He stepped off the horse and Buckskin mounted, rode through the alley and pounded forward. He saw the hoofprints at the far section of the alley. They turned on the next street away from Main, heading out of town.

Buckskin turned his mount, and far ahead where the street petered out into the countryside, he saw the rider. He was on the same sorrel-colored horse. Buckskin kicked his mount into a trot and began closing ground on the rider he hoped was Gideon Ingraham.

After ten minutes, the rider ahead curved to the right going around the town and heading down-river. Buckskin had been galloping his mount every quarter mile, then letting her walk for a quarter. He'd cut the distance between them in half. He figured he was only 300 yards behind now.

That was when the rider ahead turned and looked back. As he did, Buckskin tried to see if he was the merchant, but he couldn't. He had to be, otherwise why was he running? He got his answer a moment later when a rifle round whistled past several feet over his head.

He had his fish on the line.

Buckskin closed the gap again, then fired a rifle

round at the bouncing target ahead. Buckskin knew that shooting a rifle off a running horse was about as effective as throwing the long gun that far, but it had a good psychological effect. Ingraham hunkered down over the neck of the horse and rode faster.

He hit the river road and turned downstream. Where was he going? Was he trying to lead Buckskin into a trap? No, he hadn't had any time to set one up.

The pace slowed. No longer could Buckskin gallop his mount. She was getting tired. The nag in front of him had slowed as well and now both horses paced along at a walk, heads down, both probably breathing hard.

Buckskin swore loudly. He could walk faster than this, or run. Of course he couldn't go far that way. It could be a long chase.

They had most of the day left. The clouds increased now in thickness and the smell of rain was in the air.

They were well away from any buildings associated with Yankton. A mile back they had passed a house and barn and a try at some farming in a low place along the river. Irrigation would be easy there if the man tried.

Now there were no buildings, just a wind that whipped raw and cold off the Missouri. Buckskin looked to the west, and far across the water he could see angry clouds and patches that looked like shafts of rain coming down. Thunderstorms for sure. He urged his mount along faster but she only turned her head and looked at him in disdain.

They topped a small rise, and three or four miles ahead Buckskin could see some buildings. He couldn't tell much about them. One was larger than the rest so it could be a barn. A house and some outbuildings. Could be a small cattle operation or another farmer making a stab at it.

The road swung closer to the river here, and a rider came from some brush where Buckskin had earlier seen some smoke spiraling up. A bum maybe or some drifters. The man on the horse rode hard, and it wasn't until he was fifty yards away that Buckskin saw him lift a rifle.

Buckskin's rifle lay across his saddle and he brought it up and fired twice at the horse. He hit it with one round and the animal went down in a spray of dust and rolled over the rider. The man screamed in pain and didn't get up.

Buckskin watched him as he rode past at a walk and kept the rifle at the ready. No one else came from the smoking fire to help the injured man.

Ahead he had lost the fugitive. He searched the roadway on both sides, but could see no man and horse.

The farm buildings were now closer, and the only explanation was that Ingraham had ridden in there. Buckskin kicked the mount in the flanks and she surged into a gentle trot. He felt the first drops of rain about the same time a rifle slug drilled through the leaden sky around him. He leaned down on the side of the horse away from the buildings and rode for a patch of brush and trees 100 yards from the farmhouse.

So his quarry had come to roost. Why the farmhouse? Because of the rain? Could be. By the time Buckskin made it to the brush he was soaked through. Lightning flashed and a bolt hit a tree between Buckskin and the house. He could smell the sulfur from the strike. Thunder rolled in a continuous roar. He kicked off the mount and tied her to a tree, then worked close to the edge of the brush.

Smoke came out of the chimney. It was too soon for Ingraham to have made a fire, so someone must already have been inside. Were they hostages or confederates of Ingraham?

His answer came quickly as three rifles came through partly open windows and sent a dozen rounds into the woods where the men inside must have seen him ride in. Confederates.

How could he attack the house? Did he need to? Yes. He had three rifles against him. They were in the dry with heat and food. He was in the wet with neither. The rain came down now like it had been scooped out of the Missouri and flung in his face with a bucket.

Visibility for all of them was poor. Buckskin left his horse and moved through the brush, getting as close as he could to the house. The creek wandered a bit behind the barn but was still fifty yards away. Would they have someone in the barn? When he got behind the barn he would screen out the house. Worth a try.

Minutes later he dripped water into the dust of the barn's wooden floor. The house was only thirty yards away. A man burst out of the rear screen door of the house and raced for the outhouse. Buckskin grinned.

He would give away his position but also cut the odds by a third. Worth it. He found a convenient firing hole in the siding on the barn that faced the house, sighted in on the outhouse door and waited.

Five minutes later a man came surging out of the privy and charged toward the house. Buckskin tracked him, led him an inch and fired. The bullet and the runner met a few yards from the back door. He took the slug in the side and it slanted upwards, cutting into his heart and dropping him dead in the mud of the farmyard.

Buckskin moved from his spot by the wall and crouched low behind some two-by-four mangers as eight rifle rounds thundered into the barn. Then silence.

Buckskin moved back to the same firing hole and put three rounds through the kitchen window. Then he rolled behind some grain sacks and waited. There were no return shots. Maybe they were getting low on rounds.

He refilled the magazine on his rifle and looked at the house again. This ranch could be a property owned by Ingraham. That was why he got such instant cooperation from the men there.

Buckskin studied the layout again. From the other end of the barn, he could get to the machine shed. From there it was no more than thirty feet to the side of the house. Oil, kerosene? Both good ideas.

He went out the back door of the barn, through the slashing rain to the machinery shed, and raced around to the open front, exposing himself to fire. None came from the broken-out kitchen window.

He ran into the protection of the shed.

He found what he wanted almost at once. Two five-gallon cans. One labeled "kerosene," the other "gasoline." He wasn't sure why a farm like this would need gasoline, but sloshed the can and found it almost full. The gasoline-bomb idea that had been used against him now seemed the answer. He found some old beer bottles and some larger glass jars, but no tops.

He chose the beer bottles and filled three with gasoline from the can. Then he looked for wicks and spied some rags in a corner. He tore them up into strips, then rolled one end of a strip and pushed it into the bottle until it was tight. That left a six-inch strip of gasoline-soaked cloth as a wick.

Now if only the bottles would break on impact. He got as close as he could, lit the wick, which blazed up from the gasoline, then stepped out from the shed and threw the first bottle.

As it flew through the air he jumped back behind the protection of the building. He looked around in time to see the bottle hit the side of the house. It did not shatter.

He tried again with a second bottle. This one must have been made of thinner glass and it broke and the gasoline flames poured in through the kitchen window. The third flaming bottle also fractured against the wall of the kitchen, and the burning gasoline clung to the boards and burned brightly.

The rain stopped. One man came screaming out of the house. His pants were on fire. He rolled in the wet dirt and flailed at his burning pants until they were out.

"Stay right where you are," Buckskin barked and put a six-gun round into the dirt a foot from his head.

"Where's Ingraham?" Buckskin shouted.

"Right behind you, dead man," someone said.

"Buckskin spun and fired three times by instinct at the sound of the voice. Then he saw Ingraham slam against the wall, the shotgun in his hands lift, and both barrels fire through the roof of the machine shed.

Gideon Ingraham slumped against the wall, then slid lower, knocking down a scythe and three rakes as he went. His disbelieving eyes turned toward Buckskin. Red froth came out of his mouth as he spoke, but Buckskin could make out the words.

"You win," Ingraham said. Then he fell face forward into the dirt of the machine shed, dead before his blood could make a stain.

Chapter Twenty One

Buckskin stared at the body of Gideon Ingraham, the founder and leader of the Yankton vigilante five and shook his head. Power certainly did corrupt. He had the power and he misused it.

A sound from the farmyard caught Buckskin's attention. He went to the front of the machine shed and looked out.

The third man from the house sat on the ground keening in pain from his burned legs. Buckskin wanted to leave the man there to die, but he knew he couldn't.

Buckskin walked over and squatted beside the man. It was clear that with the seriously burned legs he could not fork a horse.

"Why did you shoot at me?" Buckskin asked.

"Ingraham owns the ranch. He said shoot so we

shot. Damn but this hurts. I never been burned before. Hope to God it rains again."

An hour later Buckskin had the man moved to the doctor's office in Yankton. He eased the man out of the buckboard and helped him walk into the office. Buckskin left him there.

Then he went to the courthouse, where he told about the farmyard shooting and Sheriff Van Dyke wrote it down. When Buckskin was done, the sheriff pushed the paper over for Buckskin to sign.

"We've been getting a blow-by-gunshot description of six of the killings the Angels committed," Van Dyke said. "Trumble is talking his head off in there. He implicated Ingraham right from the start. I'm damned surprised. I never figured he would be involved in this. Now we can go ahead and clean up a lot of things on our records." He looked at Buckskin and wiped a hand over his face.

"I know I should be thanking you for breaking up the Five Angels of Death, but it's hard. That was my job and I couldn't do it. I don't know what I'll tell the voters next month."

"Tell them what happened," Buckskin said. "Show them that you can keep the county under control now and there never will be another vigilante group here in Yankton. That should do it."

The sheriff shifted in his chair. "What about the burned one over at the doctor's office?"

"All we could have against him is assault, maybe attempted murder, but I can't prove that he fired at me. I won't press any charges if you don't. He's hurt bad enough to have learned a damned fine lesson."

"Suits me." The sheriff hesitated again, stood and

went to the window and back to his chair, then strode over and closed the door to his office and leaned against it.

"About the other thing. You said three days. It's been one. This wrap up your business in town?"

Buckskin grinned. "Almost. I still have to talk to a lady."

"We don't want no woman killings here."

"Not a chance, Sheriff. This lady is somebody's wife in Denver and I'm supposed to talk her into coming home."

"No gunplay?"

"I hope not. I'll try to be discreet and quick and get away on a downstream sternwheeler just as fast as I can."

Sheriff Van Dyke shook Buckskin's hand. "I'd appreciate that."

Outside the office, Buckskin realized he was starved. He didn't care what time it was, he wanted some food. He found an eatery he'd used before and went in for a steak and all the trimmings. It was good.

Outside he stretched, settled his six-gun in leather and walked toward his hotel. He should send a message to Evans that he was making progress finding his wife. Just another day or so and it might be a reality.

He was half a block from his hotel when a young boy ran up to him and looked at him curiously.

"Hey, mister, are you named Morgan?"

Buckskin chuckled. The gunmen hired to call him out were getting younger and younger. This one wasn't more than ten.

" 'Pears to be that I am. Why?"

"Lady gave me something to give to you." He reached inside his shirt and took out an envelope and handed it to him. His last name was written on it in a feminine hand.

Morgan nodded. "Yep, that's me. Here." He fished into his pocket and flipped a dime to the boy.

"Gee wolly gosh! Thanks a lot, mister." He ran away in the direction of the general store and its penny candy display.

Buckskin eased against a store wall, rough one-by-tens that hadn't been painted yet, and opened the envelope. The note inside on lavender paper read:

Like to see you now, whenever the boy can find you. I'll be at the Missouri Cafe having lunch, coffee or afternoon tea whichever one it takes.

The note was signed with the initial "S" on the bottom.

Sherry Crawford. Maybe Nate Hill had caught his sternwheeler south already. Buckskin continued to his hotel, washed up, checked his shave, then put on a clean shirt and town pants and a brown leather vest and set his dark brown hat on just so.

Five minutes later he found Sherry at a back booth at the cafe. She had been working on a cup of coffee. She nodded and he sat down. She had on a big hat that covered most of her face.

"Glad to see you. Nate's gone. We should talk."

"Where?"

"You mentioned a room?"

He nodded and took her hand and helped her up. They went in the side door of his hotel, up the back steps and into room 20 that he had left so quickly once before.

She looked around and frowned.

"My bedroom would have been much better, but not nearly as safe." She stared at him, her fists on her hips. "I know who you are, Buckskin Lee Morgan. You're a detective from Denver."

"True."

"Good, you admitted it. That's all I want to know right now." She walked toward him swaying her hips, her breasts thrust out. "We started something last evening we never got to finish. I'd like to see how it goes, right now."

She kissed his lips hard and caught his hand and put it over her breast. When the kiss ended her hand went down to his crotch and found the start of his erection.

"Good, I was hoping that I might get you a little excited." She sat down on the bed and looked at the place beside her. Instead Buckskin knelt in front of her and spread her legs and moved up between them so he could reach her breasts. He kissed them through the fabric, then gently unbuttoned the dress top. As soon as it came open his hand went under her chemise and caught a bare breast.

She gasped.

"Mr. Morgan, I know you probably think I'm a dance hall girl, or at lest a loose woman. I assure you that I'm not. I have made love with only two men in my life, my husband and Nate. Is that so surprising?"

"A little," he said. He pushed her dress open, lifted her chemise and smiled at the perfection of her breasts.

"Breasts are the most beautiful part of a woman, do you know that? The great artists always paint a woman's breasts. Photographers go wild over getting the breasts just right in their nude portraits and art pictures."

He bent more and kissed one breast at the base. She gasped again and her hands came down tenderly on the back of his head and neck.

He kissed around her breast softly until he reached the peak. Then he licked her nipple and saw it burgeon with hot blood and spring erect and grow as it turned a deep red.

"Oh, yes," she whispered. He moved and did the same thing to other breast and tears seeped out of her eyes. "So beautiful, so tender. No man has ever done that for me before. I love it. You make me feel so special."

"You are special. No one is like you. No one ever will be." He rose up and sat beside her. She leaned in and he held her head against his shoulder. She turned slowly.

"Please kiss me softly, just as if I were a virgin."

He kissed her with his lips barely touching hers. Electricity sparked between their lips. She drew back startled, then leaned in again for another kiss, and she sighed and lay back on the bed.

He watched her. She opened her eyes and smiled. "Not to worry, I just want to savor this moment and remember it." I can guess why you're here and I'm afraid you're right in coming. But time for that later."

She sat up and her eyes sparkled. "I've only seen two men naked. I want to make it three. May I undress you?"

Buckskin smiled and kissed her forehead. "I'd be honored if you would."

Sherry took her time. Some of his clothes she jerked off quickly. She kissed each button down his shirt, working through the hair on his chest and giggling as it tickled her nose. When she came to his underwear she paused.

"The bulge, it looks so big. My first one was old and small and never worked quite right. Nate wasn't real big, but this . . ." She grinned. "I guess I should take a look." Gently she pulled down his shorts. When his erection sprung up to freedom she gasped and sat back.

"Oh, my!" She looked at him. "Oh, my goodness." Her eyes went wide and she reached out and touched his penis. "Oh, I just don't know if there's room, I mean if he'll fit . . ."

Buckskin chuckled. "No worry there. You'll see. Now it's my turn."

He pulled her dress off her shoulders and down to her waist.

"It goes off over the top," she said. She stood and pulled the dress off and he saw she had on no petticoats, only a pair of bloomers like many of the women were wearing now. She sat on the bed and lay down, moving over to make room for him.

"Let's leave them on for right now. You know, I'm

still a little shy. I need some more encouragement."

He hovered over her, kissed her lips gently, then kissed each of her breasts and began caressing them with both hands and a feather touch. She purred softly.

His hands moved down to her belly, worked down around her muff of blonde hair to her knees, and then began a slow journey upward, stroking the soft white inner thighs gently. He kept his lips on her breasts, kissing them, caressing them, licking her nipples until she moaned softly.

"Oh, my, but that is nice," she said. He could tell her breathing had increased. She moved her hips in a slow dance.

His hands worked higher and higher and she spread her legs for him. When he reached her muff, she moaned again and her hands came down and caught his.

"Wait a minute, darling, wait a minute." She sat up and stared into his eyes, then bent to his erection and crooned softly as she kissed the purple tip. It jumped in anticipation. She kissed it again, then licked up and down the length of it.

"Yes, yes, I love him. I want him." She looked at him again, then pushed her lips around the purple head and sucked him into her mouth. His erection jumped. She smiled and stroked easily in and out on his shaft.

"Easy, Sherry. Easy, I can't take too much of that." She came off him, gave his penis a final kiss and sat up. She looked at him and then put his hands back on her crotch hair. He explored, he wandered. She gasped when he came close to her wet nether lips. He pulled back.

"Please, touch me there," she said. He moved his fingers and barely made contact with her wet center. She lifted her hips toward his hand to increase the touch. He stroked them and worked around and around until he moved and found her hard little node. He twanged it and she yelped as if she had been struck.

"What was that?" she wailed.

"This?" He strummed her clit three times and her hips began to jolt and her face went pale. She fell backwards on the bed and her whole body trembled in a climax that shook her time and time again. She wailed and crooned and her hips beat a tattoo against his hand. Her whole body shook again as spasms slanted through four, then five times.

She finished and lay there for a moment but another series of spasms shook her and she cried out and clutched at him and pounded her hips toward him, half crying, half shrilling for joy.

This time when it passed she sighed and closed her eyes and rested. He sat beside her, his hands on her breasts not moving, just holding her.

Her eyes opened after two or three minutes of furiously breathing deep and long. Her pretty face clouded and she stared at him.

"What in the world did you do?"

"You don't know, do you?"

"That's why I asked you."

"It's this little hard place here." He touched it gently. "It's like the male penis and usually highly sensitive. Yours certainly is."

"Nobody ever told me about it."

"Glad that I could. Some men don't think it's important that a woman knows. I do. I gathered that it was enjoyable for you?"

"Oh, yes!" She sat up and kissed him. "I've never felt that way before. I've had climaxes now and then, but nothing like that. I mean it was terrific, totally amazing."

She put his hand back to her crotch. "Just the lips this time so I'll want you inside me. I already do, but make me want you even more."

He massaged her soft outer lips, rimmed her vagina with his finger and then plunged it in as far as it would go.

She gasped and nodded and lifted her spread knees.

"Right now, Morgan. I want you deep inside me right now."

He was surprised how tight she was, as if she hadn't been entered much. He worked gently and soon was all the way in and she crooned softly.

"Lift your legs up around my back and lock them together," he said. She frowned at him, but did. Then he drove in hard and felt it as he touched her clit. By then he was almost as ready as she was.

He pounded against her ten times and felt her about to explode again. Quickly he stroked and met her climax with his own and they sweated and roared and squealed and then fell on the bed exhausted and needing a rest.

Five minutes later, she unwound her arms from him and sat up.

"I told you I know who you are. It took me some time to remember and it wasn't until yesterday that

I heard your first name. You had been Mr. Morgan to me, but when Nate called you Buckskin, I remembered some cases in Denver where your name was prominent in the newspapers. That's when I put it all together. If you were that Buckskin Morgan, and from Denver, you had to be the detective.

"The only reason you could be here was to kidnap me and rush me back to my husband, who can't really get it up anymore and is delighted if he fondles me for a half hour and at last gets an erection that lasts for five minutes, but that still isn't hard enough to penetrate me."

She bent and kissed him as he lay on his back. "So you see I knew what I was doing when I came here with you, and I knew you might try to kidnap me, but I didn't think that you would. Not your style. Too much of a gentleman. You'd try to persuade me to go back first.

"Then, depending on how much money Harold promised you, you might try forcing me to go back. Now I know you never would force me to do anything I didn't want to."

"Why do you have to be so beautiful, so smart and so sexy at the same time?"

"Just to bedevil you. Is it working?"

"Working perfectly. And now you've seduced me."

"I seduced you?"

"Of course. You lured me to this room. You teased me with your beautiful breasts, then chewed on my erection. You seduced me."

She laughed and he enjoyed the sound.

"So what happens now?" she asked.

"Now I present to you a list of bribes that your impotent husband will offer you to come home and be his wife even if in name only so he can hold his head up again in polite society and show you off at his parties."

"Sounds good so far. What is he offering?"

"First, your own bank account with twenty-five thousand dollars in it for your incidental needs. You'll stay at his house, be his hostess when needed, but be free to develop your own ideas, plans and projects.

"I believe he said you wanted to open a school of dance. He will pay all expenses and help you with the business end of things so it has a chance of succeeding without losing too much money."

"Yes, this is sounding good."

"He is offering you and a chaperone a trip through Europe, England and the Greek islands at your convenience. He'll pay all expenses."

"Well, now, he wouldn't do that before. I'm impressed."

"He says he knows you're a young, vibrant, needful woman and he can't supply you with the needed sexual fulfillment you crave. He will not interfere with any liaisons you might set up with young men, if you keep them out of the public eye and out of his house."

"Well, now we are getting somewhere. As you can see, I do have needs. I never actually had intercourse with anyone else while I was married to him, but I did get naked a couple of times and mess around. Yes. It sounds reasonable of him."

"Your husband says he also will buy you three

horses and give you a stable to house them in and a groom and riding instructor so you can learn to ride."

Sherry laughed. "He is serious. I know he hates horses. One bit him once and he's hated them ever since."

"Oh, the last item is a completely new wardrobe that you don't have to pay for out of your cash in the bank."

"So what do you think I'll do?" she asked.

Buckskin threw up his arms in wonder. "Who knows? You're a woman, and women are highly prone to change their mind. I'd say right now it's a tossup."

He looked down and for the first time noticed the three small moles forming a triangle on her right breast.

"Now can I start calling you Dawn, your real name?"

"Yes, you can, and yes, I'm going back to Harold, and yes, I'll hold him to every condition he's laid down, and to every bribe he's offered me. I'm getting so I hate to play poker. It isn't any fun anymore now that I know I'm better than most men who play the game as professionals."

Buckskin curled one hand around her breast and lifted an eyebrow. "Would most men include me?"

She grinned. "I can't say. But we'll have time to find that out on our long trip back to Denver. I want you to be sure to stock up on a dozen decks of new cards and a big box of poker chips as well as a whole box of food to eat."

"Done."

"Now we have a small problem."

"Problem? What problem could we have? You said you'll go back and I'm here to help you get there. We have enough money to make the trip. What's the small problem?"

"The minor little difficulty is Nate Hill. He's sworn he's going to kill you. That's even before he knows that I'm going back to Denver. He knows about my husband. He might even come to Denver to get me. What do we do now?"

Chapter Twenty Two

Buckskin scowled at Dawn. "In your note you said Nate Hill had left to go downriver."

"That's what I thought, but I saw him later. He's still in town. I don't know why he didn't leave. He's going to be missing me shortly."

"So you stay here. I'll go out and take rooms in the other hotels and register under my own name. He'll be hunting me there. It should give us time to get on board a sternwheeler."

She sat up, making her breasts dance and jiggle. Buckskin grinned at the show despite the seriousness of the situation.

"That might not be so easy," she said. "He has lots of friends around town, and he pays them to work for him. If he thinks you have any idea of running, he'll have one or two armed men watching every passenger who boards the sternwheelers each time one docks."

"Let me go register at the hotels, then we'll see what to do. Just be sure you don't leave this room. Don't under any circumstances go anywhere near the Criterion Saloon. Anything you need we'll buy on the way back to Denver."

A tear slid down her cheek. "I hate to put you in so much danger. I know he'll try to kill you one way or another. Promise me you'll be careful."

She put her arms around him and held him tightly not wanting to let go.

He kissed the back of her neck and she straightened. "You're the one I'm worried about," he said. "Don't leave the room. When I go out, lock the door, then turn the key halfway back so it stays in the lock and nobody can push it out. Make sure it's me when I come back. I'll knock once, pause and then knock three times. Understand?"

She nodded. "Knock once, pause and then three times. Yes, got it." She trembled and he held her tighter. "He knows I don't like to go out shopping because the women all whisper about me. But the barkeep will tell him I went out. He'll be curious, then furious. Nate has a terribly short temper. The last thing I want is you and him in a gunfight."

"I'll watch out for him. While I'm out, I'll check the sternwheeler dock just to see if anybody is hanging around who doesn't seem to belong there." He kissed her gently, then eased her back. "You be good, stay here and don't let anyone inside."

He dressed quickly and looked out the window. It was still mid-afternoon. A busy day. He buckled on his gun leather, checked the Colt and went to the door.

She padded on bare feet to him and hugged him tightly, her bare body pressed hard against him.

"Lady, you do that once more and I'll never get out the door." She grinned and writhed her naked body against him. He eased her away and smiled. "What a perfectly beautiful little body you have, and breasts like a Venus. No wonder Mr. Evans wants you to come home." He waggled a finger at her. "Lock the door behind me and stay here safe."

He checked the hallway, slipped out the door and heard her lock it behind him. Then Buckskin hurried down the back stairs and into the street.

It took him twenty minutes to register at the three other hotels in town. He said his luggage would be coming up soon. Then he checked the dock.

No craft was tied there. He walked casually into the ticket office building at the end of the pier and asked the clerk when the next downstream boat would be coming in.

"In about an hour if she ain't late. The *Delta Princess* ain't exactly known for her promptness. Captain don't give a damn about schedules. Says he'd rather miss the snags and the sand bars and get her here in one piece than try to keep a schedule and wind up running aground somewhere."

"Good. I'll be waiting. You see anybody loitering around outside who usually isn't there?"

"Hard to tell," the clerk said. He was about forty, balding with spectacles. He took them off now and stared out the fly-specked windows. "One gent over there by the piling. I seen him before. Seems like he goes and comes and then goes again. Three stern pushers been through and he keeps hanging around."

"Thanks." Buckskin went out the door with a cheroot in his hand. The long, thin cigar was unlit. He looked around on the dock, then saw the man by the pilings and headed his way. The man looked up and a flash of alarm washed over his face. Then he controlled it.

"Hey, stranger," Buckskin said. "Would you by any chance have a stinker or one of them new sulfur matches? Got me a smoke here and no fire."

The man by the pilings shook his head in relief that showed on his face. "Nope. No matches. I don't smoke."

Buckskin shrugged and turned. "Thanks, I'll find me some fire here somewhere."

As he walked away, Buckskin could feel the man watching him. He was a boat watcher for sure. Only he was clearly not a strong man, and had no weapon showing. More the kind of a lookout who would report what he saw rather than try to solve the problem himself.

Buckskin strolled back to town, down Main to the Van Dalton Hotel and up to the second floor. When no one was in the hall, he rapped lightly on room 20. He waited. There was no response. He took a second key to the room from his pocket and opened the door.

Sherry Crawford, who he knew now to be Dawn Evans, wasn't there. He found the scribbled note leaning against the pillow on the bed, which had been straightened and fluffed up. He snatched the note.

Hey, Buckskin. There are a few things I must have before I leave town. I'll slip up the back way at the Criterion and no one will see me. My bet is that Nate is out hunting you. I'll be back I hope before you get back. Be careful!

It wasn't signed.

He dropped on the bed, his anger with her compounded by his fear for her safety. If Nate was in such a furious mood, she wasn't safe within half a mile of the man.

He stood and checked his six-gun. He had to go find her and find her right now or his whole two-weeks adventure here might be in vain and Dawn Evans might be dead.

The first place to look was the Criterion—the back door and upstairs, not the saloon proper. A dozen images flashed through his mind as he rushed down Main to the alley behind the saloon. He could see Dawn tied to a chair as bait for him to rescue. He could see Dawn leaning out the window and vicious, bloody hands pulling her back inside.

He could see Nate Hill with a sawed-off double-barreled shotgun in each hand walking down the alley where he had been waiting for Buckskin to come.

As he stepped into the alley, it was quiet. He saw only one drunk well beyond the Criterion's back door. The stairs to the second floor were unguarded, the door at the top enticingly open a few inches.

He checked every hiding spot as he moved down the alley but found no one lurking in an ambush. When he made it to the bottom of the steps he paused and looked around. Nobody.

He pulled his Colt and went up the steps two at a time but cautiously, watching the door at the top and the one at the alley level that led into the saloon. The vision of the shotguns still bothered him.

Halfway up, he paused again and looked around. Still nothing seemed unnatural.

He worked up the last steps and peered through the four-inch slot of the open door. He saw no one in the hall. He stepped in through the door and into the long hallway.

Again, all was quiet. He moved ahead quickly, aware that his boots sent a message down the hall well ahead of him. He could see part of the living room, then something moved ahead, and he flattened against the wall.

"Morgan. I figured it had to be you. Decided to wait, and knew that you'd come to me looking for her. Your trick ain't gonna work, Morgan. I got you right where I want you."

Buckskin didn't move. He leveled the Colt at the sound at the end of the hall, now only twenty feet away, and waited.

"Ain't talking, huh? Don't blame you none. Tough damn spot. Jake is at the other end of the hall by now and I'm up here. We got ourselves a damn shooting gallery." Nate Hill laughed, his voice going high.

Dawn screamed and Buckskin took an involuntary step forward.

"Hear that, big bad detective from Denver? Think you were going to take her away from me, did you? Bastard. Kill my poker game and now try to steal my woman. Oh, hell, yes, I know about her fat old man husband in Denver.

"Hell, Morgan you're a dead sonofabitch already. I'm just trying to decide how to do it. Slow. Hell, yes, it's got to be slow. Nothing fast for a bastard like you. Knees first I'd guess with a good old forty-four slug. Sounds about right. What do you think, Morgan?"

Buckskin moved a step forward silently. His mind spun out one plan after another and he rejected them as quickly as they came. Silence was best. Then he had to get to within sight of the saloon owner before he was seen. Take him by surprise without killing him, if possible.

Another step.

Nothing from the room now fourteen feet down the hall.

"Don't think you can surprise me, gunslick. I know all about your shooting. I've been fixing up things for you here for a half hour. I'm ready. Sure, Sherry is here, so don't shoot her by mistake. Fact is, she's sitting right in front of me. Now that I have her gag in tighter she won't spit it out. Come on, big bad gunman, I'm waiting for you."

Silence again. Buckskin could see a slice of the living room. Most of it was to his left and out of sight. That's where Nate Hill was waiting. He tried to remember the room. Were there any mirrors on the wall? Any way that he could see around the corner? He couldn't remember any.

He moved two more steps, keeping his back against the wall, his Colt aimed across his body at the opening. He tried to think what kind of cover was at the end of the living room. Any massive furniture that would stop a slug? He could remember nothing that heavy.

Another step. He was ten feet from the opening. He could see more of the living room now, but no place to hide behind. He was naked.

He pulled two .45 rounds from his gun belt and held them in his left hand as he moved ahead. Three feet to the end of the hallway. More living room showed, a lamp, a couch, a small table, the phonograph sitting on another table with two wax cylinders nearby.

The shooter would be farther to the left, with Dawn. He would have a weapon zeroed in on the edge of the wall where Buckskin would have to show. Buckskin had one small advantage. Nate Hill didn't know when his attacker would roar around that corner.

All he needed was a split second. A movement of Hill's hands to shift the sights of his weapon to the left away from the hallway entrance. That fraction of a second could be Buckskin's ticket to life and winning.

He paused and listened. Only some squeaks and mumbling, probably from a gagged Dawn. He tensed, then threw the .45 rounds with his left hand at the far wall of the living room. Before they hit he had bellied down on the floor and at the impact he pushed forward around the corner with his six-gun ready at floor level.

He saw it all in a fraction of a second. It was as if all was frozen in place.

Nate Hill was sitting in a chair with a shotgun trained on the doorway, then he swung it to the left where the shells had hit. Dawn sat in another chair, her hands and feet tied and a wide gag around her mouth. Her eyes blazed with fury as she struggled against the ropes.

Buckskin's gun hand lifted the Colt, which he had cocked as he slid forward, and fired. The hurried round tore into Hill's right shoulder and he dropped the shotgun. Buckskin ducked back behind the wall as the scatter gun fired on impact with the floor, ripping double-aught buck into the floor and wall and peppering the far wall. The sound was like a pair of steam engines smashing together in a railroad tunnel. Buckskin held one ear and eased up to look around the room.

Nate had been thrown back by the slug in his shoulder and he scrambled to his feet behind Dawn's chair, hesitated a minute, then using her as a shield, pushed her chair to the left toward the door.

Buckskin charged forward. Just before he caught up to Hill, the gambler pushed the chair at him and it began to tip over with Dawn in it. Buckskin caught the chair and it took him a few seconds to right it and get it settled. Hill fled out the door. Buckskin pulled off Dawn's gag, then with his knife quickly cut her bounds.

"Get out of here, fast. Go back to the hotel room.

You have the key?" She nodded.

Then he ran to the door where Hill had vanished and peered around the jamb. A hand gun cracked, and wood chipped off the door frame just above Buckskin's head. He pulled back.

A door slammed and Buckskin surged after the man. There must be another way down from here. He ran into the next room, an empty bedroom. The window to the alley was open and Buckskin ran to it. A rope had been tied to the roofline extending past the window. Emergency exit. Nate Hill had tried to go down the rope, but his right arm wouldn't work with the slug through the shoulder and he had fallen in a heap.

He got up and turned and glared at Buckskin, who by then was going down the rope hand over hand.

Somewhere Hill had dropped his six-gun and now he ran weaponless up the alley. Three doors down, he darted into a back door to a shop. Buckskin was not far behind him. He saw a name over the door. "Trumble Leather." Stacey's place of business.

Buckskin ran up to the door and hesitated, then jerked the door open but stayed to the side against the outside wall. Two shots sent hot lead zipping through the open door, and something crashed inside. Buckskin surged through the open door and came up against a pile of leather and hides. He lay there a moment listening.

No sounds.

He moved slowly forward through this storage shed. Hides, leather, tanning liquids. Then from out of the semidarkness of the unlighted room came a figure with a bucket. Before Buckskin could dodge, the figure threw the contents of the bucket on Buckskin and raced back the other way.

Buckskin had ducked his head and pulled his arms over his face. He could only think of the acid he had used on the saddles here in the leather store.

The fluid splashed over him and he felt it sting his hand and wrist, but it was no more than that. Not acid. He exploded forward, his six-gun ready. Nate Hill would be armed now. He'd have to be more careful.

At the door into the front of the store, Buckskin stopped. He reached out and rattled the door handle. Four shots blasted through the thin wood; then he heard boots thudding on the floor as someone ran.

Buckskin opened the door and light streamed into the back room. He could see the front door of the shop standing open and there was no one in the area. He ran to the front door and looked out.

For a fleeting moment he saw Nate Hill twenty yards away walking down the boardwalk. Then two men came up in back of him, another man joined them, and a few more came until Buckskin couldn't find Hill in the crowd. He ran up the boardwalk to the gathering of a dozen men who had surrounded Hill.

"Where did Nate Hill go?" Buckskin asked.

"Haven't seen him for a couple of days," one said.

"He sure ain't here," another chimed in. "That's a fact, Nate Hill sure as hell ain't here."

Hill had said he had a lot of friends around town.

Buckskin hurried back toward the saloon. Would Hill go back there? He had no way of knowing. It could be a bad choice.

He needed to find Dawn more than Hill. Did she go back to the hotel? He ran to the alley, down it, then back to Main and in the side door of the hotel. He paused just inside but saw no one following him.

She had to be there. They would hide, then he'd shoot his way onto the next sternwheeler if he had to. They had to get away fast before Nate Hill could organize a fighting team to stop them.

He went to the second floor and checked it. No one in the hall. He tried the knob on room 20; it was locked. He heard a movement inside and a moment later the door swung open.

Nate Hill stood there glaring at Buckskin, a six-gun pointed at Dawn Evans' head as he held her close in front of him as a shield.

"Now, Buckskin Morgan, we'll get to the bottom of this. Just who the hell are you and why do you think you can take my lady away from me?"

Chapter Twenty Three

Nate Hill held the revolver firmly against Dawn Evans' head.

"Inside, Morgan, easy like and toe the door shut gently. Keep your hands up and don't make any sudden moves. I finally figured it out. You're some hot detective from Denver who's come to take my lady back to that fat old husband of hers.

"I won't let you do it. Nice and easy now, lift that hogsleg out of leather and toss it on the bed. Slow and everyone lives longer."

Buckskin did as told. When the weapon hit the bed, Nate turned the gun on Morgan. "Now go over and stand in front of the window. Right now, fancy detective, or you die where you stand."

The detective saw no other choice. He moved slowly toward the window. His only salvation was his ankle holster. That's why he wore it, but he needed a good chance to get to it.

"Now stand there while I decide what to do," Hill said. "First I figured to shoot you dead. But that might get me in trouble with the sheriff. Then I wanted to pitch you onto the next downriver sternwheeler. But then you'd dive off and come back. I'm still working on it."

"Nate, I'm through with you," Dawn said. "I'm going back to my husband. It's all settled. I'll never stay another night with you. You might as well put away the gun and go play poker in your saloon."

Hill glared at her. "Not that easy, woman. Not that easy at all. I've invested some money in you. You still owe me on that bet, and besides, I like you in my bed. You're not going anywhere even if I have to chain you to your bed."

He shoved Dawn down on the bed, and she pushed her skirt out to cover Buckskin's Colt .45.

"He's the problem. This damn detective who butted his nose into my affairs. I can't allow that. The locals are wondering why I let him go on breathing. I've got to maintain my status here to have any kind of business or any big-stakes games at all.

"I thought of shooting your balls off. That would be great, punishment, justified. But I'm not that good a shot and I could kill you. Too quick. Maybe shoot up both knees would be best. Then you could go back to Denver in a goddamned wheelchair."

Buckskin had seen Dawn settle down over the Colt like a mother hen over her chicks. Two chances, maybe. He bet that Dawn had never fired any kind of a gun, let alone a .45. He nodded at her and she tried to smile back.

"What in hell to do? First I get somebody to lock up this pretty lady in my whiskey cellar, and then I deal with the great man here, Buckskin Morgan. Don't know exactly how, but come dark we can figure out something.

"Maybe the Angels of Death could strike again, even though I've heard all of them are either dead or in jail. Hell, maybe there were six of them. Yeah, I'm getting ideas. Hanging. What would be better? First the sexy little woman here." He stopped.

"Nope, first Morgan. Tie him up. No chance of him getting frisky then. Morgan, take off the belt that holds up your pants. Do it now."

Buckskin looked at Dawn and shrugged.

"I guess I have to do what he says." His hands came down slowly and he stripped the pants belt out and tossed it to Hill. It landed three feet from him.

Hill snorted and picked it up, but kept watching Buckskin.

"Bad try, Morgan. Amateur stuff. I thought you were a real professional. Now you turn around and look out the window and put your hands behind your back."

Buckskin did so. Hill pushed the revolver in the waist of his pants and tied the belt around Buckskin's wrists to wrap them tightly together.

As Hill began the operation, Dawn slid noiselessly off the bed, caught the big gun by the barrel with both hands, and took stockinged-feet steps toward Hill, who now had his back to her.

"Damn thing's got to be tight to work," Hill said, fumbling with the leather belt.

Dawn lifted the heavy weapon over her head and slammed the butt down hard on Hill's head. The gambler gave a grunt of pain and staggered to one side.

Buckskin spun around and kicked Hill hard in the crotch. Hill doubled up and fell to the floor, bleating in pain and fury.

Buckskin pulled his belt off his wrists and jerked Hill's gun away from his belt, then took his own .45 from Dawn and bent and kissed her cheek.

"Nicely done, young lady," Buckskin said.

"Now what do we do?" Dawn asked.

"Hand me that pillow." She did so, and Buckskin stripped the pillowcase off and cut it with his knife and tore it into inch-wide strips three feet long. He used several to tie Hill's ankles together. Then he forced Hill's arms behind his back and tied his wrists together.

Hill screamed in pain and anger. "Kill me. You might as well kill me right now," he blubbered.

Buckskin took a section of the pillowcase and wrapped it tightly around Hill's mouth to gag him without causing him any danger.

Quickly Buckskin threw his clothes and other belongings in his shotgunned carpetbag. It held together, but he needed a new one.

"We're leaving?" Dawn asked.

"Yes, but we don't have any time to get your things. Sorry, too dangerous going back there. It almost got me killed the last time you tried it. Any objections?"

She shook her head.

They went out the side door of the hotel and the long way around to the boat dock. It was just past six. Two hours of daylight left. More boats should be coming down.

Inside the small ticket office, they found out that a sternwheeler should be coming past in about half an hour. Buckskin bought two tickets and said they'd wait inside.

One hard bench against the wall was the best the ticket office offered. They sat down and waited.

"Are we safe yet?" Dawn asked, her eyes looking big and vulnerable now that she was out of her element.

"No. We won't be safe until we get you into your husband's front door in Denver. I mean it. Hill has little to lose now. He'll come after us. Might even pay some pilot to take some chances and power his boat downstream faster to catch us. That is, if he doesn't get on this boat. I'll be watching every second before we pull out."

"But he's tied up and gagged in your room. He can't get away by himself. When would anyone find him?"

"That's what we don't know, can't count on, and why I'm going to be on the alert with a cocked six-gun most of the time."

"Are you that worried about me?"

"Partly. Also worried about me. I'd just as soon not wind up dead on this assignment."

"You've taken a lot of chances."

"That's what I get paid to do. One of these days the odds will catch up with me and I'll be a hair too slow, or not shoot straight enough or not be in the right place at the precise second I'm supposed to be, and I'll be a cipher, not even a small footnote in the history books."

"You're a philosopher."

"A cautious man who wants to go on living for a hundred years yet, and damning the odds."

Two men came in to buy tickets and Buckskin stood and watched them. The men never looked at him and Dawn, which was strange behavior from Buckskin's point of view. The men left the office and waited outside.

"Know those two?" Buckskin asked the ticket seller.

"Yep. Been around town for several years. Do odd jobs mostly. Not the brightest pair."

"They ever work for Nate Hill?"

"Might. They work for lots of folks."

Buckskin went back to the bench and stared at the men out the window. Should he take them here or wait until they got on board? A toss-up. Then it was too late as he heard a steamship whistle and a sternwheeler coasted toward the dock from upstream on the mighty Missouri.

Buckskin hurried Dawn on board as soon as the passengers getting off cleared the gangplank. They went to their assigned cabin on the upper deck. Then he stepped outside, locked the door, and leaned against the rail in front of the cabin and watched the others boarding. The two men he'd seen inside came up the plank just before it was pulled in.

He'd seen six people board—two man-woman

couples and the two men. Buckskin stood there wondering which would give him the best defense, standing outside the cabin where he could see anyone approach, or inside where he had protection from being picked off with a rifle.

He still had the repeating rifle he had bought in Yankton and enough ammunition. Did he advertise his alertness by carrying the weapon? He decided against it. Just where to position himself was still a question.

Nate Hill ground his hands against the bonds again and wanted to swear but couldn't. His mouth was tied shut by the gag. Where in hell was Riker? He had told him to get to room 20 here in the hotel as quickly as he could. It had been over an hour. Where were Dawn and Morgan? How could he find out? He worked his mouth until he could wet the cloth and suck some of it into his mouth and tear it with his teeth. Good.

His hands were a lost cause, tied too tightly. Morgan knew his business.

Fifteen minutes later he had the gag chewed in two and bellowed with all his might. His crotch still hurt like fire and he would have thrown up if he could. He wasn't sure how damaged his balls were, but they hurt like a red-hot poker jammed into him every few minutes.

He bellowed again, then listened. When he heard footsteps in the hall, he screamed as loud as he could. The footsteps stopped

"Help me! Help me!" he screamed again, and saw

the door jiggle. Then it came open as if someone had kicked it.

It was Riker.

He bent and cut the bindings and helped Hill stand. A moment later Hill fell on the bed grimacing in pain.

"Sorry, boss. I got the wrong hotel. Took me some time to figure out which one."

"Get down to the dock and see if the tall man and Dawn got on board any of the sternwheelers that came in during the last hour and a half. Run! Do it now. I'll be there as soon as I can."

"You don't look too good, boss."

"Shut up, Riker, and get to the dock."

Riker hurried out of the room.

Nate Hill lay back on the bed. Another half hour and he'd be able to walk again. Damn but that hurt. He'd never been kicked in the crotch before. He never wanted to be kicked there again.

He sat up gingerly. Buckskin Morgan. The man was dead, he just didn't know it yet. He'd get him if he had to track him all the way to Omaha or Denver. He had to kill the man.

Buckskin Morgan found the spot he wanted on the *Missouri Queen*. He sat on a pile of heavy rope just in front of the starboard smoke stack facing back along the cabins. His back was protected. No one could see him coming from the bow, and he had an excellent field of fire in front of the cabin where Dawn rested behind the locked door.

He sat there with the rifle at his feet pointing barrel forward, ready to be picked up and fired in a half second. For the moment he felt safe, but he knew he couldn't hold this position all the way to Omaha.

He hadn't seen the two men since they had boarded. They could have bought steerage passage below and rested on or around the freight on the main deck. He was certain they didn't have one or two cabins on his side of the ship. He waited.

About an hour downstream, they pulled into the landing at Caruthers' Bend and took on wood to burn in the firebox that stoked the boilers to make the steam.

He left the rifle under some coils of rope and went to the side of the ship to watch. The two men who had bought tickets in Yankton got off. Good. He watched until the gangplank came up, but no one came on board. The sun was down. The ship would keep moving at night, but probably at a slower pace. This far down on the river it was deep enough and wide enough that most boats traveled it at night, if the pilot knew that stretch of the river. Some pilots specialized in parts of the river, some took their boats all the way down to St. Louis.

Buckskin felt relieved. Maybe Nate Hill hadn't worked himself free in time to get a man on board this ship. If so they had an advantage. There were other ways to get to Omaha, but he didn't think any would be faster.

Nate himself could be on the next sternwheeler, two or three hours behind them. There was a chance that that boat could be faster or didn't have to make as many stops and could catch the *Missouri Queen* at one of the ports down the way. If so, it would be a simple task for Hill to wait for the right ship, come aboard and try to do his foul deed then.

Speculation. Pure guesswork. But Buckskin had to figure out the worst possible situations so he could be ready for them.

He took one more look at the shoreline slipping away as the big ship moved into the current and the dusk. He took the rifle and went to the cabin where Dawn was and knocked on the door.

He identified himself and she let him in. He closed the door quickly and locked it. He wished it had a bolt of some kind. Locks could be opened.

"We're away safely so far," he said.

Dawn smiled and unbuttoned the white blouse she wore. "About time. It's been a hard day and I need some tender loving care."

"I could hold you until you go to sleep."

She made a face at him. "You do and I'll tell my husband how mean and cruel you were to me. Come over here."

She sat on the bunk and held out her arms. "Do what you did this afternoon. That was fantastic."

"Somebody could break in here at any time and try to gun us both down."

She smiled and lit a lamp. "But you don't think anyone will, do you? Otherwise you'd be back on deck with the rifle and watching."

Buckskin chuckled. "You got me there." He sat down beside her and finished the unbuttoning job and took off her blouse. She had no chemise under it. For a moment he watched her breasts. So beautiful, so perfect, it was a shame that they would sag and wither with age.

He petted them and Dawn gasped.

"I know it sounds silly, but the first time you touched me there made me remember all the times I'd been told not to let boys touch my breasts. Silly, I know. Kiss them, then I'll be in the mood again."

They undressed each other slowly, gently, with a lot of kisses and heavy breathing. When they both sat on the bed naked, she looked at him in the soft light of the kerosene lamp and smiled. Her face turned sober, and then she looked at him shyly with a little-girl grin.

"Isn't there more than one . . ." She stopped and lifted her brows. "It's still hard for me to talk about it. I'm not all that inexperienced but"—she took a big breath and looked up at him with the touch of a frown—"isn't there more than one position to do it?"

"To make love?"

"Yes."

"There are. Some Orientals claim there are a hundred and twenty one different positions for sexual intercourse, but most of them are combinations of others."

"A hundred and . . ." She began to laugh. "I think for right now just one other way would be plenty."

"I'll be glad to show you when you're ready." He kissed her then, long and deep, and she sighed. They stretched out on the bunk taking up almost all of it. She rolled against him and her hand found his crotch where his erection was full and pulsating.

He warmed her up as he had before, realizing she wasn't nearly as experienced as she wanted to believe. When she began to moan softly and reach for his erection, he rolled her on top of him as he lay on his back.

"This is another position," he said.

"Up here? I thought you had to be on top. I don't know why. Will it work?"

He lifted her gently and held his penis upward and found her moist entryway and then let her down easily on his shaft.

"Oh, my," she crooned. "Oh, my goodness sakes!"

Soon he had her resting on his pelvic bones and he was fully inserted and she laughed like a schoolgirl.

"It really will work this way?" She frowned. "But how can you move?"

"That's part of the fun of it. You get to do most of the moving." He pushed his hips upward and she met him, then lifted up as he moved down and she grinned.

"Oh, yes, I'm going to like this."

He wasn't sure if he touched her clit or not this way but he stroked steadily and smiled when she began to heat up to the boiling point. She erupted and the spasms were just as strong and as many as before.

She squealed and moaned and kissed him all over his face as she came out of the climax. Then she fell on him like a just-shot elk. She came alert a moment later. "Hey, your turn. You didn't get your turn."

He took his turn in a dozen swift strokes, and

they both rested. A few minutes later they parted and lay there holding each other.

"You really think that Nate will still try to get you and me, or will he give up when he knows we're on board a boat?"

"Not sure. But I have to figure that he's coming. He might chase us all the way to Denver. Your house isn't exactly a hard one to find."

"Yes, I was thinking of that. Daddy can put out some guards, real ones with rifles, patrolling the front and back of our estate."

"That will help."

Buckskin sat up and pulled on his clothes. "I want to take a turn around the deck and see what I can see. I don't want any surprises come morning."

He made sure she locked the door, took only his six-gun, and worked his way from shadow to shadow along the upper deck. He wasn't concerned about the main deck. Too many places to hide and ambush someone down there. He found nothing suspicious on the Hurricane deck at the bow or the boiler deck toward the stern.

He went back to the cabin, made sure he saw no one watching him, and slipped inside and locked the door.

"Everything all right?" she asked.

He nodded, pulled off his boots and sat down on the bed beside her. "Right now it looks fine, but it's a long way from here to Denver."

Buckskin slept two hours at a time, then took a quick look outside. At five in the morning he went to sleep again and didn't awaken until he felt the craft nudge a pier. He pulled on his clothes and boots and strapped on his gun. He was at the rail before anyone left the boat.

One of the couples walked down the gangplank. The crew off-loaded some freight and took on some more. Then the whistle sounded and the boat pulled away from the dock.

Buckskin let out a held breath as the boat headed into the channel. Now he believed that they really might have escaped from Nate Hill after all.

At the next stop, Buckskin saw there was food available, so he dashed off, bought a basket and enough food to last them for a day, mostly sandwiches and fruit, and hurried back just before they pulled the plank.

For the first time that morning, they sat out on deck in chairs and watched the shore roll by. One of the crewmen had told him they should arrive at Omaha sometime after noon.

"He said we passed Sioux City, Iowa, during the night. He told me we were moving only about half speed in the dark because of the problem of snags. Now we're making up time, and he figured we'd get there sometime around one o'clock this afternoon."

They munched on sandwiches and talked and laughed a lot. She told him some of the great things she planned to do, but the best of all was a school of dance. She'd hire a good ballet mistress with lots of experience and start building a company. She might have students at first and then one or two professionals, but eventually she wanted to have a real ballet company.

Buckskin nodded but kept watching the shoreline and wondering about Omaha. If Nate Hill was there, he'd make his move somewhere between the boat landing docks and the train station. Buckskin had to be ready.

Chapter Twenty Four

It was just after ten o'clock that morning when Buckskin took a stroll around the Hurricane deck near the bow of the ship, always keeping sight of Dawn sitting outside their cabin. He had just leaned on the rail when he heard running steps and looked up in time only to throw up his arms as a man hurtled toward him in a running charge.

Buckskin bent enough to take the force of the large man's weight on his shoulders and hip, and bounce him away. Then the man came in with a two-foot club and swung it viciously.

Buckskin darted out of the way of the club and dug for his six-gun before the man could start another swing. But the man didn't swing the club again, he threw it just as Buckskin's Colt cleared leather. The heavy club hit his right forearm, making him drop the six-gun.

He spun and attacked the man, who he saw was as tall as he was but heavier with an untrimmed full beard and deep-set dark eyes and shaggy black hair.

Buckskin landed two hard fists to the man's cheek and jaw, driving him back a moment. Then the big man charged, head down. Buckskin skipped sideways and threw out a foot, tripping him.

The bearded one fell hard on his stomach, and Buckskin was on top of him before he could move. He grabbed one of the man's thick arms and twisted it behind his back, pushing it up hard until the man barked in pain.

"Why?" Buckskin asked.

"Fuck you."

"Who sent you?"

"The devil himself." The man gave a bellow of anger and heaved his hips upward, throwing Buckskin off, and he rolled to the side and leaped to his feet. Buckskin saw his Colt a dozen feet away. He bent and pulled the .32 from his ankle holster and showed it to the man.

"You want to argue with a six-gun, little friend?"

The man turned to run. Buckskin fired at his legs, hit one, and the bearded man rolled to the deck and stayed down.

Buckskin squatted in front of him but out of reach. "One of them stingers in your eyeball is going to mess up your brain just all to pieces. Now, you want to tell me who sent you?"

"Damn, my leg hurts. Didn't get paid enough to

get shot or get killed. Hell, yes, I'll tell you. Got a telegram and fifty dollars to get on this boat at Sioux City and take care of you. Dump you overboard, then bring the woman back to Yankton where I'd get another hundred dollars."

"Telegram?"

"Yeah. Somebody strung a line up to Yankton. Not a lot of folks know about it."

"You swim good, little friend?" Buckskin asked.

"Damn, no. Rather wait for Omaha."

"Rather see you swim to shore. We're not more than two hundred yards out. That shouldn't be any problem for you."

"I'll drown myself."

"Tough luck. You should have thought about that when you took on the job. You want to get over the rail now, or do you want another slug in your leg?"

The big man stood, stared hard at Buckskin and climbed the rail, then dove cleanly into the muddy waters of the Missouri. No shout went up. Probably the pilot and none of the crew saw it. They tended to mind their own business.

Buckskin saw the swimmer as he headed for shore with a steady overhand crawl stroke. He looked like an excellent swimmer. He'd make it to shore with no problem.

The telegram. Buckskin realized now that he should have thought of that. The wires were stretching out all over the west, making communication easier than ever. In this case that ease of getting messages from one point to another was going to cause him more trouble. If Nate Hill had sent an assassin from Sioux City, he certainly would have alerted someone in Omaha too, just in case the first man missed.

He frowned, wondering where Nate Hill himself was. Back in Yankton, Dakota Territory, or on a sternwheeler chasing them down the Missouri?

He went back to where Dawn stood by the deck chair. She must have seen the whole thing. She hurried to meet him as he walked toward her. She hugged him tightly, then they went inside the cabin.

"One man. Nate evidently sent a telegram to him in Sioux City and he came on board last night."

"He swam to shore?"

"Looked like he was good in the water. No real problem there one way or the other. What I'm wondering about is Omaha. It's a good bet that Nate will have someone looking for us in Omaha. What we'll do is split up. The man there will be looking for the two of us together. You keep your hat on to hide your face and I'll be well behind you with my bag. It should work until we get to the train. Then I'll sit behind your seat."

"You think Nate will keep chasing us?"

"I do. I don't think he'll give up in Omaha. We may have to settle this in Denver."

"Oh, no. We can't put Harold in any danger. He isn't used to it. Promise me that he won't be hurt in any way."

"I can't. But I'll do the best that I can to keep him safe. We may meet Nate well before Denver. Who can tell? We should be into the harbor at Omaha in an hour or two. Remember, we go off the boat separately, we don't speak or even look at each other.

I'll carry my bag and you keep your face down."

She nodded. "I'll be glad when all this is over." She watched him a minute, then nodded. "I know, I know. I brought this all on myself by running away. Everyone has to grow up a little sometime. I guess this was my time."

"We'll hope so. You have a pocket in that skirt anywhere?"

She showed him one on her right side. He gave her two five-dollar bills and a twenty. "Put these in the bottom of your pocket and use one to hire a cab to take you to the railroad station. I'll be in a cab right behind you. I'll leave my brown hat in my bag and wear an older gray one I have. That might help throw off the watcher.

"Remember, he'll be a professional criminal. He won't mind hurting you to get me. That's his main object. Nate won't want you hurt, but at the final moment this man or men might think it's needed."

He reached down and took the small revolver from his ankle holster and gave it to her. "Keep this in your pocket. You may need to keep your hand on it so it doesn't become obvious. You know how to use it. Cock the hammer with your thumb, then aim and pull the trigger."

Her brows went up and for a moment her eyes showed fear. Then she held the weapon, brought it up and aimed it at the small window, then nodded and put it in her pocket.

"Yes, I can do that, if I need to help you or to keep away from this man or men in Omaha." She looked up at him and shivered. "Just be sure you don't lose me."

"I won't. I can run as fast as these horses walk through Omaha. When you get to the rail station, go in and buy a one-way ticket to Omaha and ask where you catch the train and what time it leaves. I might be standing in line behind you or maybe in front of you. Don't talk to me, don't even look at me. Keep your eyes looking down and shield your face."

She sighed. "There will be someone there hunting us, won't there?"

"Yes, I'm certain of it. I didn't think Nate would be so tenacious, but evidently his standing in town will be seriously hurt if he loses you."

An hour later at the sternwheeler dock in Omaha, Buckskin stood at the rail and watched Dawn walk toward the main-deck gangplank and go down. He was four passengers behind her. He scanned the dozen people at the dock but saw no one he'd classify as a criminal intent on murder.

He tarried at the dock a moment looking around, saw Dawn get into a one-horse hack at the curb. He went that way, hailed another cab and told him to follow the cab ahead to the railroad depot.

"I know a shorter way," the cabby said. Buckskin lifted his six-gun from leather and showed it to the driver.

"Follow that cab ahead or hope your widow will remember you more than a week after you're six feet into the good Nebraska soil. Understand?"

The man gulped and said he'd keep right on the rear wheels of the rig ahead.

At the rail station, he paid the cabby, thanked him and walked into the depot a dozen feet behind

Dawn. She looked around and went to the ticket counter.

It happened quickly. Two men came from a group of people in another line, hoisted Dawn by the arms and carried her toward a door at the far end of the station.

Buckskin charged, slammed his fist into the shoulder of the first man and pushed him to one side. He punched the second man in the jaw, blasting him away, then he caught Dawn's hand and ran into the train yard.

Passengers had begun to gather waiting for a train to come in. Buckskin pushed into the group and ducked down to prevent the attackers from spotting him. Dawn's face had flushed and her eyes shone bright.

Buckskin asked one of the people in the group where the train they waited for was going. He said Columbus, Grand Island, Denver eventually. Buckskin thanked him and ducked lower as he saw one of the snatchers come through the entryway.

The man looked one way, then the other and walked toward the end of the group. Buckskin had Dawn take her hat off and he pitched it to one side, then walked in the same direction the ambusher had taken.

Buckskin got behind the man and touched him on the shoulder. He turned around and his eyes widened. Buckskin hit him with a left jab in the face, then a right fist that crashed into the point of his chin and knocked him down. Buckskin picked him up by the shoulders and dragged him to one side.

A few curious people came up.

"My friend here is drunk. Would you watch him for a minute while I go get him some coffee?"

A woman snorted. "You hit him. I saw you hit him."

"True," Buckskin said. "When he gets drunk he gets violent. Lucky he didn't start shooting. I'll take his revolver so he doesn't hurt anyone."

The train came rolling in hissing and steaming, and most of the people headed for the cars. Buckskin went with them, found hatless Dawn about where he had left her.

"Let's go. No sense hiding now. One of them is down, I don't know where the other one is." They hurried to the train and stepped up onto the platform of the last car and went inside. They took two seats at the front of the car, and Buckskin went back to the platform and watched the terminal. He didn't see the other man. A moment later the train began to roll forward and he went back to the front seats. Dawn was still there.

He had her move to the window seat and slid in beside her.

"So Nate Hill has struck again. Now we should be fairly safe the rest of the way into Denver. We have about five hundred and fifty miles, more or less. Going to take some time. We'll probably stop in Columbus to eat something."

"I remember those places. Fast in and out if you're lucky," Dawn said.

"We'll survive. This train can make forty miles an hour. If it makes regular stops it still should average thirty miles in an hour over the run.

"That means it'll take us fifteen hours to get to Denver," Dawn said. "I'm good with figures."

Buckskin grinned. "You certainly are."

She laughed. "I wish we'd had time to get a compartment. Then I'd show you how much I appreciate what you've done for me."

"I know, you showed me that once or twice already."

"Yeah, but another two or three times would be good."

Buckskin squeezed her hand and she sighed. He watched the others in the car. Nobody seemed the slightest bit interested in them. He saw the conductor coming. He changed seats with Dawn so she was on the aisle and pushed three twenty-dollar bills into her hand.

"Tell the conductor we didn't have time to get tickets, and ask him if this will cover two to Denver. Tell him you don't need any change and smile your prettiest."

The conductor smiled as soon as he saw Dawn. He stopped in front of her.

"Ticket, miss."

"Oh, goodness. My friend and I didn't have time to get them before we got on. Made it by a whisker." She smiled at him. "I have this, will it pay for two tickets to Denver?" She handed him the bills, and he nodded.

"Yes."

"We don't need any change. Just the tickets. Thanks. You're a very nice person."

He tore off tickets from a roll in his small bag and gave her two, then pocketed the sixty dollars.

Buckskin figured the conductor made himself about a ten-dollar profit. He moved on up the aisle asking for tickets and Buckskin began to relax.

They would have no more problems until Denver. He wasn't sure how he knew it. A gut feeling he had. He wanted it to end in Denver. No more stalking by Nate Hill. The yards just below the train station would be ideal. In clear view of the station, not any other people around. He'd work on the idea.

At the stop in Columbus they bought food to eat on the train, then settled in for the long ride the length of Nebraska. Without any washouts or delays, it would be nearly morning before they pulled into Denver. About five A.M. they should arrive, but that was figuring ideal conditions, which almost never happened on the railroad tracks these days.

The afternoon wore on, and the scenery didn't change much. Small settlements had sprouted along the rail tracks, and in some places they saw extensive farming. They bought more food for supper at one of the stops, then they ate and watched it grow dark.

Dawn slept. Buckskin watched the inside of the car. New people arrived and familiar faces left on most stops. Then the lights went out in the car and it rolled along through the night. No reduced speed on the rails.

Buckskin dozed. He came awake when a man walking up the aisle fell against the seat and Dawn mumbled something. Buckskin pushed the man away and saw that he was drunk. He straightened him up and aimed him down the aisle swaying between the seats.

The sun came up and Buckskin watched it through heavy lids and red eyes. The train came to a stop in the middle of nowhere. The conductor said it was a minor washout and should be fixed in four hours. Buckskin dozed and came awake and dozed several times during the delay.

Finally they were rolling again. An hour later they came into the outskirts of Denver and Buckskin roused Dawn. She yawned and growled at him, then kissed him on the lips and sat back smiling.

"I had a wonderful night's sleep. How about you?"

"Like a log," he lied. Now he watched the passengers with less interest. If they had been in Nate's pay they would have attacked in the middle of the night.

He had only to worry about the train station. Their delay could put another train right behind them from Omaha. He asked the conductor about it. The man preened his moustache and nodded.

"Took us nearly six hours to get moving again. Which means old nine-eighty-four should be now"—he looked at his watch—"Lordy, nine-eighty-four should be about ten minutes behind us. Tom is really gonna razz me about this run."

Buckskin watched the familiar streets flash by as the train slowed and came into the station. Yes, the yards just to the south would be best. He and Dawn there waiting for someone, and that someone would be Nate Hill.

As soon as the train stopped and the porter put down the step, Dawn and Buckskin stepped off the train and walked quickly toward the engine, then into the triangle of unused ground between the tracks and the depot and the train switching yard. Buckskin figured this would be the best spot to be seen and to take care of Nate Hill.

They watched their train pull on through, and as soon as it cleared the station another steam engine rolled in with its string of passenger cars.

Buckskin watched closely, but from nearly 100 yards away the faces were only blobs over clothes. One man started to walk toward them, and Buckskin tensed. The man turned away and left the area.

Ten minutes later all the passengers had left, the train pulled on through, and he could hear another engine approaching.

"Wrong. I guess I was wrong. I figured he'd be on that train right after ours and that we'd have a meeting right here."

"Maybe he never left Yankton," Dawn said. "Let's go home."

They went into the station and out to the street. Half a dozen hacks stood there waiting. Some called to him, but he passed them. A rather shabby hack sat at the end of the line, the driver apparently snoozing in his seat.

Buckskin gave the rig a shake, but got only a wave from the driver and a crusty call that could have meant anything.

Buckskin handed Dawn aboard and then stepped in himself. Dawn gave the address and the man mumbled it back, unwound himself, and without even looking at them slapped the reins on the back of the tired-looking horse and they moved out into the morning traffic.

It was slightly after ten. Buckskin scanned the sidewalks and streets for any possible danger. He knew the area, and when the driver turned the wrong way to reach the expensive houses and small estates in the upper reaches of Denver, he yelled at the driver with the correct street.

Again the driver yelled back something and turned at the next corner, and Buckskin settled back. There were several routes to get to the street of millionaires.

Five minutes later, Buckskin was sure they were going the wrong way. They were in a sparsely settled area, with only a few houses per block. They were halfway out of town.

Buckskin stood and hit the driver on the shoulder on his high seat.

"Hey, now I know you're taking us the wrong way," he yelled at the driver. The horse stopped, the driver turned, and the black muzzle of a .44 came with him. He threw off the old hat he wore and Buckskin stared at Nate Hill.

"On the contrary, I'm going exactly the right way. We're here, in fact. Both of you, out of the rig. I'm tired of chasing you two. Get out now or I'll kill you both where you sit."

He motioned with the weapon. "Morgan, keep both your hands where I can see them. I'd hate to waste more than one round on you. Out!"

He watched them carefully, and slid out of the buggy himself. "Walk over to those trees. That looks like a good spot so your bodies won't be found for a while."

Buckskin still had his Colt. But he'd never known

a man to live who tried to outdraw a weapon already aimed at him. He had to wait.

They entered the small patch of trees and Hill called again.

"Far enough. Sherry, I was gonna give you one more chance to come back to me, but hell, when you hit me over the head I quit that idea. Too bad. You were good at poker and not bad in bed, but I'll find a better partner for both. Looks like it's about time."

Buckskin dove to the left into the soft ground, grabbing for his six-gun. He got it out of leather about the time he hit the dirt and rolled to his right, pinning his right hand and gun under his body a moment.

He heard one shot, then a second, and then a smaller sound of a shot. He came up with his weapon and aimed and fired all in a split second at Hill, who stood looking at Dawn with a strange expression. Buckskin's bullet hit Hill in the side and spun him around. The second shot from the Colt took him in the chest and slammed him backwards, the gun slipping from his fingers.

Buckskin ran up and covered the man. He was dead. He looked then at Dawn, who stood stiffly, her right hand extended with the .32 caliber revolver in her hand. She looked at Buckskin and uttered a small cry.

"I shot him! I shot him!" She mumbled the words and then crumpled to the ground.

Ten minutes later they had it sorted out and were on their way toward the Evans estate in the Bountiful section of Denver. Dawn had pulled the .32 when Buckskin dove and got off one shot at Hill and hit him in his shoulder. The shot had so surprised him that he didn't get off another one at Buckskin.

Dawn sat well on her side of the buggy. She looked at Buckskin from time to time. She sighed and shook her head.

"Is this all over now? Will there be any more assassins after us?"

"I'd say it's all over. Nate Hill played himself for the final attacker in case the others failed. He must have come in on that train right after we did. He might have seen us standing out there and decided to try the cabby routine. If we didn't pick his cab, he'd simply follow us and start shooting."

"But it was safer to take us out in the less populated area."

"True." Buckskin watched her. "Are you ready to see your husband and to accept his terms?"

"Oh, yes, more than ready. I'll be able to live with them. I had my fling. I tried out gambling and found it grew boring after a while. If the money isn't important, it means nothing."

"The dance studio?"

"It's my first project. I'll start tomorrow by finding a place to buy that I can turn into a dance studio and practice hall. A rather large room with no pillars or posts."

"Good."

She directed him to her home. When they arrived, she sent one of the servants to go to her husband's office and tell him that she was home and waiting for him.

Buckskin sat in the front hall waiting. Dawn hurried to her bedroom, where she brushed her hair, washed her face, put on a touch of rouge and lip color, then slipped into the gown her husband liked the best. She came down the steps when she heard a rig pull up in front.

Harold Evans rushed through the front door, glanced at Buckskin sitting there, then ran to the open stairway where Dawn had waited for him halfway down. She now came the rest of the way like a queen and held out her cheek for Evans to kiss.

"I'm back to stay, Harold. I understand your conditions and your stipulations and offers, and I accept everything. Mr. Morgan has been most resourceful. Men chased us down the Missouri, over the railroad tracks, and one man even held a gun to our heads right here in Denver. But there is no more threat."

Harold Evans wiped moisture from his eyes, gazed at his wife a moment longer, then retreated to the hallway.

"Mr. Morgan. If you'll come by my office tomorrow, I'll see that the rest of our contract is completed. Shall we say about ten o'clock?"

Buckskin nodded, gave a short wave at Dawn and hurried out the door. Suddenly he wanted to check his mail. See what Clare Johnson had to tell him about what had happened at the hotel. Clare. Yes, he would consider her seriously. But he also was wondering what kind of job offers he'd had, or what he might pick.

Clare might have a suggestion. Clare always had a suggestion. He hurried now, drove the cab back to the railway station where its owner was waiting for it. Then he walked along the familiar streets toward his hotel room which was his office. He hurried now, wondering just what kind of job offers he might have and where he would go on his next assignment.